Praise for
Learning Not to Drown

"A thought-provoker that will leave readers
contemplating the line between family
loyalty and self-preservation."
—*Kirkus Reviews*

"Readers will be inspired."
—*Booklist*

"Uplifting."
—*Publishers Weekly*

"Powerful messages . . . A worthwhile read."
—*Library Media Connection*

Learning not to drown.

A novel by Anna Shinoda.

atheneum

NEW YORK LONDON TORONTO
SYDNEY NEW DELHI

An imprint of Simon & Schuster Children's Publishing Division
1230 Avenue of the Americas, New York, New York 10020

For information about special discounts for bulk
purchases, please contact Simon & Schuster Special Sales
at 1-866-506-1949 or business@simonandschuster.com.
The Simon & Schuster Speakers Bureau can bring authors to your
live event. For more information or to book an event, contact the
Simon & Schuster Speakers Bureau at 1-866-248-3049 or visit
our website at www.simonspeakers.com.
Also available in an Atheneum hardcover edition
The text for this book is set in Mrs Eaves.
Manufactured in the United States of America
First Atheneum paperback edition May 2019
2 4 6 8 10 9 7 5 3
The Library of Congress has cataloged the hardcover edition as follows:
Shinoda, Anna.
Learning not to drown / Anna Shinoda. — 1st ed.
       p.   cm.
Summary: Clare, seventeen, has always stood up for her eldest
brother, Luke, despite his many jail stints but when her mother
takes Clare's hard-earned savings to post bail for Luke, Clare
begins to understand truths about her brother and her family.
ISBN 978-1-4169-9393-3 (hc)
ISBN 978-1-4424-9668-2 (eBook)
ISBN 978-1-5344-3948-1 (pbk)
[1. Self-actualization (Psychology)—Fiction. 2. Brothers and sisters—Fiction.
3. Family life—Fiction. 4. Secrets—Fiction. 5. Criminals—Fiction.
6. Drug abuse—Fiction.] I. Title.
PZ7.S55722Le 2013
[Fic]—dc23   2012051502

If you cannot get rid of the family skeleton,
you may as well make it dance.

—George Bernard Shaw

Acknowledgments

I was only able to come so far in writing Clare's story on my own. There are many people to thank for their support and insight.

I'll start with my best friend and husband, Mike, who not only provides me with encouragement and support but who is also an excellent brainstorming partner and critique buddy.

Caitlyn Dlouhy, who believed not only in my book but also in my ability to improve it, and gave me the essential feedback I needed in order to make it better than I thought possible.

Amazing agent Jennie Dunham, who found the perfect house and the perfect editor.

Kim Turrisi, Lin Oliver, and everyone over at SCBWI.

Jean O'Neill and Vanessa Lasdon. Encouragement. Support. Advice. A quiet place to write. Best critique group ever. I can't thank you enough.

Keith Hunter. Irreplaceable. I miss you.

All my friends and family who have shown me support or helped me with details or shared their own stories with me, especially: Otis, Abba and Jojo, Tracy Nathan, Tony Cupstid, Mark Wakefield, Lisa Ling and Paul Song, Pam and Chris Zam, Jordan Berliant, Michael Green, Ryan Demarti, Jonathan Schwartz, Karen Ellison, Danny Hayes, Laura Elliot, Laura Villandre,

Kymm Britton, Paul Crichton, Katy Hershberger, Dee Anderson, Bobby Kim, George Hundleby, Bruce Thompson, Jim Digby, Dave and Linsey, Brad and Elisa, Chester and Talinda, Joe and Heidi, Rob and Erika, Miriam, Megan, Laurel, Blanca, Donna, Muto, Jason, my parents, Jeff, Bill, Tammy, Zita, George, and the rest of my family.

Mrs. Smith, for teaching me everything I need to know about knitting and a whole lot more about compassion and unconditional love. You were the best honorary grandmother.

My two favorite creative writing teachers: Mike Buctha, who encouraged all things writing when I was in middle school and high school, and Joann Rocklin, who taught the class that inspired me to return to doing the thing I love most.

Sue and Carolyn, who helped me hold hands with my own skeletons.

Edwin Ushiro, for the swimmer he painted inspired by Clare. And the talented Kelia Anne MacCluskey for allowing us to use her photo for the hardcover edition.

Also thanks to all the people over at Atheneum who helped turn my manuscript into an actual book.

And to you. Thank you for reading. You're awesome, and I'm glad to have been able to share this with you.

Learning not to drown.

THEN: Age Eleven

The front door window was broken.

I could see the clear, jagged edges that held to the frame.

Slowly I got off my bike. Rolled it to the tree next to the house, my hands turning white from gripping the handlebars. I leaned my bike against the trunk, my eyes still on the window.

I moved closer, then closer. My shoes crushed the glass on the ground into smaller pieces. Inspecting the shards that clung to the frame, I paused only for a few seconds before I turned the doorknob and walked inside.

The drops on the linoleum floor were round. In sixth-grade art class I had tried, again and again, to draw a perfect circle. I couldn't do it without the compass attached to my pencil, stabbing the paper in the center. My freehand circles were always wavy, lopsided. I didn't think it was possible to make a perfect circle without the compass. But here, right in front of me, were perfectly round, bright red droplets. Mom always said that we had thin blood. That's how I knew it was one of us.

I could have gone back outside. Waited at a neighbor's until I was sure Dad was home from work. He was used to blood. He was used to corpses.

But I didn't. I don't know why, but I followed the droplets.

They were a much better trail than breadcrumbs. The blood would stain the floor, stain the carpet. It wouldn't be picked by birds. We'd always be able to follow it.

The sharp sounds of an argument and a nasty smell—body odor and alcohol, and another that I couldn't recognize—stopped me for a moment. Maybe I should have left then.

Curiosity gave me bravery. I turned the corner.

Chapter 1:

Family Skeleton

NOW

Skeletons don't like to stay in closets.

Most families try to lock them tightly away, buried beneath smiles and posed family pictures. But our Family Skeleton follows me closely with his long, graceful stride.

I guess people in my town think they have a pretty clear picture of Skeleton. Their whispers have haunted me most of the seventeen years of my life, stalking me almost as closely as he does: prison, prison, prison. Shame, shame, shame.

They don't see him like I do. His eye sockets expand and shrink. His cartoon jaw morphs from smiles to frowns, from serious to surprise. He's at least six feet tall, and when his bones stretch, he can dunk a basketball without his big toe coming off the ground. He's quite talented.

When he wants to relax, he lounges in a silk smoking jacket with a Cuban cigar and drinks brandy from a warm snifter. He might have a drinking problem, but I don't want to be presumptuous.

I think Mom, Dad, Peter, and Luke see Skeleton

clearly. After all, they are my family. Although I can't be sure, since Mom and Dad rarely talk about him, and Peter leaves the room whenever he appears.

Skeleton is the constant reminder of the crimes committed by my brother Luke. I'm used to Skeleton's taunts, his lanky fingers pointing, the click of his bones when he cartwheels across the room. I'm used to him reminding me he will always be a part of my life story. He will always be there to warn that every action has a reaction, every crime has a consequence.

And the more he hangs around, the more my reputation decays.

Skeleton didn't always exist—our family photo album shows me what reality was like before he started to appear. But I was too young then to own that memory now, a pre-Skeleton memory. *My* reality, *my* memories are like spinning pieces of a jigsaw puzzle that never make a complete picture.

And I can't help but think, maybe, if Skeleton would go away, we could have perfect again.

Chapter 2:

What Perfect Looked Like

THEN: Ages Two and Four

Our family photo album always sat in the living room on the lower shelf of the square dark wood coffee table, available for anyone to look at anytime. When I did, I always turned to the same page—the pictures giving me the memory I didn't have, the memory of what perfect felt like.

In the photos I am two years old, and my little-girl curls peek from under the brim of a pink sun hat. Warm sand is under my legs. Mom sits next to me in a navy-blue bathing suit and bug-eyed sunglasses, with a bright yellow shovel and bucket between us. I look out toward the water with a fascinated stare at Dad; Luke, age fourteen; and Peter, age six—all swimming—my hands together in a clap. Under the picture, my mother wrote in swirling handwriting: *Clare couldn't wait to get into the water with her brothers!*

The next picture was an action shot of Dad holding me in the lake, both hands splashing, water drops suspended in air, my eyes shut and mouth open in surprised bliss. Luke is mid-laugh with an arm around Peter as Luke's hand shields them both from the splash.

There was a photo of Luke and Peter, kneeling next to a large sand castle—*The Masterpiece!*—Peter filling the moat with water from the yellow bucket. Squatting next to Luke, I pull his arm with one hand while pointing at the rising water with the other.

The last was a group shot of Mom and Dad kneeling behind us, me squinting and smiling between my brothers. With the lake as the background, the descending sun on our faces left our shadows long in the sand. Mom wrote: *None of us wanted the day to end!*

That family, together and happy, not wanting the day to end, is one I know only from those pictures.

Two years later Luke went away.

My first *real* memory was of a nightmare. A nightmare in full color. The air an icy blue.

There was the house—just like ours, even with our yellow-flower cups. It was so quiet, the refrigerator didn't even growl. I walked through the halls, feeling the carpet squish between my toes as I called for my parents, for Peter and Luke.

The sound was pulled into the walls.

I looked up, up at Mom's pictures. My bare toe hit something solid and cold. Peter. Frozen. Frozen with his eyelids open, the eyeballs missing.

Ran through the house. Found Mom, then Dad. All frozen. All missing eyes. When I put my hand to my face, my skin was hard and cold. My fingers found the holes where my eyes had once been. I stopped moving, my feet ice-cubed in the carpet. Where was Luke? I waited for him to come save us.

He never did.

Grandma Tovin was staying with us when I had that nightmare. I barely have any other memories of her, since she died when I was five. That night she woke me up and held me. My hands clutched the side of her nightgown and wouldn't let go. Grandma pulled her favorite rosary out of her pocket—the one with dark red beads—and told me that when she had a bad dream, she liked to pray. So together we said Hail Marys, my fingers rubbing each bead. When we were done, I was still so scared, she let me sleep on the hide-a-bed in the living room with her for the rest of the night. But I didn't want Grandma—or Mom or Dad or Peter. I wanted Luke, and Luke was gone.

The next morning Grandma told Dad that I must have somehow watched one of his garbage scary movies. And that sweets before bed cause nightmares. When Skeleton heard this, he bent in laughter, holding his ribs so they wouldn't shake off. Then, done laughing, he pointed proudly at himself. Grandma ignored Skeleton, hung her favorite rosary in my room. She told me that if I had another nightmare and she wasn't there, I could hold it and pray and it would protect me. But it didn't work. The nightmares kept coming. And Luke was never there to save me.

Chapter 3:

Interruption

NOW

"When you mince the garlic, make sure it's really tiny," my mother says as she hands me a cutting board.

I pull a knife from the top drawer. "What's for dinner?"

"Chicken and rice with broccoli. After you're done with the garlic, chop half an onion."

"Sounds good." I study Mom for a second. She's concentrating on the rice, slowly stirring it in the pan to coat each kernel evenly with olive oil. Her brow is smooth. Shoulders back and relaxed. It's a good time to ask.

"I saw Drea's mom today at school. She told me more about their trip this summer—the one where they're touring colleges." I start slowly, peeling the dry skin off the garlic clove. "Two weeks, six campuses. All in California and Oregon. They invited me along."

"Oh, Clare. I don't think so." She answers so quickly, like she didn't even listen to what I asked.

Still. An "I don't think so" isn't a complete no.

I try again.

"But, Mom." The knife slices effortlessly through the garlic. I stop to reposition my fingers out of the way.

"I've gotten a ton of brochures from different schools. It's confusing. I really need to see what's out there in person."

"What about your summer job and saving for college? Don't you think that is more important?"

I knew she was going to say that.

"I called Lucille Jordan and talked to her. She says that if we choose the right time, I can have two weeks off. And if I pick up extra shifts, it won't really affect how much I earn this summer."

Mom looks down at my cutting board. "The garlic needs to be little bit smaller." Then, "And how much would this trip cost you? Transportation, food, lodging?"

"Ms. P said they're still working out all the details, but it won't cost too much. I don't have to worry about hotel rooms since we'll just get an extra cot for me. And she's driving, so I'd just have to pitch in for gas."

Mom wipes her hands on the kitchen towel. "Clare Bear, I just don't see the point. There are perfectly good colleges within driving distance of here. Your money will go further if you live at home. Get your AA from the community college, like Peter. Then look at universities for the last two years. It's smarter, Clare. Don't waste your hard-earned money on a trip looking at schools we can't afford." Her voice lowers at the end, edging on compassion. I frown. It *is* logical. Financially the smartest thing to do is to stay at home and go to the local CC. I swallow that thought and hold it for a moment, allowing it to swirl inside me. I feel queasy. Almost instantly. Living at home until I'm twenty.

I just can't do it.

I need to go on this trip. I need to get away. One last try. I take a second to compose my thoughts. Ready.

Riiiinnng.

Interrupted.

Mom hands me her wooden spoon. "Keep stirring the rice—when it's golden, add the chicken stock." She reaches for the phone.

Maybe I can ask Dad. Maybe he could convince Mom. Yeah, right. It'll be canned lecture 101 about how there's a perfectly good school forty-five minutes away.

"Yes, I'll accept the charges," Mom says.

It's Luke. It has to be. Who else calls collect?

The rice has turned from white to yellow, some of the grains already golden brown. Careful not to spill, I stir the chicken stock in as my mother's voice, suddenly bright, cries out, "Luke? Hi!"

I tap her on the shoulder and quietly say, "I want to say hello." She nods. Then points my attention to the stove. Individual bubbles slowly start to rise up though the rice. Boiling now. I stir it one last time and turn the heat down, covering the pan.

"A few days early? That's wonderful! So I'll be there to pick you up on the twenty-seventh." Back to slicing, I grab an onion, smiling. It sounds like we'll be seeing Luke sooner than expected.

"What do you mean?" Despite Mom's even tone, the vein in her forehead has surfaced. I catch her eyes for a second. She turns to face the wall, as if that will keep me from hearing the rest of her conversation. Pretending not to listen, I cut into the onion, letting the eye-burning odor release.

"Luke, I think it's best if you come straight home. Who is this friend you're planning to stay with?"

I slice quickly, then stand back to give my eyes a break. "What kind of work?"

There's nothing left to prepare for dinner. Wanting to stay nearby, I wash the cutting board and knife, fidgeting with drying it longer than I need to, taking in as much as I can from our kitchen side of the conversation.

"Yes, the job sounds like a good opportunity. But, Luke, don't you think it would be best to be with your family, not this so-called friend, who you don't know anything about?" I want more information. I want to hear Luke's voice and find out from *him* all the details. Cautiously I tap Mom on the shoulder. She waves me away.

I take two steps toward the living room and stop to listen as she says, "Fine. When will we see you?" She sighs. Pauses. "Stay out of trouble, and get home as soon as you can. I love you." Another pause. "Good-bye."

Before I even think to stop her, she hangs up the phone.

"Clare. Get back into this kitchen." Her tone is sharp. "I did not say you were done helping me with dinner. Do you think these dishes are going to do themselves?"

I clench my jaw and return. Lower the dishwasher door and pull out the plates. The vein in her forehead is pulsating now. Any chance I had to convince her to let me go on the trip with Drea is now gone.

Mom pulls out a pan, then slams the cabinet door. She should be *happy*. Getting out early and a job lined up? Isn't that a good thing? Even if Luke can't come home right away?

She's angry enough that I probably should keep quiet, but she got to talk to Luke and I didn't.

"How's Luke?" I ask.

"Fine." She drops the pan onto the stovetop. The clank echoes, filling the room.

"He's getting out early? That's good, right?"

"Yes." She turns the burner on high; the flames shoot up, engulfing the steel in wisps of blue.

"When will he be home?" I dare to ask, stacking the plates as I put them away.

"Eventually."

I'm tired of her one-word answers. "What kind of job did he get? Did he say when he was going to call back? I wanted to talk to him." I pout.

"You can't have everything you want," she practically yells at me. Olive oil and garlic and onions hit the pan, hissing from the heat. I clamp my mouth shut and start to load the bowls and cups piled in the sink, my own anger brewing. Mom could at least answer a few questions for me. "Speaking of which," she continues, "you will not be going with Drea and her mother this summer. No ifs, ands, or buts. And don't even think of asking your father. The subject is closed. Finish the dishes and get out of my kitchen."

My mother continues to bang cabinet doors and slam drawers shut as she cooks. One call from Luke could have put Mom in a better mood, then maybe I could have convinced her to let me go on this trip. I feel my anger shifting from Mom to Luke. He set her off and ruined my chances.

On the way out of the kitchen, I make eye contact with Skeleton. He raises his hand in salutation. Just a little wave to let me know he's here. He's been watching. I ignore him and hurry to my room.

The ruckus in the kitchen slowly quiets to, at last, silence. I know the chicken is in the oven, the rice is simmering, the broccoli steaming. And I also know that Mom is now in the living room, standing in front of her Christmas ornament collection. Handcrafted by her father out of glass, silver, and crystal over open flame. Etched and tapped with fine details. Papa used the skills he had practiced for more than ten years to create the perfect five ornaments as a gift for Granny when my mother was born. And when Luke was born, Granny passed the gift along to Mom. She leaves them out on the oak bookcase to admire year-round, displayed on a graceful miniature silver tree. Just above eye level, the perfect height for Mom to be able to unhook each ornament with ease and meticulously shine it before gently rehanging each treasure. She looks insane when she does it—the ritual of laying out five different cloths and glass cleaners and vinegar, the tin of silver polish, the white gloves, the way the corners of her mouth tip up just slightly as her brow tilts down in concentration. Peter used to lick his fingers and leave a single print on each ornament. Then the two of us would bet each other

M&M's on how long it would take her to make them perfect again.

I know she is staring at all five ornaments now, noting the dust spots and smudges. She is checking her watch, maybe looking over her shoulder at the kitchen. The risk of ruining dinner will pull her away. But if Peter and I were to make a bet right now, I'd put ten M&M's down that the ornaments will be gleaming by tomorrow morning.

Sitting on my bed, I glare at the stack of college brochures on my desk. It's ridiculous that Mom won't let me go on the trip. She probably thinks that by keeping me home, I'll end up doing exactly what she wants: living here and commuting to Crappy CC or Shithole State. It's not going to happen. . . . But neither is the trip. No way will Mom change her mind. If Luke hadn't called, maybe I could have persuaded her. Or if he had called and said exactly what Mom wanted to hear: "I'm out early; I have a good job lined up and will be renting a house across the street from you, so you'll always know what I'm doing, and I've met a nice Catholic girl to marry and start a family with." HA! Like *that* would ever happen.

My cell phone buzzes in my pocket. A text from Drea: "Still on?"

"As planned," I text back, and toss my phone onto my bed. If Mom had said yes to the trip, I wouldn't have risked losing that opportunity by sneaking out tonight. Now . . . forget it. I'm going.

Only five hours. Five hours until I'm out of here. I hate this house and I hate my mom and I hate Luke for calling at the wrong time. *Wrong place at the wrong time.* Luke is always in the wrong place at the wrong time. My fingers tap on my knees, little spikes of angry energy. Even watching my fish tranquilly swimming circles in my aquarium isn't doing anything to calm me down.

To quiet my hands I grab a half-knitted beanie from my bedside table and squeeze the skein of mohair yarn. Snow white to contrast with Skye's black hair. I loop the yarn over the needle and start a new row of stitches. I'll be done with hers by tonight, which leaves just Drea's and Omar's to go. It's weird, knitting hats when it's so hot, with Beanie Day so many months off. But I need to get them done now, so I can knit blankets with the leftover yarn for the kids at the shelter before the temperature drops.

The needles make a quiet click as each stitch slips off, reminding me of Granny sitting in her rocking chair when Papa was in one of his moods. Clicking and rocking—a little island of calm making something beautiful.

Click. Click. Click. I cast off the final stitches, then go to my bookcase and grab the *Knit Slouchy Beanies* magazine I picked up at a yard sale for the pattern I'm sure Drea will love. And there was one in there that Luke might like too.

Luke. Luke will not be coming home immediately. Disappointment instantly swirls, overtaking any anger I had left. It's been so long since I've seen him. Close to four years. Couldn't he at least come home for a visit? Just a quick one? Then start his new job?

I know I'm being selfish. If Luke came home, he

could lose his opportunity. He's twenty-nine years old. He'll need to make money. Need the structure of a schedule, as my father always says.

Any job is important, but with the *right* job maybe he'll stay out of prison, Skeleton will go away, the whispers will stop, and my favorite memories of Luke will snap together perfectly with the present, making a picture I can see and understand. It sounds impossible, but I have to hope.

With the right job, this time it could be different.

Chapter 4:

Wins and Losses

THEN: Age Six

Luke didn't have to work anymore, so we stayed at the lake late, wading into the water after the lifeguard had gone home. He carefully led me by the hand toward the forbidden side, the swamp.

"Mommy doesn't want me to go over here," I said, clutching Luke's hand tighter, feeling my toes sinking deep into the mud. "And neither do the lifeguards. They blow their whistles whenever anyone gets too close."

"Do you know why they don't want us over here?" Luke bent down, his nose touching mine.

"Because we'll drown," I told him, looking down at the water, embarrassed. "I still can't swim." Most of my friends could at least dog-paddle.

"You can't?" Luke asked. His mouth dropped open, like he was shocked by this information. "Well, wanna learn right now?"

"In the swamp?" I crinkled my nose. "Yuck."

"Okay. Later. But quit worrying. I won't let you drown." Luke gave my hand an extra squeeze.

"The truth is"—Luke led me farther into the swamp—"the best frogs are on this side of the lake. If you wanna win the Frog-Jumping Contest, this is the place to get 'em."

"Oohhh!" I *did* want to win. I wanted to get the first-place trophy, and the free tickets for the games booths, but mostly I wanted to be in the parade, riding in back of Lucille Jordan's fancy convertible. Mandy Jordan took all her friends for a ride on her birthday. Not me. I wasn't invited to her party. Mandy's friends said it felt like flying and that they were like movie stars. I wanted to try it too. And I could . . . if I won the Frog-Jumping Contest.

Looking around, Luke pointed out different frogs, sleeping in the muck.

"Which one is the winner?" he asked me.

I scanned the mud. Pointed at the biggest frog I saw.

"Shhh." Luke signaled with one finger against his lip. Cautiously he lifted the frog out of the mud and into my hand. Its body was soft and slimy, and it didn't even try to get away. I watched the space under its chin get big and small, big and small. It was cute.

Once we'd waded back to shore, I carefully set the frog down on the grass. He took an instant gigantic leap, racing toward the lake. "Let's name him Speedy!" I said as Luke swooped in to pick him up just before the water's edge.

He was fast! We could win! But as I put Speedy in my beach pail, adding some reeds from the lakeside, a rock, and some muddy water, I remembered Mom.

"Won't Mommy be mad? You know she doesn't like animals."

"Don't worry, Squeakers." Luke winked at me. "I'll talk to her. She won't be mad for long."

When we brought Speedy home, Mom's upper lip disappeared. "Frogs are vile. Besides, you'll kill it. What are you going to feed it? Luke, you will be returning the frog to the lake immediately. No ifs, ands, or buts."

"But, Ma," Luke protested. "Ma. Let her keep it until Saturday. You know, the Frog-Jumping Contest at Patriot Days. We have a winner here."

Peter looked into the pail. "Doesn't look like a winner to me," he grumbled.

"I said no, Luke," she said, ignoring Peter.

"Come on, Ma," Luke cooed, wrapping an arm around her. "It's only a few days." Mom's angry forehead vein was slowly disappearing. Luke was doing it! He was convincing her it was okay.

Peter put his finger in the pail and touched the frog, then picked him up.

"Back in the pail," Mom instructed. Peter dropped him back in.

"Hey—watch it. We need to protect those legs!" Luke warned. His brown eyes flicked from Mom over to Dad, who was relaxing in front of the TV.

"Hey, Pop," Luke said, "come look at what Clare and I found."

"What's that?" Dad pushed himself out of his easy chair with a grunt. "Aha! A frog. I was on a walk this evening when I spotted one smashed on the road. A big one. Flatter than a potato chip. Guts everywhere. That's how it goes. Frogs and cars just don't mix. I had a baggie in my pocket so I scooped it up." He grinned wickedly at me. "It's in the back of my truck, if you want to see it. . . ."

"Stop it!" I covered my ears until Dad stopped talking.

"I really wish you'd leave your work stories at work," Mom said, shaking her head. "So, what do you think of this?" She motioned to the frog with her hand.

After inspecting it, Dad nodded.

"Looks like a fine jumper. Make sure you feed it a few crickets. Oh, and cover the pail with chicken wire so he doesn't escape. And so the raccoons don't get him." Dad had made the final decision. We were keeping Speedy until after the race.

"Maybe . . . ," I whispered softly to Speedy. "Maybe if you win, Mommy will love you and let me keep you forever."

After dinner, when Peter groaned to Luke that it wasn't fair that he'd taken me to get a frog and not him, Luke told him he needed to toughen up. Then, putting Peter in a headlock, Luke wrestled him to the floor. I jumped up on the couch and put my hands over my face, peeking through my shaking fingers as I waited for it to be over, wishing for Mom and Dad to come in and break up the fight. Peter was laughing at first, saying "stop" between giggles, his arms pushing and legs kicking. But then Luke sat on Peter's belly, pinned his hands to the ground over his head with one hand, and started tapping on his chest with his other fist.

Peter wasn't laughing anymore.

"I can't breathe!" Peter yelled.

"Then how are you talking?" Luke laughed.

"Stop!" The tears came. Luke stopped.

Later that night I overheard Mom talking to Dad. "He's *too* rough with him. He left a bruise on his chest! Peter's only ten. And Luke is eighteen—he's old enough to know better," Mom said. "It's gotten worse. He's learned violence there, more than anything else."

"I'll talk to him," Dad said.

Saturday was hot. Lucille Jordan, the president of the chamber of commerce, hosed off the black asphalt several times before the race began, taking great care not to get one drop of water on her red checkered shirt and white shorts. I liked her outfit. I didn't like mine. I was wearing boy clothes. I hadn't even been born yet when Luke had worn them, but I know he did, because there was a picture of him in the same red shorts and blue shirt on Mom's desk. And the pocket in the shirt was stretched out and saggy from when Peter used to shove rocks into it. Why couldn't I have had sisters instead?

Ready, set, and go. Speedy started hopping as soon as I set him down. Other frogs were jumping to the left and right. Some went backward. Not Speedy. He jumped straight down the asphalt. Past the finish line. Through the parking lot and into the stream just beyond.

Luke and I ran after him, but Speedy had disappeared into the reeds and water. When I started to cry, Luke hugged me tight and said, "Awww, Squeaks. Speedy's gonna be real happy in that river. I bet he even finds a lady frog to be his girlfriend." He wiped my tears with the bottom of his T-shirt. "I've got an idea. After we get your trophy, I'll win you a goldfish. You can name it Speedy."

No more tears. Just like always, Luke made me feel better.

After Mom took a million pictures of me holding my shimmering frog trophy, it was time to check in for the parade. Finally I was going to get my turn in the convertible! Lucille Jordan was smiling so big, I could see her molars. "Well, hello, Clare. Ready for your special ride?"

I nodded.

"Mandy and I will be up front—you know my daughter, Mandy—I think you're in the same class this year." Lucille's smile seemed to be getting bigger. "Mayor Bowman—our grand marshall—and you get to ride in the back."

Luke lifted me onto the back of the convertible.

"Hello there, little Miss Clare. Congratulations." Mayor Bowman was already in place. He tapped the seat next to him, inviting me to sit. "Luke Tovin. Staying out of trouble, I hope?"

Skeleton arrived, leaping into the back of the car and taking the spot next to me. I looked at my shoes, wishing he'd disappear.

"Yes, sir, I am," Luke replied as he opened the car door to climb in.

"Where are you going?" Lucille asked him.

Skeleton wrapped his arm around my shoulders, pressed his bony teeth to my cheek. I wiggled away as I said, "Luke helped me catch Speedy. Can he come too?"

"Oh, Clare, sweetie. I don't think so." Lucille's mouth was smiling, but her blue eyes were worried. Skeleton mimicked her, his eye sockets getting wider and wider. "No room."

I moved as close to the mayor as I could. There was plenty of space if Skeleton moved out of the way.

"Look! I made room," I said.

Lucille coughed, her face turned red. Skeleton motioned for her to lean in closer, to say more.

Wringing her long fingers together, she stared at Luke. Then she moved right next to his ear and growled in a low voice only we could hear, "Luke, do you really think that people want to see you in our parade?"

What Lucille said didn't make sense. Why wouldn't people want to see Luke in the parade? Uncomfortable, I slid away from the mayor and reached out for my brother, suddenly wishing I hadn't won the Frog-Jumping Contest. When he leaned over toward me, I whispered, "Maybe we should let someone else ride in the parade."

"Naw, Squeaks," Luke said. "You look good sitting there." He slowly stepped back, out of the car, and closed the door. With his hands up like a frame, he closed one eye and peered through the hole at me. "That's gonna make one pretty picture." He dropped his arms and scratched his head. "There's one problem. If I get into that car with you, I'm not gonna be able to see you in the parade." He shrugged. "Think you can ride by yourself so I can watch with Ma and Pop?"

Mayor Bowman patted my back and offered, "I'll help you hold the trophy up."

I looked at Mandy and Lucille. They didn't want Luke to be there. I was pretty sure they didn't want me to be there either. But the mayor was nice. And I really, really wanted to go for the ride.

"Okay," I told Luke.

"Well, then, let's get started," Lucille said as she sat in the driver's seat.

"Next year you should let the Patriot Days Queen ride in our car instead of the Frog-Jumping Contest winner," Mandy said from the front. Then she added under her breath, "I bet she has warts too."

Luke stuck his tongue out at Mandy's hair, perfect red curls and all. Skeleton pulled a curl down, watched it bounce up. Pulled another. Watched it bounce. I wanted to laugh. But I also wanted him to stop. He already brought enough attention.

"You wave like the princess that you are," Luke said as he started to walk away. "Look for me in the crowd, okay?"

Luke had said I was a princess. I sat up straight, cupped my fingers, and waved back and forth slowly. Just like all the famous people in the Rose Parade.

I don't know if it really felt like flying, but I definitely felt like a movie star.

By the time we headed home with my trophy and the four goldfish Luke had won for me, I forgot how uncomfortable I'd been when Lucille had been mean to

Luke. And I forgot even more when Mom was excited to see the fish. "We had aquariums back when your father and I were first married. I bet I still have everything we need."

Mom and Luke climbed the ladder to the forbidden attic and brought down a fish tank, complete with a heater, filter, fake plants, and rocks. Mom even agreed my room would be the best place for the fish.

Luke, Peter, and I named them Speedy, Junior, Rex, and Clyde. I fell asleep watching them swim back and forth, back and forth. The best night-light ever.

But the next morning Luke said he was getting restless. By the time the sun had set, he'd left the house with one duffel bag of his stuff. When I cried, Mom told me, "Adults aren't supposed to live with their parents. They're supposed to keep a job and take care of themselves." Then, smoothing my hair, she added, "I'm sure he'll visit soon."

Skeleton shook his head. He was sorry to see Luke go too.

Chapter 5:

Sneaking Out

NOW

At dinner I keep waiting for Mom to mention Luke's call to Dad and Peter, but she steers the conversation to concentrate on what each of us did that day. Her voice is, in fact, unnaturally cheerful. Everything is set up joyful, joyful, joyful, but all I can feel is her underlying anxiety and unrealistic expectations for everything to be perfect. I'd do anything to not have to sit through dinner with her.

As our meal draws to a close, Peter stretches his long arms out in front of him, cracking his knuckles while he announces, "I'm going to be out late tonight. Don't wait up for me." I shift uncomfortably. He must be planning to go to the same party that I have to sneak out to attend. The difference is Mom's set of rules. He's allowed to be out all night. I'm not even allowed to go.

"And where are you going?" Mom asks.

"A bonfire with my friends." He looks over to me, his thin lips curving into a smirk. He's preparing to ruin my night.

"Are you done with your dish?" I change the subject

and try to save myself by standing up and offering to take Dad's plate.

"Yep. Here you go."

"What kind of bonfire? No drugs or drinking, I presume." Mom pulls the conversation back to where I don't want it to be.

"No. Nothing like that," Peter lies. Hands me his plate. "It's the unofficial bonfire the juniors throw for the seniors." I freeze. "Clare. You're a junior. You're going, right?"

"No." I blink at him a few times. Jerk. Why is my discomfort his pleasure? "I'm beat from finals this week. Besides, it doesn't even start until after my curfew."

Mom's long stare could freeze an ocean. She's deciding whether to believe me or not.

"That's too bad," Peter says. "Everyone else will be there. Mom, you should let her go."

"I don't think that is anyplace for a young woman to be." Mom's answer snaps at the same time I say, "It's okay. I'd rather sleep."

I've only been sneaking out for the past nine months or so, but I know to do it right. There are rules to keep from getting caught. Rule number one: Never let parents know that there is any reason to sneak out. This means not asking permission to do anything that they may possibly say no to.

But now I have a dilemma. Knowing that Mom and Dad are both aware of the party tonight, the only sure way to not get caught is to stay in. Which I would consider if it weren't the end-of-the-year bonfire, if I hadn't promised Drea I'd be there, if Mom had agreed to let me go check out college campuses this summer, if Luke's phone call hadn't made Skeleton appear. Escaping to my bedroom isn't enough tonight. I need to get out.

"Thanks a lot, butthole," I hiss to Peter as we stand side by side loading the dishwasher. I peer toward Mom in the open adjacent living room. She's polishing her crystal bell ornament—that was fast. I bet she couldn't wait for dinner to end.

"Just doing my job as older brother." He lightly punches me in the arm. "Besides, what if she had said yes? Then you could have gone without sneaking out. It would be liberating."

"You know that's never going to happen. You just screwed me," I say.

He snaps the towel in the air, then tosses it onto the counter. On his way out of the kitchen, he turns. "See you tonight, Clare."

For me, sneaking out is never like in the movies. There's no climbing out windows or tiptoeing down the hall past where my parents are sleeping, or where they're entertaining or whatever in the adjoining living room. And I don't know anyone who thinks their parents are stupid enough to fall for tricks like putting a bunch of pillows down the middle of the bed to look like a body.

After following my regular nighttime routine, I lie awake in bed listening to the sounds of our TV blasting.

At around ten forty-five I hear Mom push my door open a crack and whisper good night. A half hour later Dad finally wakes up from his after-dinner TV nap and heads down the hall, stopping by my room to plant a kiss on my forehead while I pretend to be sound asleep. I wait until it is safe to assume they are both sleeping before I send a quick text message to Drea. "Ready in 15." I get out of bed and change out of my pajamas into a fitted tank top. Then I slide on my tightest jeans, checking my butt in the mirror. With a steady but quick hand, I apply my favorite green eye shadow—Drea says it makes my brown eyes pop—and pull my hair back into a ponytail. I put on my sneakers and grab my black hoodie in case it gets cool.

One last step before I leave my room. A note on my pillow: *Mom and Dad, I couldn't sleep, so I went for a walk. Be back by 3:00 a.m.* Getting caught sneaking out would be bad, but having the police called because my parents suspected a kidnapping would be worse. A lot worse.

The front door is the farthest from my parents' room, so that's the exit door I aim for. I'm dodging creaks like they are bombs, being watchful of every step, every breath. Slipping out silently into the full-mooned night.

Carefully I press the door shut. Freedom! Drea's headlights shine at the end of the block. But I still need to be quiet. My parents' bedroom window is wide open, and my neighbors are practically spies for my mom and dad.

I cross the street immediately, wanting to avoid Mrs. Brachett's eyes. She's one of those weird nocturnal old ladies. Good thing I do; she's sitting next to her open window reading a book.

I recross two doors down—don't want to run into Rambo, who barks at anything that moves. Almost there.

"Let's go!" I tell Drea as I jump into her car. Sneakout successful. I can relax until it's time to sneak back in.

We drive out of town, up the winding roads to the campgrounds.

I glance over at Drea's curls and makeup. "You look great."

"Well, I should. I've been taming this hair for the last hour and a half."

Drea's got one of those moms who would rather know her kid's going to a party, even if there might be beer there. Her only rule is she insists on knowing where we are and that we call her if we're not sober enough to drive home. I wish Ms. P were my mom.

"Who do you think will be there?" I ask.

"EVERYONE. Omar, Chase, Skye, Ryan." She stops to grin at me. There's no one at school that I really have a crush on, except maybe Ryan Delgado. Although he's dating Mandy—and that's enough to make me wonder what's wrong with him—he still interests me. It doesn't hurt that he's gorgeous, even with his crooked nose that on anyone else's face might look ugly. On him it's perfect. Just a reminder of how athletic he is.

We weave past Lookout Ridge.

"Whoa. Check out all the cars at Lookout tonight." Drea slows down. "Anyone we know?"

I glance at the couples parked along the road, cars facing the view of stars above and city lights below.

"Don't think so. Oh. Wait. Lala's Love Mobile," I say, twisting around to catch another glimpse.

"That's a big surprise." Drea rolls her eyes, then changes the subject. "Off topic." Her voice raises with excitement. "My mom's getting the schedule for our trip all figured out; four colleges I like, and the two she thinks you and I should 'give a chance.' And she needs to know which colleges you'd want to add. Tonight would be cool, but you can let me know tomorrow."

My heart sinks. It's not "our" summer trip anymore. It doesn't matter which colleges I want to see. And now I have to disappoint Drea.

When I don't say anything, Drea asks, "So . . . what do you think? You can pick out some schools you know I can't get into. It'd still be fun for me to visit them."

"It doesn't matter what I think, okay?" I say in a burst, realizing too late that I sound angry at Drea. "I mean, I told my mom, and she's completely against it. She even shut down asking my dad." I pause, thinking about telling Drea how Mom might have been considering it . . . before my brother called. But that could bring Skeleton into the car. I say instead, "I got the typical lecture: Why would I waste good money moving out when I could go to a perfectly fine community college?"

"That college is a hole. You're not really considering it, are you?"

"No," I say. "My bestest friend, Drea, is going to scope out a good school for me."

"Are you sure you trust me?" Drea gives me a devilish grin as she pulls over behind a long line of parked cars.

"Of course. At least I trust your report of campus life," I reply.

Hiking up the dirt road, counting the cars on the way—thirty-seven so far—we head toward the red-hot ash that flies beyond the treetops. Drea's dark skin looks almost blue in the full moon's pale glow as she walks beside me. The knobby pines and gnarled oak trees have shed their usual sinister look for a fairy-tale forest. We pass the last car. Fifty-three. Between those and the ones parked down at Lookout, I doubt anyone between the ages of fourteen and eighteen is home tonight.

I take a deep breath in—it feels so good to be out of the house.

The road turns right, but we turn left to where a crowd huddles near the blazing bonfire. More people line the edge of the clearing, leaning against the trees, smoke rising from the red tips of cigarettes waving in their hands. And then, beyond the line of trees, there are the silhouettes of classmates looking for more privacy in the woods.

I look back toward the bonfire, my eyes landing immediately on Peter, less than two steps away, guarding a massive ice chest. Really? Of all the people here, *my brother* has to be one of the first I see?

"Peter! What a surprise. Never thought we'd see you here!" Drea greets him, flashing a sympathetic grin at some blond girl who's practically licking him. "Remind me. How long ago did you graduate? Four years?"

"Three, Drea. And I'm guessing that you might graduate next year. If you try really hard." Peter takes a chug from the Coors in his hand. Turning to me, he says, "The real surprise is seeing my little baby sister here. It's past bedtime. Mommy and Daddy would be very upset to know you were out at a party."

"And I'm sure they'd think it's fine that their sweet boy Peter is the bartender," I say. Peter loves showing off that he's old enough to buy beer, and he doesn't mind the profit he makes by doing it either.

"That's me. I try to contribute to the kids in any way I can." He glances down to his blonde, who's now looking bored.

Drea hands Peter five dollars. He slips it into his pocket, then dips his arms into the ice chest and holds out two beers. "You're welcome."

Drea and I grab the cans and look past Peter. On the far side of the fire, we spot our friends. Omar gives a nod, and the two-headed love monster, Chase and Skye, wave us over. It's getting worse. Even their hands are synchronized.

Making our way to them, we say hi to a few kids we know. A cluster of Cranberry Hill girls are eyeing us, following our movements. Once they realize it's just Drea and me, they go back to chattering in a close circle.

It becomes quickly clear that the party's been going on for a while, by the amount of glazed eyes and slurred hellos we encounter. But when we join our own circle of friends, Skye informs us we haven't missed much, and our typical banter begins. Summer plans, Lala's absence from the party, and a friendly argument between Omar and Chase about who will end up as valedictorian dominates most of our conversation until our attention is drawn to the right of us, where a sophomore stumbles to remain standing, a constant flow shooting from his zipper.

"At least he's aimed for the trees. Kind of." The fire warms my left side, leaving the other exposed to the cool night air. I pull my hoodie on.

Drea crinkles her nose. "He must be really wasted to piss in front of everyone."

"Not as wasted as she is." One of the girls from ASB sits on the ground, laughing each time she fails to stand up.

"Classy," Omar comments, his thumbs pointing to the girl. "What a mess."

"I'll tell you what's a mess." Peeing Sophomore staggers over, his words thick. "There's a dead squirrel. Over there." He points toward the sky, then the bonfire, then the ground. "It's gross."

"What did it die from?" Drea asks. "Your piss?"

I pinch my nose and swallow hard. His damp left pant leg is dangerously close to me.

"I'm gonna get another beer," he says, heading first toward, then away from the leaping flames.

"Better call your dad, Clare," Omar teases.

"How high is a dead squirrel on his priority list? If we call it in tonight, what time of day will he come to pick it up tomorrow?" asks Chase, his blue eyes lit up. I smile. Here we go. The jokes about Dad never get old—not to my friends, not even to me.

"I smell a wager!" Omar raises his eyebrows. "Who's in? Five bucks says the pickup happens by noon tomorrow."

"Noon? No way." Skye shakes her head. "When we found a dead cat in our backyard at ten o'clock one night, he came right away to do it."

"You got the friends-and-family treatment," I reply wryly.

"Did he bring the giant spatula?" Chase scoops his fist in the air, pantomiming tossing a pancake and catching it.

"Catula!" Omar cracks up at his own joke. "Your mom doesn't use the Catula in the kitchen, does she?"

"Only when you come over," I manage to say through my laugh.

"Let's call it in." Skye pulls her cell phone from her jeans pocket; her almond-shaped eyes disappear as she smiles mischievously.

"Don't." I give her a look. "My dad might come right now to get it."

"And then he'll start hanging out all buddy-buddy with us," Drea adds.

"And share his corpse-cleanup stories," Omar says, reverently lowering his ball cap to his heart.

"To my dad," I say, raising my beer can, "keeping Sovereign Forest clean, one dead animal at a time!"

"Hear, hear!" Chase and Omar shout.

Skye puts away her phone. "Okay. I won't call now. But I promise, I'm calling when I leave."

"Five bucks says the pickup happens between ten and

eleven a.m.," Chase says, pulling his wallet from his Manchester United sweatshirt.

"I'll put five in for three p.m."

I turn my head, although I already know the voice belongs to Ryan. His usually messy hair is mostly hidden by a beanie tonight, making his hazel eyes stand out even more. Surprisingly, Mandy isn't hanging on him, boa constrictor style. I look around, expecting to see her close behind, but she's nowhere to be seen. It makes me relax a little. When Mandy and I cross paths, she usually does her best to make Skeleton appear.

"Nice, Ryan!" Chase takes the cash as Omar adds Ryan's name to the list of bets he's typing into his cell phone. "Who else wants in?"

As Chase and Omar collect money from our friends, I shake my head and take another sip. Beer's almost done, but I keep the can anyway, like a security blanket. It's the perfect way to avoid being asked "Where's your drink?" which almost always leads to another full beer landing in my hand. I don't want to be the stupid one, like the girl who couldn't stand up—now puking in the bushes—or the sophomore socializing with a pee-soaked pant leg. Besides, it's almost impossible to sneak back in intoxicated. I learned that from Peter. One morning my freshman year, when I was leaving for school, I found him sleeping with his back pressed against the house. He told me he couldn't find the keyhole because it kept moving. So he'd slept outside. His hands were like ice blocks. I dragged him inside, insisting that he take a shower before Mom woke up and wondered if we had opened our own brewery. I got the water running hot before I left.

Mom caught him right before he made it into the bathroom. She didn't care that he'd been out all night, but she was furious he was drunk. He was stuck painting the house every weekend for a whole month.

That was two years ago. I look over toward Peter. He's making out with the blonde, one hand up her shirt. I think I might throw up, no beer necessary.

"Need a refill?" Ryan asks, suddenly standing right next to me.

"Nope. I'm good." I hold up my can. He smiles and leans against the nearest tree trunk. Settling in. Getting comfortable. Looking at me. I'm suddenly hyperaware of my appearance. Is anything stuck in my teeth? Did my ridiculously long and random eyebrow hair grow since I trimmed it two nights ago? Why didn't I think of these things when I was getting ready?

"Having fun?" he asks. It's not like it's the first time he's talked to me. Ryan floats from one group of friends to the next, unaware or uncaring of the invisible but present hierarchy of popularity. But this is the first conversation that I've ever had with Ryan alone.

"Yep." Ugh. Can't I think of anything to say other than "nope" and "yep"?

"Tonight's pretty chill, but tomorrow night's going to be crazy. You gonna be there?"

"Yep." Shit. There I go again. Quick. Make conversation. "So. Big plans for the summer?"

"Yeah. I'm going down to Baja to surf Seven Sisters

with some buddies of mine from Venice. I can't wait. I hate living away from the ocean."

"That's sounds really amazing. Have a good time." Have a good time? *Have a good time?* Of course he's going to have a good time. Why did I say that? Why can't I think of something more original? Think. Normal conversation. "I love the ocean. I love swimming." I sound like a stupid robot: "I love. I love." Say something that doesn't start that way. "One day I'll want to go scuba diving. I'm even thinking of majoring in marine biology."

"Do you surf?" He puts his drink down and stretches his hands toward the fire. It's a little too far away to really feel the heat. He steps forward, and I follow.

"No. I mean, I'm pretty bad in sports. But I snowboard. Kind of. I'm not great, but I can link turns and get down the mountain." Good job, Clare. You almost said a sentence in there.

"We should ride together next winter. Do you ever go backcountry?"

I laugh. "No. And I don't think I want to. You're on a crazy different level from me."

"So, what are you doing this summer?" he says, letting himself slip to the ground to sit down. I lower myself to the dirt patch next to him, fidgeting with the tab on my beer can. I wish I had something as interesting as a surf trip to Mexico to talk about.

"The same old stuff. Just going to be here around town. Lifeguarding at the lake. Again. Filling out college and scholarship applications and preparing for the next AP tests." Is it too nerdy that I just confessed to studying over the summer? Smart can be sexy. To some guys. I think. I hope.

"That's cool. I don't know if I'm going to do the college thing. I haven't figured that out yet." Ryan shakes his head. "I'd like to just travel. You know? Everyone is in a rush to start working. By the time you retire, you're old. Why not do the stuff you want to do right out of high school and save the career for later?"

"I guess I never thought of it that way," I say. I'm having a vision of what that would be like. Hopping on a plane, maybe even with Ryan, landing somewhere beautiful and taking the time to just explore. Not caring about which college is going to get me the best job, the best paycheck. It's a fantasy. But I sit with it for a moment and try to believe it's possible.

"There has to be a way to make it happen, right?" His tone has changed, evidence that he knows reality will trump his idea. Avoiding my eyes, he grabs a long stick and puts the tip of it into the edge of the fire. It smokes for a second, then lights.

"You'd think somehow." I pause and try to come up with something witty, something to make him laugh. When nothing surfaces, I go with practical. "Are you good enough to go pro?"

"Nah." He pulls the stick out of the fire, watching the flame slowly work its way toward his hand.

"You could open a surf shop," I suggest, shoving my hands into my pockets.

"But then I'd have to do math." As the flame grows, Ryan gives up and throws it into the bonfire. We sit for a second in silence, before my brain finds the right thing to say.

"Then I see only one option for you. You can travel the world. Get paid to do it. And you will get to wear an awesome outfit every day." I lift my lips into a teasing smile. "Flight attendant."

He laughs. "Can't I at least be a pilot?"

"Sure. But you might have to do math."

"I'll get to wear the swanky hat, right? It's a good trade," he says, laughing again. This is fantastic. *This* is what I needed tonight. Ryan shrugs, then adds, "Maybe it's a good idea. My dad is always telling me that I need to start thinking of my 'life plan.'" He puts his fingers up as quotes. "I don't know. I guess I don't want to choose the wrong thing. Why are you thinking marine biology?"

"The ocean is . . . incredible. Fascinating. Mysterious. I'd love to explore it. And I like all the crazy creatures. But. It's not like I know that's what I want to do for sure. It just feels like it might be a good idea."

"With your grades, you can do anything. That's pretty rad. To have all your options open." I watch as Ryan grabs another long stick to put into the fire. I've always thought of him as so happy, so relaxed. It's strange to think that he's as unsure about what to do as the rest of us. Maybe even more because school isn't his thing. Then it hits me—Ryan knows I have good grades, which means he's at least aware of me. I'm about to say something else, when my cell phone vibrates in my pocket. My reminder alarm. It's time to leave so I can sneak back in before my parents wake up.

Drea's standing next to Omar. It looks like Chase and Skye are already gone. Even the bonfire has shrunk.

"It was great talking to you," I say to Ryan. "But I've got to go."

"Yeah," he agrees, "it looks like the party's over. See you around, Clare."

"Good night."

I join Drea. As we walk away from the fire, a chilled breeze creeps through my sweatshirt. The full moon has set. Even the trees nearest the dirt road blend to a menacing black. We automatically quicken our pace without saying a word to each other.

In less than fifteen minutes my night out is over.

Drea drops me off at my regular spot a few doors down. I walk hastily to my house, slide my key in, open the door, fight with the key to get it back out of the lock. Try to close the door quietly, grimace at the loud click the latch makes as it shuts. Tiptoeing down the hall to my bedroom, I accidently hit a squeaky floorboard on my way. Damn.

Gently I turn my doorknob and push the door open. Carefully close it. Turn on my desk lamp. And scream.

My mom sits on my bed, tightly wrapped in her robe. Her thin arms are crossed against her chest.

"Are you trying to wake the whole house, Clare?"

"You scared me," I whisper.

"Not as much as you scared me." She stands up.

I keep my eyes down, away from her glare. I see her slippers have worn through; one of her toes is peeking out the end. I'll have to remember at Christmas that she needs new ones.

"Sneaking in at three o'clock in the morning. After you told me that you were not going to the party tonight because you were too tired. I believed your lie." My mother stands up and puts her finger under my chin, pressing hard on the bone. Raising my head. With her other hand she shakes the note. "Then this: 'I couldn't sleep, so I went for a walk.' Did you really think I would fall for that? I was a teenager once too. I'm not stupid."

"Sorry," I whisper, looking into her eyes, red and swollen from the early hour.

"Young lady"—Mom grabs my arm tight, pulling me in—"do I smell beer? You've been drinking, too?"

"I had one. Just one."

"Liar." Mom leans in close to my face, her sharp nose practically touching mine, her night breath melting my skin. "Sneaking out. Drinking. Lying. What's next, Clare?"

Skeleton makes his entrance, twirling through the doorway, dramatically tossing his hat to the hook on the wall. He sits on my desk to watch the show.

I tell my eyes to stop watering. I swallow hard and look to my fish tank. Angelfish gracefully weave through the pearl grass.

Think fish. Think swimming underwater, bubbles and bright colors. I exhale, imagining the air escaping my mouth and floating to the surface.

"You're grounded. For a month. No car. No phone. No computer. No TV. No friends." Mom holds her hand out. "Give me your car keys and your cell phone." Skeleton shakes his finger. *Shame, shame.*

"What about school tomorrow? I need to drive to school." My keys dangle in the air, suspended by two fingers over Mom's cupped-hand fire pit.

"Fine. But you'll be grounded for the whole summer if you don't come home immediately after."

"I have to work at graduation. Junior honor guard. Remember?"

"Graduation ends at nine thirty. I expect you home by ten p.m. sharp. Not one minute late." Mom and her holey slipper are at the door. "Did you hear me, young lady? Not one minute late."

"Yes, Mom."

I pull on my pajamas and sink into bed.

A month! She's never grounded me for that long before. And it's the first month of summer! I'll miss the party tomorrow night. Miss the opportunity to see Ryan again.

But as I try to go to sleep, it's not the thought of being grounded that keeps me awake—it's my mother's words and everything they imply: "Sneaking out. Drinking. Lying. What's next, Clare?"

Chapter 6:
Why?

THEN: Age Seven

"Why is Luke in jail, Mommy?" I raced in the front door. I'd been waiting almost all day to ask her.

"Who said he's in jail?" Mom stood up from the couch and helped me take my backpack off.

"Mandy Jordan. She told everyone at recess that her mom says Luke is in jail because he's a bad guy." I bit my lip. "She said he doesn't even deserve bread and water."

"You shouldn't listen to what other people say," Mom said.

"I thought that he was visiting Granny. But some other kids said it's true. That he's in jail. And jail is where they put the bad people. Why is he in jail? Is Luke bad?" I bit harder.

Mom gave me a long look. "He was in the wrong place at the wrong time," she said, pulling me into her lap.

"So he's not at Granny's?" I started to cry. "What did he do?"

"I told you. He was in the wrong place at the wrong time." She grabbed a tissue and wiped the tears off my cheeks.

"When can he come home?" I asked.

"He'll be back by Easter," she said. Easter! That was almost a whole year away! Before I could say anything else, Mom asked, "What do you have for homework?"

"A spelling worksheet, and some math, I think," I said.

"Well, you'd better get started." She steered me toward the kitchen table.

I had more questions, but I knew Mom didn't want to talk anymore.

At least I had an answer. Something to say when Mandy started picking on me again. "Mandy, Luke was in the wrong place at the wrong time. That doesn't mean he did anything bad."

It felt good, to have that answer. For a little while. But then I started thinking more about it. Luke was in the wrong place at the wrong time. Someone can go to jail for that? Does that mean he wasn't supposed to be in jail and someone else was? Did he do something bad by accident? And what about me? What if I was in the wrong place at the wrong time?

Then—everywhere I went—I thought, Could it happen to me? At school: Will I have to go to the principal's office if the person next to me cheats, because I am in the wrong place? In the grocery store: If someone steals something while I am here, will I go to jail because I am in the store at the wrong time?

I was afraid to say anything to Mom or Dad about it. I could tell Mom didn't like talking about it, and I didn't want to make her sad. Or mad. If I asked the wrong question at the wrong time, I'd be stuck grounded or have to do more chores. So I kept my lips tightly shut, the fear of going to jail—even though I'd done nothing wrong—filling my mind and growing, growing, growing.

Chapter 7:

The Costumes We Wear

NOW

"This frickin' thing's made for a girl," Omar says. "Guess you'll have to wear it."

"Nice try. You're the one who volunteered for this." I yank on the zipper, trying to pull it past Omar's wide shoulders, moving it about a centimeter. "Hmmm. Looks like you're stuck. Literally. Zipper's not moving. Up or down."

"Promise me you'll cut me out of this the second graduation is over." Omar shakes his fist to the sky as dramatically as he can. "I can't live life as Stanley the Squirrel."

"Um, sure," I say, concentrating on getting him *into* the costume. "On three, you suck in." Pulling the matted fake fur together with one hand, I grip the zipper with the other.

"Ready? One, Two, Three." Yank. Zip. He's in. I pull the extra-extra-extra-large gown over his huge, furry arms, slip the paws onto his hands, and pop Stanley's head over Omar's own. "Great. You're all ready."

"Aren't you forgetting something important?" Omar sounds like he's in the bottom of a well.

"Oh, right, the cap. Voilà!"

I guide Omar out of the storage closet, and we fall into formation with the eight other junior honor guard members—bridesmaids of the senior class. The seniors are giggling and singing songs, a cloud of alcohol and weed cologne following them.

Graduation is as boring as cleaning the kitchen floor with a toothbrush. Unless you're the person graduating. I'm not. I'm the idiot in the middle of the field, holding the Fighting Squirrels' purple and teal flag, on two hours of sleep. To keep from fainting from exhaustion, I practically lean on the flagpole, wondering if I look like a polar bear in my billowing white gown.

Know what I need? Something dramatic. Someone streaking through the ceremony, a pack of wild wolves carrying the principal away, a gigantic earthquake swallowing the field whole. But my only entertainment at this bore-fest is Omar's overly dramatic mimed congratulations to each grad.

Only a hundred and one more diplomas to go.

After the ceremony, grads are hugging and grinning, arms around necks and waists as flashes spark and cameras click. Aunts and uncles, grandparents, parents, godparents, brothers, sisters, cousins, nieces, nephews, neighbors, all gathered to wish them well.

"We're so proud."

"Way to go!"

"You made it!"

Everything they say is so predictable.

One more year, that will be me. Thinking about it makes me feel jittery. Life after graduation, life as an adult, life without my parents' rules. What will *that* be like? Of course, thinking about the actual graduation is enough to make my stomach eat itself. Mom will have rules, probably more than usual on that day. Peter will most likely be drunk and hitting on my friends. Then there's Dad, talking about dead animals as casually as most people talk about the weather. On second thought, maybe I won't go. But then I remember Luke. Luke will defuse Dad's weird comments with a joke and convince Mom to drop a few rules, just for the day. Luke will be there. He will. It'll be my *graduation*. Of course he'll be there.

Skeleton taps me on the shoulder, reminding me that he, also, will be there for the joyous event.

Maybe when I'm done with high school, when I move away to college, maybe then Skeleton will finally leave me alone. For now I ignore him, walking toward my car and away from the scene.

"Clare. Wait!" Omar the squirrel runs after me, his shouts muffled by the massive stuffed head. "You promised to get me out of this thing!"

I rush over, grab the zipper, and with one yank, free him from the costume, saying, "Okay, bye. See you later."

"That was fast," Omar remarks as he pulls off his head. "Wait, you're not seriously going home?"

"I am seriously grounded, and will be for the rest of my life if I'm late. Have fun for me tonight." I turn and run for my car, hearing Omar yell "See ya later" after me.

. . .

Home five minutes early. The house is quiet.

"I'm here," I announce to the living room, glancing in to see Dad sitting on the couch watching TV and Mom with her glass ball ornament in one hand, her polishing rag in the other. A spot in my chest tightens. Again? She just cleaned them last night. What set her off this time? Maybe Peter just smudged them up this morning to mess with her. I hope.

"How was graduation?" Mom asks in a calm, even tone. She cradles the ball in the nest of one gloved hand. Bringing it up to the light, she slowly turns it, the metal hanger between a pinched thumb and forefinger, the nest less than an inch below. A safety net. She squints and pulls it in closer for inspection. Shines a spot. Holds it back out toward the light. One more turn. Satisfied, she returns it to the bottom of the metal Christmas tree hanger to join the other four. Good God, I hope my friends never walk into my house when she's doing this.

"Fine," I answer, walking quickly to my bedroom. I don't want to deal with her or Dad. I just want to go to sleep.

I hear her voice as my bedroom door shuts. "Don't forget to leave your car keys on my desk tonight. Don't forget you're grounded." Like I could.

Too bad Mom doesn't allow locks on any of the doors inside the house. I'd love to turn one to make sure my stupid family leaves me alone tonight.

I drop my backpack and grab my fish food. Taking the biggest flake of food out of the container, I pinch it between my fingers. As soon as my fingertips come near the water, Brutus rushes to the surface. He nibbles from the flake before the rest even realize it's feeding time. I sprinkle in more food. As I watch the angels eat, my brain flips back to thinking about graduation. And college. I worry about the money side of it the most. My high school counselors say I have really great SAT scores, good grades, decent participation in extracurricular activities, fours on the two AP tests I already took. Any college would want me. I wish I could convince my parents to consider that: ANY college would want me.

Feeling dejected, I put the cap back on the fish food and sink into bed. Something rustles.

Mail. Probably a brochure from a college. I roll over and grab it. A letter? Only one person I know writes letters. Luke!

Dear Squeaks,

How's my favorite sister? Your last letter was hilarious! I don't laugh much here, so I read it over about 50 times. Thanks for that.

I've been looking at the pictures you sent of your new fish. Without knowing their personalities, naming them was tricky, but they look like a Raymond and a Sushi to me. That's right. Sushi. Don't complain—you asked for it!

Congrats on the SAT scores. Wow, Clare. I'm really proud of you.

I've been taking welding classes here, so I might be able to get a good job when I'm done. Keep your fingers crossed for me, okay?

I can't wait to see you. My parole review is coming up, so I could be home in less than a month. I'll call and let you know.

I miss you and love you lots,
Luke

The parole review must have been yesterday—that would be the reason for the phone call. Obviously it went well, since he's getting out early. I just wish he were coming home immediately.

I read the letter over again, trying to imagine him writing it. But it's hard—he hasn't given me many details. I don't know what his cell is like or who he shares it with or how much time he has to spend there each day. It's good to hear he's taking classes—not all the prisons he's been in offer that type of program.

This letter is full of mostly good things, like most of his letters. Concentrating on the positive things he has going for him, writing more about me and what's going on at home than what he's going through being there. I know it has to be hard, and even though he doesn't say it outright, I can feel how lonely he is when I read the line "I don't laugh much here."

I pick up the box on my desk. Run my hands along the edges, sanded smooth and stained dark, the seams perfectly aligned.

It was the last gift given to me on my eighth birthday.

I opened it after all the guests had left and the balloons were drooping. Luke said the box was for my treasures. His fingertips, still stained the color of the wood, ran over the rounded edges, curved corners.

I held the lock tight. It could protect my treasures. Even from Peter? Yes, even from Peter.

Sawdust and stain fumes clung to Luke's shirt. I can still smell them faintly when I now press my nose to the inside of the lid.

Thirteen years of my relationship with my brother live inside the box, most of it in prison-approved pre-stamped envelopes. Letters worn thin, the pencil marks faded and rubbed into the paper, my finger oils as much a part of the letters as Luke's words.

I must have written him hundreds of times, beginning in first grade when my little hands wrote short, misspelled words in fractured sentences, missing punctuation and capitalization. Luke has sent *me* exactly thirty-eight letters, including this one, and Christmas and birthday cards. Each kept in its original envelope. The earliest praised me for my good marks in school, said how proud he was that the teacher thought I was good at paying attention.

I pull out one from the first grade. *Wow, little Squeakers, you are growing so fast! I wish I were home to see you in the school play. I've shown everyone the photo of you as the snowflake. My friends agree that I have the cutest little sister. Don't grow too much more before I can see you again.* This letter is especially worn. I was cute. Luke and his friends said so.

Shifting through the pile, I don't have to open the

envelopes to know what he has written in most of them, but the desire to read them sidetracks my need for rest.

One more. I'll read one more, then go to sleep. I blindly grab a letter and open it. *I bet the applesauce tasted even better since you helped with it! Eat an apple for me, Squeakers. And take good care of our tree so I can have lots next year.* I swallow, remembering how Mom had to explain to me that we couldn't just mail an apple to Luke. How, to make me feel better, she took pictures of us picking apples to send to him instead. But he'll be home this year when the apples are ripe.

I add my new letter to the box, carefully close and lock it.

As I lie down to sleep, a vision of Luke walking through the front door appears behind my closed eyes. I miss him so bad, my heart actually aches.

But then there's the other side of his return, the whispers—*prison, prison, prison, shame, shame, shame*—the glowering looks. No wonder Luke doesn't plan to come home immediately. It dawns on me: It's better for him to go where he has a blank slate. Where people can get to know him like I know him. A place where the present overrides the past. And real second chances exist.

Push all of it *out* of my mind. Too tired to think anymore about it tonight.

Chapter 8:

Blue Circles

THEN: Age Seven

I overheard Mom tell Dad that Luke was getting out of prison on March 23. I circled the date on my calendar, circled it in bright blue, sky blue, the happiest color I could find.

Writing Luke a letter, I listed all the things we would do as soon as he came home. I wanted to play in the park and show him how high I could swing. I wanted to teach him charades because we'd just learned it in class. I wanted to help Mom make his favorite meal: beef Stroganoff and peach pie.

March 23, March 23, circled in blue.

March 23 came. March 23 ended, at midnight, with me awake in my bed, waiting for him to come home.

March 24 started, at midnight, and eventually I fell asleep, waiting for Luke to come home.

On March 24 Mom told me that Luke was probably visiting with friends and that he'd be home soon.

On March 25 I wondered why Luke's friends were more important than me, and I cried when I had to go to bed.

On March 26 I threw my stuffed animals at my

calendar and scribbled over March 23 in black, black ink.

On March 27 I sat next to the door, looking at Mom's clock on her desk. When the little hand hit five, Luke would be home. When the little hand hit six, Luke would be home.

On March 28 I was scared that they hadn't let Luke out of prison, or that he had been hurt, like hit by a car. Maybe we should call all the hospitals between the prison and here. Maybe we should call the prison to make sure he left.

On March 29 I gave up.

On March 30 he came home. He didn't know why I crossed my arms and turned around when he appeared.

He asked, "Why is Squeakers mad at me?"

I cried. He hadn't come home right away. He didn't know why I was mad at him.

He pulled me onto his lap and said, "Do you know why I call you Squeakers? No, huh. You were too little to remember, right? Well, when Ma brought you back from the hospital, right after you were born, you took one look at me and squeaked. Like you were saying hello. And I said 'Clare' was too serious a name for cute little you, and you know what you did? You squeaked at me again, like you were agreeing. Still mad, Squeaks?"

"Why didn't you come home on March twenty-third?"

"I had some stuff to take care of, and I don't have a car, so I had to hitchhike."

"Hitchhike?"

"You ever see the people walking down the street with

their thumbs up? They're looking for a ride somewhere."

"Mom says not to pick them up. Mom says those
people are dangerous."

"Maybe some, but is your brother Luke dangerous?"

Laughter. Luke, dangerous? That was a silly idea.

"No, not me. I just need a ride, that's it. And someone was nice and they picked me up and brought me to
you. It took a few extra days. That's all. I'm here now.
So why don't you teach me how to play this charades
game you wrote me about."

Like always, and like magic, Luke made me feel
better. Special. Smart and funny and cute. I drew a big,
bright blue circle, sky blue, the happiest color I could
find, around March 30.

And hoped this time he would be home for good.

Chapter 9:
Half-Safe

NOW

"Crap!" I forgot to set my alarm! I jump out of bed—pee, brush teeth, flick waterproof mascara on, pull hair into a ponytail. Throw on my bathing suit, deodorant, a pair of shorts and a tank top. Grab my work bag, sunscreen, and a towel. I look at my watch. Thirteen minutes. Not bad. I see my car keys on my dresser. Really? I forgot to leave them on Mom's desk last night. But . . . I'd rather be grounded for an extra day than be late for work. I snatch the keys and run out the door.

In my car. Turn the key. Nothing. Turn it again. Still nothing. The battery must be dead.

"Crap!" I shout again and scramble out of the car. Stupid thing is *always* breaking down. Maybe because it's a million years old and I bought it for six hundred bucks.

"Why today?" I growl, sliding my fingers under the edge of the hood to find the latch. It opens with a groan. I stare down in shock.

The battery isn't dead; it's gone.

"Good morning, sunshine." Dad appears, sipping coffee, a suspiciously greasy hand cradling his mug. "Is something the matter?"

Like he doesn't know.

"My battery," I say, pointing to the abyss, "seems to be missing."

He grins even wider. "That can't be. Let me see." He cranks his neck to the side, pretending to take a long look under the hood. "Well, look at that. It does appear that your battery is gone."

"You wouldn't happen to have had anything to do with this?" I ask through gritted teeth.

"Maybe this wouldn't have happened if you'd left your keys on Mom's desk last night," he says, shrugging.

"DAD! This is so unfair. I have to go to work. I'm going to be late!"

He laughs. I'm crazy angry, and he's laughing.

"You think it's *funny*? BEFORE you pulled my battery out of my car, did you think for one moment that I might be fired for being late?"

"Is Clare Bear getting upset?" Dad laughs harder. "Come on. It's funny. Admit it!"

"It's not funny, Dad." And don't call me "Clare Bear"; you know I hate that. Now my stupid eyes start to water. Don't cry. I slump to the ground. "How am I supposed to get to work on time?"

"Ride your bike."

"My bike?" He wants me to ride my bike? It's probably a black widow nest by now. I haven't ridden that thing in years.

"Yes, your bike. You know, Old Faithful or Superbike or . . . what was it that you used to call it?" Dad gulps his coffee like a camel.

Bike-a-saurus Hex. My parents bought it way too big for me. And they chose green. Chunky-vomit green. It was a curse to have to ride it.

"Bike-bye? Bike, Bike? Motor-bikel?" Keep guessing, Dad. Keep pretending like you don't remember.

"Tell you what, Clare Bear," Dad says as he slams my hood shut. "I was just on my way to work. I'll give you a ride." He puts his coffee mug down on the edge of the driveway. "And tomorrow you can leave with enough time to take . . . Bike-a-saurus."

His eyebrows jump up and down. I don't smile.

"Clare." Dad gallantly opens the passenger door of his truck for me. Saunters to the driver's side. Pulls his work jumpsuit from the back and whistles as he steps into it. He always looks more like he's wearing a costume than a uniform. I used to tell everyone at school he was a superhero. Mandy Jordan was the one who broke the news to me that Dad picked up dead animals for a living. It would have been so much easier if my parents had just told me that instead of letting me be publicly humiliated by my archenemy.

"Dad, I'm going to be late." I tap my watch, irritated.

"Okay, okay." He jumps in and shuts his door. "All buckled in?"

"Yes. Can we go now? Please?" After clicking his seat belt, he backs out of the driveway.

Finally.

Barely two blocks down he slams on the brakes, coming to a stop next to a raccoon roadkill. "Look at that!" Dad fishes at my feet for something. Grabs his clipboard and scans it. "Not even called in yet."

"Can you pick it up after you drop me off at work?" I plead.

He taps his pen on the clipboard.

"Well . . . I guess." And mercifully he steps on the gas. "Do me a favor, Clare Bear," he says, handing me the pen. "Write up the address and put 'roadkill' in the second column." His clipboard falls onto my lap. Gross. No telling how many times he has touched this after handling a dead animal. I hold the pen at the very tip.

"Speaking of dead animals," he says, staring ahead, "yesterday I picked up a dead squirrel at the campgrounds past Lookout Ridge."

"Big surprise," I say, trying to keep my voice light. "You pick up a hundred a day."

"Not up in the campgrounds. No. Plus, this one was called in. Called in the middle of the night. The voice sounded a little familiar too."

"Hmm," I say, trying to sound indifferent. "Every voice sounds familiar to you. We live in a town with population nothing." Dad's clipboard is still on my lap. The bet. I glance down. *Lookout Campground Squirrel pickup: 10:14 a.m.*

"Yeah. I guess I know everyone around here. Especially your friends." Get to the point, Dad. "When I picked it up, I was pretty surprised to see a lot of trash up there. Looks like someone had a pretty good party: beer cans, cigarette butts, tiny empty baggies. Wouldn't happen to be the same party you were at the other night?"

Silent. Frozen. I know what the deer in headlights thinks right before getting hit: Something bad is going to happen, and I can't do anything to stop it.

Dad brings the truck to a stop just outside the gated entrance to the lake. "Tell you what, Clare. As part of your punishment for sneaking out, you'll be picking up the trash at that campsite after work today. You do that, and we won't have to tell the ranger, or the sheriff, where your secret party spot is. Okay?"

I don't have time to argue. It wouldn't change anything anyway. I grab my bag. And slam his piece-of-shit-truck door as hard as I can.

While running for the lifeguard post, I imagine Dad's truck falling apart as the door slams, leaving him sitting on the seat, holding the steering wheel, attached to nothing. A confused frown across his face. Cartoon style.

I glance down at my watch. Breathe a sigh of relief. I'm perfectly on time.

"Clare. Late on the first day? It is eight thirty-five and you are supposed to be here at eight thirty sharp." Lucille Jordan's plastic face tries to smile. Why does Mandy's mom have to be my boss? I'm surprised Lucille even allowed them to hire me. She swirls the cup in her hand and takes a small sip out of the straw before continuing. "I hope this isn't going to be a habit of yours."

"Sorry. My watch says I'm on time. I'll set it five—no, ten—minutes back."

"Why don't you do that," she says, sarcasm lacing her voice.

I rush through my morning duties, concentrating

on checking the safety equipment instead of wallowing in how crappy my day has been already.

Before my butt hits the chair on the too-short life-guard stand, a dozen kids jump into the water with elated screams.

The lake's kinda gross, but it's the only body of water in our dumpy town bigger than a bathtub. Fed by snow runoff and a natural spring, it was originally a huge mud hole that fed into a large stream. Then someone thought it was a good idea to define two sides of the lake with a concrete slab. They dug out the mud hole, and the stream shrunk to a brook as the lake filled. They planted grass. Great mountains of sand were brought in to create a beach on the shallow side. Tractors groomed the beach until it was smooth and flawless.

And then, what did they do?

They left the last side natural: the swamp. A place where the mud is so thick, it grabs your feet and pulls you in to your knees. Tall weeds tangle to the surface. Sharp reeds grow wild, sticking out of the muck that seeps into the woods, where rattlesnakes live and poison oak grows.

Half-man-made, half-natural. Half-safe.

Splashing and screams on the shallow side of the rope turn my head. Mandy's little brother, Chris, is jumping high into the air, using both hands to push a little girl's head underwater.

I feel the water going up her nose. The hands pushing on her head, moving with her as she tries to find a way back up. Hear his laughter.

I blow my whistle. Point at Chris: beckon him to me with a single finger. As he lets go a little red head pops out of the water, coughing and wheezing.

Chris wades to the side while I jump in to check on Redhead.

"Are you okay?" She lifts her arms. My hands lock under her armpits, and I pick her up, pull her out of the lake, and wrap her in my towel.

"Chris." I use my stern voice. "It's the first day. The whole summer isn't going to be like this, is it?" Damn it. I sound like Lucille Jordan.

"What? I wasn't doing anything wrong!" Chris throws his arms into an overexaggerated shrug. "We were just playing."

And *he* sounds like Peter.

"That's not playing, Chris. It's dangerous. She could drown. You get to sit with me for ten minutes."

"Hey," he protests, splashing his arms down angrily. "I'm supposed to get a warning first."

"You got all the warnings you needed last year. Ten-minute time-out for the first offense; fifteen for the second. And you're going home on the third."

"I'm telling my mom you didn't give me a warning," Chris says. "Hey, Mom!" he yells. Lucille Jordan chats with her friends, lounging under a huge blue sun hat, looking like something out of an expensive alcohol ad.

"Not now, honey. Mommy's busy," she shouts back.

"But Moooom."

"I said, not now."

Chris scowls at his mother. Defeated, he climbs out

of the water and sits on the edge of the lake, pulling his legs to his chest in perfect pout position.

"You sure you're okay?" I ask Redhead again.

"Yep." She hands me my towel and jumps back into the water. Soon she's singing and splashing and playing.

"Man, this stinks," Chris mumbles. I look at him. The real problem is that he's too old to be stuck in the shallow end. I remember exactly how that feels.

"Don't you want to be able to swim in the deep end this year?" I ask.

"Leave me alone."

"It's a really simple test. You could pass after taking some lessons."

"Shut up," he mutters.

"What was that?" I use my stern voice again.

"Nothing." Chris slumps forward and groans.

We sit in silence for a few minutes.

"Bet you didn't know that I couldn't even float until I was eleven years old."

Chris turns his blond head and stares. "You lie."

"It's true. And I didn't learn to swim until a year after that."

"And you're a lifeguard now? Yeah, right."

"Believe what you want." I pause. It would probably be pretty fun seeing him learn. "I can teach you."

"I don't need a stupid teacher."

"Fine." That's it for the talking. For the rest of the ten minutes, we stare at the lake.

• • •

Chris seems to be behaving after his time-out, so I go on autopilot. I'm taking in the sun and the splashes and the glimmering water. I've never been hypnotized, but I imagine it'd feel like this.

"Cllllllaaare." Drea's nose is almost touching mine. "Some kid's gonna drown on your watch. Where the hell were you at?"

"I was concentrating on the water." I look down at my watch. Noon. Already?

"Whatever, crazy. Listen, the party last night was awesome. Mandy puked, like, eight times, and still stumbled around for at least forty-five minutes thinking she was all hot. Vomit breath and chunks in her hair. Ryan eventually convinced her it was time to go home. But . . . once he got her all tucked in, he was back at the party."

"No Mandy?"

"Uh-huh." Drea grabs my whistle and blows it hard, yelling, "Hey. No dunking, jerk."

She spreads a towel and sits down next to my chair. Even though I'm grounded, at least I work at the summer hangout. That's going to save my sanity.

"Anyone else planning to show up today?" I ask, hoping she'll say Ryan. Without Mandy.

"Nah—not with all the drinking last night. But I think Chase, Skye, and Omar are going to come by tomorrow. And they're dying to know who won the bet. You get the squirrel pickup time?"

"Yep. Can you send a group text for me? Squirrel pickup time: ten fourteen a.m."

"Okay," Drea says. "Remind me—how much longer will I have to be your messenger?"

Peter appears. Sunglasses on and a soccer ball tucked under his toned arm.

"Twenty-nine more days," I answer Drea. Ignoring my brother. "And, on top of it, thanks to a certain phone call made to my dad, I'll be cleaning up the party from two nights ago."

"Bullshit!" Drea exclaims.

"I hope whoever wins gives me a tip for all the extra pain and misery I'm going through."

Drea's phone chimes. She reads her text, then says, "Hit Chase up. He won the bet."

"I think it's pretty funny." Peter tosses the ball into the air and starts juggling it from one knee to the other. "You know Dad's going to make you separate the trash from the recyclables. It's going to take you forever."

"Thanks for rubbing it in, jerk." I take my eyes off the lake to glare at him.

"Peter, you should get the brother-of-the-year award," Drea says, then adds, "Oh. Wait. No, my mistake. The asshole-of-the-year award. That's the one."

"So witty, Drea. You should be a comedian."

Drea's phone chimes again, breaking up their banter.

I turn to Peter and say, "You're right. This is going to take forever. Can you be a really nice big brother and come help me clean up this afternoon? Pretty please?"

"No way."

"Please? Come on, Peter. I need help." Peter is

impossible to predict. Sometimes he can be decent, even nice. Why not today?

"I'm not an idiot."

"Peter. Please?" One more shot. "Luke would. He'd help me in a second."

"Luke," Peter scoffs. "Luke's not here, and I'm not Luke." He kicks the ball high into the air, catches it, and tucks it under his right arm.

"I wish he were. At least he knows how to be a good, supportive brother."

"If Luke is your idea of a good, supportive brother, your brain is fucked." Peter slips his sunglasses on. "See ya, Clare." He walks away, dribbling the ball between his feet.

"Well, that was a dick thing to say," Drea says.

"Typical Peter," I reply. He was right about one thing. It is going to take me forever to clean the party mess up. "Any way I can convince my favorite friend in the whole wide world to come help?"

Drea sighs. Her brow knits up in a look of sympathy. For a second I'm afraid she'll say no.

"I'm sure I could think of a thousand reasons not to. But. Since I am your favorite friend in the whole wide world, I'll help. If we come across any used condoms, I'm not touching them, even if I'm wearing a toxic-waste cleanup suit. That's all you."

Chapter 10:
Filtered

THEN: Age Eight

"Hey, buttface." Peter was the first awake after me. I squirmed in my seat at the table as I crunched my Lucky Charms, wishing they'd put more marshmallows in the box.

"Quit calling me that." I never had a better comeback.

"Whatever you say, assmunch." Peter pulled back the curtain of the sliding glass door a little and peeked out. "WOOOOW!" he said, grabbing my chair and wiggling it. "Clare, you are NEVER going to believe it. It SNOWED last night."

"Snowed? Really?" I jumped up to run to the door. Then stopped.

"You can't trick me, Peter," I said. "It's summer. It can't snow in summer."

Peter piously placed his hands together. "It must be a miracle! I just saw a real miracle."

I raised an eyebrow and looked toward the door. In science we had learned that a snowstorm required temperatures of thirty-two degrees or lower. It was summer, but the house did feel chilly that morning. And at church they talked about miracles all the time. Mom and Dad would be so proud to have children who'd seen a miracle. Besides, I *wanted* it to snow in summer. Snow meant sledding, snow caves, jumping off the porch and landing waist deep.

"This is so COOL." Peter peered behind the curtain again, then looked at me. "Fine. If you don't believe me, look for yourself."

Looking seemed okay. Cautiously approaching, I expected Peter to drop a huge spider in my hair, or maybe trip me. I pulled back the curtain and scanned the yard, expecting to see white, sparkling white, everywhere.

SMACK! Peter knocked my face into the glass door.

"HAHAHAHA. You are so stupid. I can't believe you fell for that. Snow in summer. A miracle. What a dumbass!"

Sobbing, I ran to my room. Wiped my nose to check for blood, then crumpled onto my bed. I was so stupid. Why did I always fall for Peter's tricks?

I thought about going to Mom, crawling under the covers with her and crying, telling her how awful Peter was. But Mom did not like to be woken up. And the day before, when Peter had tripped me, Mom had snapped at him to leave me alone and had double-snapped at me for being a tattletale.

If Luke had been there, Peter wouldn't have tricked me. Because Luke would've been awake with me, eating cereal and asking about my plans for the day. If Peter called me a name, Luke would give him one look, and

Peter would mutter "Sorry" and leave the room. But I hadn't seen Luke for months. Right before Christmas he'd just disappeared. I'd gotten a letter from him on Valentine's Day asking me to be his pen pal. Even though he'd written that he loved and missed me, he still hadn't come home. Not even for Easter or the Fourth of July.

And he wasn't there to protect me from Peter when I needed him the most.

Chapter II:

Stagnant

NOW

It's sad to see the leftovers of a party. Only ashes remain in the bonfire pit. Marlboro butts and empty Coors cans lie with pine needles and pinecones. How did the forest survive our night?

"Okay, kiddos." Dad hands us each two bags and a pair of rubber gloves. "Trash in one bag, recyclables in the other. Go to work."

I snatch the bags from him, still pissed off, until I notice in amazement that my father is putting on gloves and bending to pick up a beer can. I thought this was *my* punishment.

"You're going to help?" I ask.

Dad nods.

"Thanks," I mutter. I'd expected him to sit in the truck and take a nap, or go hunting for more dead animals.

Drea works in circles around the fire pit while Dad stands in it, picking out charred cans. I follow a trail of trash to the outskirts of the clearing where two hiking paths meet.

"Man, this sucks," I say aloud, realizing the chore is bigger than I even imagined.

Squirrels chatter loudly as I step off the trail, pursuing the shiny aluminum deeper into the forest. Light trickles down through the trees, but where it doesn't, it's dark, making it feel later than my watch tells me it is. I reach the end of the can trail. The bonfire pit is pretty far away—I've wandered farther than I thought. Hairs on my arms stand on end. I hurry back to the path, noticing each chirp, snap, and rustle. Then I freeze. Someone is walking toward me from the other hiking trail. Tall. Male. Making big strides.

He's probably just a hiker. I'll walk toward the clearing, even if it means turning my back on him.

"Hi," he calls out before I have a chance to move.

"H—," I say nervously. I clear my throat and try again. "Hi."

"Nice day for a walk. . . . Hey, I know you." He steps forward. "You're Luke Tovin's little sister, right?" He smiles. "I'm an old buddy of his." Steps closer. How could he be one of Luke's friends? His face is lined in wrinkles and he's missing a tooth on the left side. His nose is raw, like mine looks after a day of snowboarding. He looks way too old to be a friend of Luke's.

I spy Skeleton out of the corner of my eye, peeking from behind a nearby tree trunk.

"Oh, yep. That's me," I say, silently willing the man to go away, to not get any closer. "I'd shake your hand, but . . ." I see him take in the trash bag in one hand, the glove on the other.

"You picking up the woods for a charity project or somethin'?"

"Something like that," I mutter. Step out to pass him. A wide step. Skeleton peers out from behind the tree again, bones trembling.

"Need any help?" The man bends down to pick up a can I missed. Gives it a little shake next to his ear. "Got to see if anything's left. Don't want good beer to go to waste."

Gross. He laughs. Looking up the trail, I see Dad bending and standing, picking, picking, picking, his back toward me.

"How is Luke, anyway?" the man says.

"Good. I'll be seeing him soon. I can tell him I ran into you." I step back. Skeleton grabs a branch, pulls himself up to the next, climbing fast. He stops at a high branch and looks down, a death grip on the tree trunk. Motions for me to start climbing.

"We used to party up here too, you know." He steps forward again. The empty beer can still in his hand. "You've grown up quite a bit since I last saw you." His eyes travel down my chest to my legs.

Definitely not one of Luke's good friends. Skeleton's bones are rattling, rattling. Too afraid to turn and run, I look up toward the clearing. I see Dad. He's so far away. But I have to try.

"If you know Luke, you must know my dad. I'm sure he'd want to say hi. HEY, DAD! OVER HERE!" I shout and wave, see my father look my way, his hand shading his eyes. He drops his bag and walks toward me, a speed walk that borders on a jog. Luke's friend takes a few steps back.

"Hi, sir. Name's Dan. I'm a friend of Luke's." He puts his hand out.

"I know who you are," Dad says, wrapping his arm around me instead of shaking Dan's hand—which drops, then travels to scratch his head.

"I was just helping your daughter out here." Dan drops the can into my trash bag.

Dad pulls me close.

"Luke out of the slammer?" Dan smiles wide. Dad clenches his jaw.

"Soon."

"Great. Tell him to come say hi when he's out." He pauses. When we don't say anything else, he adds, "Well, I'd better continue on my hike."

As Dad watches him stroll down the trail, he says, "I think it's clean enough here. Why don't you and Drea work with me around the bonfire."

His hand on my back steers me to the clearing. I want to thank him for coming to get me, but I don't say a word, and neither does Dad. It's better that way. Then neither one of us has to admit that maybe I was in danger, and neither one of us has to admit we've been in danger before. A memory starts to surface, starting with a vision of a broken window—but I quickly push it away.

After the clearing is clean, we drop Drea off at her house and return home.

Dad opens the back of the truck and drags out a medium-size box.

"Get the front door for me, will ya, Clare?" he asks.

"What's in the box?" I prop the door open with my leg as he struggles to bring it in and plops it on the coffee table.

"Fire safe," he says, slicing the top of the box open. I hold the packaging as he pulls the safe out. It's rectangular and small enough to just barely fit into my backpack. Dad unlocks the door with the key and stares inside. I'm impressed by how thick the walls of it are. It won't hold a lot. It seems like a waste of money. We really don't own much that is considered valuable.

Mom joins us just as I sink deep into the couch, enjoying how the soft cushion feels on my tired body.

"What are you going to put in here?" I ask.

"Valuables. Important papers," Dad says. "In case of fire," he adds.

Mom looks at the safe and then at me. Her lips thin out.

"You didn't make your bed this morning," she says to me. She's still pissed. It doesn't matter to her that I have no cell phone; no car; no rights to the TV, computer, or land line; or that my back is aching and I have the scent of stale cigarette butts and beer stuck in my nose from picking up trash for the past two hours. "Go make it now."

"Can't I relax for a second?" I can't hide the irritation in my voice.

"Idle hands," Mom says. My brain immediately completes the sentence: . . . are the devil's playground. Her favorite saying.

"But why do I have to make my bed? I'm going to sleep in it in a couple of hours."

"Don't argue with me, young lady."

I push off the couch and stomp to my room.

Forget that. I shower, eat dinner in silence, and go to bed, reveling in how messy it is. But that small victory is short-lived because I can't stop thinking about the guy in the woods—I try to lie on my stomach, then my side, then on my back. Stare forward. Keep eyes open, because when they close, I can see him, his disturbing eyes traveling over my body. I can see him with Luke. Stop. Don't think about the possibilities of what Luke could have done hanging out with a guy like that. My heart palpitates, my breathing thin at the top of my chest. I try to take some deeper breaths, push the air all the way down into my lungs. Keep my eyes open until they shut on their own.

Icy blue air. Grass soft between my toes. Moist. Our yard, usually dull and boring, with only dirt and a few tall trees, transformed with foxglove, hollyhock, lavender, roses. All open to the moon. I turn back toward the house. Warm glow in each window. Home. Outside, the flowers are too bright, the grass too soft, the greens too green. "Walk confidently," I whisper, but my legs and feet run, arms pump. In the door. Lock it.

The house feels wrong. Food on plates. No one to eat it. No one in the family room, the television blaring a bright cartoon, blankets crinkled on the couch, pillows haphazard. Washer swooshing. Dryer droning.

Bathtubs filled, steaming hot and ready. And my room. Everything in place.

I will be safe in my bed.

Jump in with both feet. No mattress, no pillows, no blankets.

Decaying bodies, dead but alive. Clammy hands seize my ankles.

Scream.

Leap out of the bed with strong legs that catapult me across the room. My body hits the floor. Hard.

My small blue night-light beacons to me, and I quickly crawl along. Using the doorframe as a guide, I feel the wall until I find the light switch. Illumination.

No decaying bodies. No corpse hands. No icy blue air. Nothing but my room. Stagnant and dark as ever.

Just a nightmare, a nightmare. Not real, not real. I clench my hand to my chest, wishing in some way that I could smash my fingers through the skin and manually help my heart slow.

I need to be distracted. Stop, mind. Forget the nightmare. Stop and think of anything else. Anything. Like . . . the color of my walls.

Eggplant. I don't like the vegetable. I don't like the color. I prefer something lighter—something that wouldn't steal the sunshine even on the brightest days. Like sky blue or maybe buttery yellow or apple green. It would be nice to wake in the middle of a nightmare to a room painted in bright colors. The room was this color when it belonged to Luke, the same color as it had been when my parents had bought this house more than twenty years ago. It'll probably be the same when they die. I wish Mom would let me paint it, but she's got something against paint. Or maybe she has something against change in general.

The only thing that's not stagnant in the whole entire house is my fish tank. I flip on the light.

My one sucker fish is currently feasting on the NO FISHING sign. The angels are suspended, almost as if the light has frozen them in a moment of surprise.

After my goldfish died, I bought bala sharks. Which did great for a long time. Then, one by one, my bala sharks committed suicide by jumping out of the tank, drowning on the carpet.

I chose angelfish next, a school of four to prevent aggressive behavior, as advised by Luke, who, for a few months, was the fish expert at Tank Goodness. He loved that job. I wonder if they would even consider hiring him again.

As the angels adjust to the light, they begin to slowly move. I take my finger and put it up to the glass. Sushi instantly finds it, follows my finger as I move it up and down and across the front of the tank. The nightmare is feeling far enough away that I can start to think about reality.

Check through the sheets and blanket, look under the bed. It's safe. I sit down, pushing my legs under the covers, grabbing my knitting. The *clink, clink* of the needles and concentrating on counting stitches keeps out the nightmare that wants to replay in my mind. Drea's beanie is really looking nice. It's the first time

I've added beads to anything, and I'm happy to see it's coming out great.

When I feel like I can barely keep my eyes open, I put my knitting on my bedside table and lie down on my back.

Seventeen is way too old for nightmares and fears of the dark. I keep the lights on anyway.

Chapter 12:

All Hallows' Eve

THEN: Age Eight

"Are you really going to take us trick-or-treating?" I held as still as I could while Luke adjusted my crown. I couldn't believe he was home.

"Aye, Princess Squeakerrrrrs." Already in character with pirate eye patch on, Luke was going to make tonight more fun than most Halloweens. I couldn't remember the last time he'd been home in October.

"Have a good time," Mom called out, not looking up from some very serious work-type papers she was reading in front of the fire.

Luke's rough hand clamped onto my chin, moving my head from side to side, checking that my crown was on straight. Then we went out the door. Luke held his hook out to Peter, but he squirmed away, too old to hold hands, even on a dark All Hallows' Eve. Or maybe he was still mad that Mom wouldn't let him trick-or-treat with his friends so he was stuck with us.

At the first stop, Mrs. Brachett answered the door, saying, "A princess, how cute; and let's see here, a monster . . . and a pirate. . . . Luke Tovin . . . how appropriate," making Skeleton appear, jumping out from behind the bush next to me.

We grabbed apples off the trees that lined the streets, taking big bites of the free fruit as we walked from house to house, Luke and Peter competing to see who could hit the most stop signs with cores and bruised apples from the ground.

After getting treats from a dozen or so houses, we stopped in front of Mr. Kirkland's place. I raised an *Are we really doing this?* eyebrow at Luke. He grinned a pirate grin and rapped his hook against the door.

Mr. Kirkland swung the door open. "I suppose you kids are looking for a handout. Trick or treat. Humph. Here," he said, dropping apples into our bags. Apples?

"Argh. This here be no treat, me matie," Luke protested.

"Consider it a treat that I don't call the police and report you as trespassers." Mr. Kirkland slammed the door in our faces.

Once on the street Luke dropped his hook into his candy bag and grabbed Peter's arm.

"The name of the game is TRICK orrrrr treat. Free apples be no treat. This one deserves a trick," Luke continued in pirate slang. "Argh. A good pirate is always prepared." He pulled a six-pack carton of eggs from the bottom of his treat bag.

"Are you crazy?" Peter exclaimed through his monster mask. "Mr. Jerkland is still mad about the flowers you ran over with your friend's ATV."

"Argh. No man livin' or dead can prove that there

accusation." Luke walked behind a bush. "And me thinks you best follow, unless you want to be caught eggin' Ol' Jerkland's abode."

We scurried behind the bush. Luke wound up and took the first shot at the front door, centered, right next to the handle. *SPLAT!* He put an egg into the palm of both my hand and Peter's. Was it okay to do this?

"Come on, thar, Peterrrr, Squeakerrrrrrs," Luke said. "Do it not fer me but fer all yer maties gettin' free apples from the grumpiest ol' fart on the high seas."

Peter shrugged and nodded at me. I threw as hard as I could, and hit only the path. Peter wound his arm back. His throw smashed the egg against the window. Uh-oh.

"RUN!" Luke yelled, grabbing my hand. We dashed around trees, jumped over bushes, heard Mr. Kirkland open his front door and yell, "Goddamned rotten kids! Where are you? I'm calling the police. This is vandalism!"

We ran for two blocks before collapsing behind a fence, laughing.

"That was so cool," Peter said, ripping off his mask. "But, man, was Jerkland mad. Do you think he's actually going to report us to the police?"

"Nah. Even if he does," Luke reasoned, "they won't care. Besides, we're not gonna be the only ones who egg his place tonight. Nice arm, Peter. Just like your big brother, eh?"

I saw Peter's smile dip before he could pull his mask back on. Luke didn't notice. He was looking at me.

"Hey, Squeaks," Luke said, "that was a lot of fun, right?"

I nodded.

"Sometimes, when things are fun, grown-ups get mad and don't like it. You know, like when you play too loud in the house. So don't tell Ma or Pop, okay? We'll keep this between the three of us," Luke told me.

"Okay. Can we go get more candy now?"

"Sure thing," Luke said, helping me to my feet, then held out a hand that Peter ignored. Mask back on. Hook back on. Crown straightened. "We'll trick-or-treat our way to the gas station, and I'll get you guys some hot cocoa."

Bags full of loot, we arrived at Mountain Mini Mart. As the bell jingled our arrival, the cashier looked up.

"What do you want, Luke?" Her voice sounded angry. Why would she be mad?

"Just here to buy some hot chocolates for my kid sister and brother. And get a few items every pirate needs." He gestured at the liquor. "That's all."

Skeleton pointed at our bags, elbowed the cashier sharply in the ribs.

"Leave your bags at the front," she ordered. "And you"—she pointed at Peter, saying, "mask off."

Luke nodded, throwing his bag onto the counter, whispering "It's okay" into my ear. The cashier followed us, watching Luke's hands, my hands, Peter's hands. Keeping close, even when the bell rang to announce other customers. They had candy bags and masks on, but she didn't tell *them* to leave their stuff at the front and take their costumes off. Why was she being so unfair?

Skeleton strolled with us, knocking down some chips,

making it look like my skirt was to blame. I rushed to pick them up. The cashier's angry eyes looked from me to Luke to Peter, eventually glaring at Luke.

Peter helped me fill up my hot chocolate cup, while Luke grabbed a bottle of rum with a pirate on the front. We all met at the counter, where Luke paid for our drinks, bought some cigarettes, and we collected our candy loot. I was relieved when we exited.

"Why was she so rude?" I asked Luke, sipping my hot cocoa.

"Because"—he winked at me with his one showing eye—"she doesn't have a little sister nearly as cute as you."

I looked to Peter to give me an answer—a real answer—but he shook his head and stared at his flashlight's round beam on the ground. I stomped my feet out of frustration. But there were more houses, more candy. It was Halloween night; I couldn't be mad for long.

Chapter 13:

Balance

NOW

I stand with my toes curled over the edge of the diving board. Aside from the dark circles under my eyes, the only residue from the last nightmare is an occasional vision of the corpse hands wrapping around my feet. I shake it away.

It's quiet this early: no kids, no adults. The smooth surface of the water reflects the gnarled branches of the oak trees, the peaked tops of the spruces, the thin lines of the reeds, and a silhouette of me. It gives the illusion that I could dive into an alternate world, maybe one where I could live with Drea and her mother, where Ryan and I dated, Mandy didn't exist, where I never had nightmares, where Peter was always in a good mood, and Luke was Luke but . . . better.

One. Two. Three. My feet spring from the board. My hands, in a diamond over my head, cut through the air, then the lake's surface. Water so cold it's shocking sends my heart racing. I surface, brushing my stray hairs away from my eyes before going into a front crawl. Long, powerful strokes, my legs kicking behind me, propelling me forward. I wish my school had a swim team. I'd love to compete. Maybe I'd even be good at it.

Before I know it, the water is getting thicker. I'm almost to the swamp. I dive down and flip, doing a double underwater pull before my lungs force me to surface. Then it's back to the crawl. My body is already warmer and the sun on my back feels incredible.

I switch to breaststroke for the second lap. Halfway through I'm feeling tired. This lap will be it. I turn back toward the diving board and freeze.

Someone else is in the lake. Someone on . . . a surf-board? On the lake?

I swim closer for a better look.

It's Ryan, belly-down on a huge board, zipped into a skintight wetsuit. He pops up from his stomach onto his knees.

"Clare?" he asks. "Is that you?"

Treading water, I greet him, "Hey."

"Hop on," he says, making room on the front of the board for me.

I struggle to pull myself up, almost tipping us into the water. But eventually I sit facing him.

"So . . . looking to catch some ripples on the lake?" I joke.

He smiles. "Nah. This board's for paddling. It's been a minute since I last surfed, and I don't want my shoulders to be so worked the first day out that I'm ruined for the rest of the trip."

"Makes sense."

"It's pretty awesome out here this early."

"My favorite part of the day." As I say this, I give an involuntary shiver. Now that I've stopped moving, the sun isn't strong enough to battle the lake's early morning chill.

"I can't believe you're in this insanely freezing water without a wetsuit," he says. "You're tough."

I laugh at the thought of me being tough and pull my arms around my chest, rub my hands against my triceps in an attempt to warm them up, and tell him, "There's nothing better in my world than swimming, even if it's in this ice bucket."

"I can get that. For me it's surfing." He pats the board with both hands. "Hey . . . you wanna try standing on this beast?"

I look down at the board, then the water. How different will it be from snowboarding? I'll fall. That's for sure. And I'll probably look like a complete oaf. But there's no one here but me and Ryan. I'd rather try and fail than be timid. After all, he thinks I'm tough.

"Ummm. I guess?"

"Awesome! Turn around so you're facing front and scoot down toward me a bit."

I turn around carefully. The board sways to each side a little as I attempt to back up.

"Stay center. It won't wobble so much. Okay, stop right there. I'm going to stand up first, then I'll help you." The board sways again for a second. Then he's standing behind me. "Get into a kind of push-up position. Yep—like that. From there you'll pop up onto your feet. I'm going to help you stand. Ready? Push and pop up!"

My feet hit the board, and for a second I'm standing,

Ryan behind me, supporting me with his hands on my hips.

Then the board flies to the right, our bodies to the left.

When I surface, Ryan is already swimming toward his board.

"For your first time up, it was pretty killer. You just got too close to the edge with your left foot. Let's do it again."

I swim over and pull myself up.

Lying on the board, I take a second to focus. Push and pop up. Ryan's hand on my hips, the board under my feet. My landing is sturdier this time.

"Awesome!" he says into my ear. I can feel his body inches from mine. "Now just think of this but on the ocean." Determined to stay standing as long as possible, to keep this moment as long as possible, I stare toward the shore, trying to keep my concentration, keep my balance. A few families have set up towels on the beach. "And if you have to fall, just kind of fall backward, or kick the board away, like this." He hooks his arm around my waist, and we tumble into the lake.

As we surface, we're both laughing.

I pull myself onto the board a third time and glance down at my watch. Eight twenty.

"I need to get to the lifeguard stand."

"I'll give you a ride."

I sit toward the board's nose as Ryan lies behind me, paddling us to shore. As we near the beach, I see a group of Cranberry Hill girls descending like a swarm of bees, chattering loudly into one high-pitched hum. I'm shocked to see them here this early, until my eyes land on Mandy, her ridiculously huge camera slung around her neck. Ever since she became the official yearbook photographer, she lugs that thing almost everywhere. I know it must be a pretty amazing camera. Probably top-of-the-line. Professional. Her parents bought it for her as a congratulations gift for being selected. At school she follows her friends around, creating random photo shoots anywhere on campus. Our next yearbook will look like a contrived department store catalog, featuring her friends modeling all the back-to-school must-haves.

Mandy looks out at us. Her arms cross her chest as she waits for us to dock on the sand. Ryan on his board with another girl? I have ruined her morning photo shoot. No way I am going to get in her path.

"I'm going to swim from here," I tell Ryan. "Thanks."

I dive off the side and swim directly to the lifeguard stand. Luckily, Mandy and her gang wait on the shore for Ryan instead of going after me.

Lala is sitting next to the stand, admiring the swirls painted on her nails.

"Hey!" I greet her, pulling my towel out of my bag. I wrap it tightly around my body. "Did I mess up? I thought today I had the opening shift?"

"No, baby doll, you didn't mess up," she says, adjusting her necklace. "I'm just early because my mother decided to vacuum at the crack of dawn. I couldn't go back to sleep, so I came here to check on the social scene."

From the corner of my eye, I can see Ryan hoisting up his board, Mandy angrily pointing to me, can hear bits like "girlfriend" "treated like shit" "can't believe." Cranking my super-ears up, I can hear him saying, "It was only a surf lesson" and "She's a friend."

"Trouble in paradise," Lala says, nodding in their direction. "Put on the moves, baby doll. I bet you can break them up by the end of the week."

"That's not what I'm trying to do." The truth: I'd love for them to break up. But not if I cause it. I don't think I could date him after that without feeling guilty.

She shrugs. "Whatever, little flirt. I'm going to see what's going on at the tennis courts. See you."

Ryan, with his board under his arm, heads for the parking lot, Mandy scrambling after him, still yelling. Ryan says in an even tone, "Let me know when you chill out. I'm outta here."

I look back to the lake, feeling confused, mulling over Lala's words.

"*What* do you think you're doing?" Crap. Mandy's perfect face is distorted in anger, inches from mine. "Trying to steal Ryan?" She gives a harsh laugh. "Stealing. That's a typical Tovin move. Stay away from my boyfriend. Or I promise to make your life more miserable than it already is."

She struts away before I have time to react. She wasted her breath. I do not and will not steal. Ever.

. . .

I can't concentrate on working, with Mandy planted on a towel less than fifty yards from me, her friends taking turns sending me death looks.

"Helllllooooo," Chris says, waving his chubby hands at me. "I just dunked that redheaded kid again. Don't you care?"

I'm a bad lifeguard.

"Why are you telling me this, Chris?" I say. "Do you *want* to be in trouble?"

"I don't know." What a weird kid.

"Ooookaaaay." I look over the property again. Is it two yet?

"I'm bored," Chris says, filling a bucket with water, dumping it out, filling it up again.

I look at him, then at the other boys his age off in the deep end of the lake. I decide to try suggesting the swim lessons again.

"You'd have a lot of fun in the deep end. There's the diving board, the island. Your friends . . . ," I say.

He glares.

"The offer to teach you still stands. Greg, Manny, Sarah. I got them all swimming in a few weeks."

"I told you before. I don't need a stupid teacher."

"Okay, Chris. Just so you know, most days I show up forty-five minutes before I start work to swim. If you want to learn, I'll be here."

"Whatever," Chris says, running away with his bucket full of lake water. He sprints across the lawn, charging through the group of girls around Mandy. Then he dumps the icy water right on his sister's face.

"You little brat!" She takes a swipe at him. Too fast, he runs away. It's petty, I know, but I love seeing Mandy tormented.

She complains loudly about her magazine—"ruined, completely ruined." Her hair—"Does he realize how long it takes to blow out my hair?" And the smell of the water—"Disgusting. I smell like swamp." She rolls up her towel, shoves it into her bag, and storms past me to the exit. I sigh in relief. My eyes and brain are back on the water.

A half hour later Lala reappears.

"Hey, baby doll," she says, her metal bracelets clinking as she rubs sunscreen on. "Your shift is up."

Two o'clock. I have to be home in an hour. Mom made me write my work schedule for the week on her calendar. I padded it on each end. That way I can still swim in the morning and have almost an hour to relax with my friends before going home. I have to stick to the lake, though. If she or Dad ever shows up and I'm not here, it'll be another month grounded for me.

I spread out my towel on the grass and pull my sack lunch out of my bag. Chris walks by with a slice of pizza from the Swimmer's Snack Shack. The bread and cheese and oregano smell so good, but eating here costs me an hour of work each time. Lunch from home is free.

"Hey, Clare," Skye says as she and Chase walk toward me with rackets in hand. "Have time for a quick tennis match? Chase and I want to play doubles, him and me against Omar and you. You game?"

I look at my watch and sigh. "Sorry. I need to finish lunch and get back home. I have only about a half hour." Besides, I'm awful at tennis. Maybe as bad as Omar. Chase and Skye should just play each other.

"Then, lunch it is," Skye says, pulling a sandwich from her bag.

We sit in a circle on the grass. Laughing and talking. I've missed out on a party, a movie night, and will be still grounded when they go camping over the weekend and down to the beach next week. But at least I have them now.

The next thirty minutes fly past. I grudgingly pick up my stuff and pedal toward home.

Summer is the season of yard sales. I bike past each one, slowing down enough to get a good idea of what they might have. Broken chairs, homemade candles, lemonade, dishes, toys, lots of stuffed animals, a treadmill, and . . . yarn? I pull the brakes and hop off my bike, lean it against the nearest tree. There's a whole box of yarn, all different colors, mostly medium weight, and a few skeins of yellow thick chenille. I'm pretty sure if I get the whole box, I can make one kid-size blanket out of the chenille and maybe three baby blankets out of the rest.

"Twenty-five cents a skein or two dollars if you'll take the whole box."

"Deal." We shove it all into a couple of plastic bags so I can hang them off the handlebars. Man, I miss my car. On the way home, I have to stop every few minutes to adjust the bags.

I wheel Bike-a-saurus into our front yard and lean it against a pine tree. Through the kitchen window I can see Mom on the phone. Talking with her hands as much as with her mouth. I open the door and quietly walk in.

"I know you need the help. I'll fly out," she says, her left hand in the air. "But it'll have to be in the fall." A pause. "Well, a plane ticket is just not something that we've budgeted for, so I'll need to save for that. Besides, Luke is coming home soon, and I'm looking forward to spending some quality time with him. How about September or October?" Another pause. "I'll try. Okay, Mom. I love you too."

She hangs up the phone and looks at me.

"Granny?" I ask. She nods. "How is she?"

"Restless. She wants to get the house fixed up so she can sell it and move into a retirement home condo."

"Granny wants to move to a *condo*?" I feel dizzy, like someone just told me gravity no longer exists. Granny's house and Granny feel like one inseparable thing to me. Even though I rarely get to go see her, I know that she is in that house, stuffed with curtains she's hand-sewn and blankets she's knitted, the back porch built by Dad and Papa before I was born, Papa's workshop in the barn, the small chicken coup, and rows of vegetables in the garden.

"The house is just too much work since your grandfather died. I'm actually surprised she's stayed there this long." Mom gives my shoulder a squeeze. "It's a good thing. She'll be around people her age. There'll be help when she needs to get to a doctor's appointment or wants to go grocery shopping. Anyway, I'll be going out there this fall to get the house ready to sell."

I can't imagine never going to the farm again, so I find myself saying, "Can I go? I'll help."

"We can barely afford my plane ticket, Clare, but thanks. Besides, you'll be back in school by then." She waits a beat, then asks, "What's on the agenda for today?"

"Homework. AP history summer assignment."

For a second I think she's going to add something to my to-do list. Clean the bathroom or scrub the kitchen floor. But instead she says "Study hard" as she leaves the room.

Before pulling out my history book, I sit on my bed and sift through my newly purchased bags of yarn. If I work it right, I think I can make a violet baby blanket with flowers in three shades of pink, another with blue and green stripes, and a rainbow one with the rest. Granny has a great book of patterns for using up odds and ends of yarn. Maybe she can mail it to me.

As I cast on each purple stitch, I imagine the baby that this blanket might go to. Maybe a newborn, all squishy and tiny. Or a little one-year-old just learning to walk. I think of her mama and wonder if, like me, she's waiting for someone she loves to be out of prison. And I slide the stitches on a little faster, because of all the things she has to think about, at least with this blanket she won't have to worry about her baby being warm.

A knock, and my door starts to open. I fumble with my knitting, dropping it onto my bed and picking up my history book.

"Clare, do you think you can park your bike in the backyard from now on? It's such an eyesore," Mom says.

"Sure," I agree, looking back down to my history book.

"What are you working on?" She motions to my needles.

"Another beanie," I lie. It's ridiculous, I know, but I've never told anyone I make blankets for the homeless shelter. Not even Drea.

"Okay. Well, when you take a break, please move that bike."

After she leaves, I put my knitting away, thinking about how the first time I walked into Loving Hearts Homeless Shelter, Peggy at the front desk looked up at me and said, "How may I help you?" There was not one look in her eye of suspicion or judgment.

I don't tell anyone that I knit like crazy year-round and drive the forty-five minutes to Loving Hearts at least twice a winter. I don't tell anyone, so I never have to worry about Skeleton following me there.

Chapter 14:
Creation and Destruction

Granny's hands moved fast. *Click, click, click, click, click.* I stared as the string of heart-red yarn became a scarf just for me.

"When I grow up, will you teach me how to do that?" I asked.

"No." She looked up and smiled at me, but her fingers didn't stop. "But I can teach you now."

"Now? I want to make a blanket," I told her. "A blue one, with sunshine-yellow flowers."

She put down her needles and dug into her knitting bag. "Let's start with something simple. How about a scarf for one of your dollies? We'll use this yarn, so it matches yours. I'll get it started for you."

I watched her loop ten stitches onto a set of big needles. Then she guided my hands. I mumbled aloud with each stitch, "Needle into loop, yarn over, slip, and slide."

The front door creaked open, but I didn't even look up. It was probably just Peter coming home from Evan's house. I hoped he went straight to his room.

But the footsteps stopped right in front of us.

"LUKE!" I shouted, jumping up. "Look! I'm knitting. This is going to be a scarf for my doll."

"Wow, Squeakers! Let me see." He picked up my little scarf already two lines long and said, "You did this? Nah . . . it must have been Granny."

After giving me and Granny hugs, Luke announced he was going to be home for a while.

"Yay!" Granny never came for visits, and now Luke was there too! Maybe he'd stay a long time instead of just a few days.

It was the best week ever! Granny helped me finish my doll's scarf, and we started on a hat to match. She even gave me my own knitting needles. Luke and I went to the lake and made a sand castle, and every night we watched a movie. I was so happy it was summer, because I didn't have school to ruin my fun. But the week came to an end, and Granny had to go home.

At the airport she gave me three quarters.

Once home, I ran to my room to put them into my bank on the dresser.

Where was Piggy? She was there yesterday, right next to my ballerina music box, when I found two nickels and three pennies between the cushions of the couch. But now the bank was gone.

Maybe Luke could help me find her. I shouted for him and ran around the house, but he wasn't anywhere.

So I looked for Piggy by myself, everywhere. Imagined she got tired of staying in one place and somehow her pink body, fat with change, leapt from my dresser and ran out of my room. It was stupid, but the only other thought was that someone had taken her. I'd rather believe in magic, even though a piggy bank coming to life was a pretty creepy idea. I kept looking.

No Piggy anywhere.

I went outside and searched the backyard. She wasn't in the flowerbed with the snapdragons or under my favorite apple tree. Maybe in the front? There on the road: bright pink pieces. I ran to the edge of the yard. What had happened? I squinted my eyes, looking to see if I could find any of my coins on the street. None. They were all gone. Someone had taken Piggy. And smashed her. And they'd taken my coins, too.

Dad helped me pick up the pieces, but he couldn't put them together, making jokes about Humpty Dumpty each time he tried. He promised to get me a new bank and gave me all the change in his pocket: two quarters, a dime, and six pennies. I'd had a lot more in there than that.

I waited for Luke to come home, imagining we'd become detectives to find out what had happened.

But Luke didn't come home that night. Or the next night. Or the next week. And Mom and Dad and Peter didn't want to help me solve the case. Maybe one of them had broken Piggy. It wasn't Granny, and it couldn't have been Luke. Luke would never have done that to me.

A few months later, my ear tight to the bedroom door, I heard Mom and Dad whisper about Luke going to jail, twenty-three months, eighteen with good behavior.

"Was he in the wrong place at the wrong time, again?"

I asked my fish, contemplating whether the question was worth getting in trouble for eavesdropping for.

But I knew it would be best not to ask, even though I really wanted to know more, because I doubted that Luke could be so unlucky as to be in the wrong place at the wrong time *again*.

Chapter 15:

Rain

NOW

I wake up hardly believing it's the Fourth of July weekend already. Summer is moving fast.

BOOM! CRACK! BOOM!

Who in the hell is setting off fireworks at six in the morning? I moan and pull my pillow over my head. I have a half hour more to sleep.

Then I realize: My room is still dark. Too dark for six a.m.

There is another *BOOM*. I roll over to my window and pull back the curtains.

Thick clouds fill the sky, touching the treetops. Rain pushes the leaves of the apple tree down, making it look as tired as I feel. The sky brightens with a lightning strike. One one thousand, two one thousand, three one—*BOOM!*

Wow, that's close, I think, slamming my window shut. No work for me today. The lake is closed if there're thunderstorms. No picnics, no fireworks, no Fourth of July. No phone, no Internet, no TV, no friends, no nothing. I am stranded. I slide into my bed and go back to sleep until 8 a.m.

"You guys have it easy," I say to my fish, dropping in their flakes. They race to the surface, gulp the food down. The tank is looking dirty—algae is growing on the glass, pebbles, and NO FISHING sign.

Raymond is the last to finish eating; his black spotted nose pecks around the rocks for flakes that may have sunk. As he roots around, I take out their castle and the NO FISHING sign and place them into my fish bucket.

I barely register the phone ringing. It's just after eight in the morning, so I know it's not one of my friends calling. Besides, they all know I'm grounded.

Scrubbing the sides of the tank with a sponge on a wooden rod, I watch the glass clear as the water becomes murky. I empty a quarter of the tank with a siphon, change the filter, replace the castle and sign. All that I have left to do is add more water and treatment solutions to make sure the pH is right.

"Clare." Mom opens my door as she knocks. "That was Lucille calling. The lake is closed today. So since you aren't working, I have a job here that I want you to do." She looks at my fish tank, my wet arms, and adds, "You can finish that later."

Wiping my arms with an old towel, I follow her to the living room. Couldn't I at least have breakfast first? She points at the faded spots on the carpet that lead to the front door. "I'd like for you to work on getting these stains out."

Skeleton slides into the room, sipping his brandy, using a closed umbrella as a cane.

"Mom." Is she senile? "I've already tried everything to get those stains out."

"Well, I bought this new pet-stain remover, so try that." She hands me a bottle and an old scrub brush. Skeleton taps the spots on the carpet with his umbrella, flapping his jaws open and shut, open and shut.

"I think this stuff was made for fresh stains. These are at least six years old." My hands are shaking. My stomach knots up, rotten inside.

"Try it again and see." She starts to walk away. Turns around to look back. "Are you still in your pajamas? Really, Clare. It's almost nine. Wasting the day away in bed." She pauses. "Speaking of which, I don't think I saw your bed made."

If I stay in this house much longer, I'll go crazy for sure. One more year. One more year and I'm free. College. Dorms. I just need to make sure I've got enough money saved to move out as soon as I graduate. The lake being closed today is *not* helping my college fund.

After making my bed and pulling on an old T-shirt and some ragged cutoff jean shorts, I do a few things to procrastinate. Add water and treatments to the fish tank. Eat a bowl of cereal and drink a mug of coffee. Then decide to have a glass of orange-mango juice as well.

As I tilt my drinking glass for the last time, I grimace, knowing I can't put it off any longer. Mom will freak out if she doesn't see me on my hands and knees with brush in hand soon.

I spray and scrub. Spray and scrub. A half hour later the only thing I've managed to do is saturate the carpet in a gross fake-orange smell. The stains haven't gotten even one percent lighter. My only hope is to scrub so hard that I wear a hole right through the carpet. *Then* the stains will be gone.

Peter walks in from his room, heading to the front door. He stops midstride when he sees me on the floor.

"What. Did. You. Do?" he asks.

I shrug. "It's raining. I can't work. I guess she needs to keep my hands busy?"

"I'm glad I'm out of here," he says, moving toward the door. "If Mom asks, I'm at Evan's watching the Dodger game." Then he stops, licks all five fingers on his right hand, and plants them one by one on each of Mom's ornaments. I'm not sure if he just potentially made my life worse, but I am strangely satisfied knowing the ornaments are no longer perfect.

Twenty minutes and one lunch break later, it's still raining and I'm wondering how long I need to pretend to scrub before Mom will be satisfied that I tried. Skeleton is settled in Dad's easy chair, sipping his brandy, reading the paper, occasionally looking down at me, frowning and pointing his umbrella at the spots leading from the front door to the living room. He wants me to remember. Scrubbing furiously at the carpet, I look away from him, trying to concentrate on *anything* else. Of course my brain goes straight to Ryan. He's in Venice now, but the four days before he left, he was at the lake at the same time I swam. And despite my promise to stay away from him, I found myself standing on his board every morning. Using a paddleboard oar, I was even able to do a lap without falling. And Mandy was never there, so after our morning swim and paddle, we'd sit on the side of the lake and chat for a minute before I had to work. Which was awesome. The more I get to know Ryan, the more I like him. He invited me to visit him in Venice. Even if I weren't grounded, I'm not sure I'd go. After all, isn't that a trip his girlfriend should go on with him? I'm not his girlfriend, and I'm not trying to be. Okay, maybe I am. But I'm not trying to *steal* him from Mandy. I'm just enjoying his company as a friend. For now. Of course, if they ever break up . . .

I'm so lost in my thoughts, I barely hear the front door opening.

"Squeaks?" I look up. Pause with the scrub brush in hand. Luke is standing right next to me, his shoes firmly planted on the bloodstains I wish could disappear.

Chapter 16:
Perfect Circles

THEN: Age Eleven

The front door window was broken.

I could see the clear, jagged edges that held to the frame.

Slowly I got off my bike. Rolled it to the tree next to the house, my hands turning white from gripping the handlebars. I leaned my bike against the trunk, my eyes still on the window.

I moved closer, then closer. My shoes crushed the glass on the ground into smaller pieces. Inspecting the shards that clung to the frame, I paused only for a few seconds before I turned the doorknob and walked inside.

The drops on the linoleum floor were round. In sixth-grade art class I had tried, again and again, to draw a perfect circle. I couldn't do it without the compass attached to my pencil, stabbing the paper in the center. My freehand circles were always wavy, lopsided. I didn't think it was possible to make a perfect circle without the compass. But here, right in front of me, were perfectly round, bright red droplets. Mom always said that we had thin blood. That's how I knew it was one of us.

I could have gone back outside. Waited at a neighbor's until I was sure Dad was home from work. He was used to blood. He was used to corpses.

But I didn't. I don't know why, but I followed the droplets.

They were a much better trail than breadcrumbs. The blood would stain the floor, stain the carpet. It wouldn't be picked by birds. We'd always be able to follow it.

The sharp sounds of an argument and a nasty smell—body odor and alcohol, and another that I couldn't recognize—stopped me for a moment. Maybe I should have left then.

Curiosity gave me bravery. I turned the corner.

Chapter 17:

Homecoming

NOW

I look down at the stains and up at Luke in disbelief, hundreds of thoughts filling my head at once. Is it really Luke standing in front of me? It's been almost four years, but he looks old, more like forty than twenty-nine. His face is leathery, wrinkled in spots. The Virgin Mary that I remember as so bright on his arm is now faded, the blue tattooed lines blurring into his skin.

"How's my little Squeaks?" Luke's long arms reach toward me before I even say hello. He's unaware of his feet, how they step on the faded spots. The tiny hairs on my neck start to rise, then fall. He doesn't remember. I can tell.

I stumble to stand, dropping my scrub brush. Luke sweeps me up with both arms, pressing my breath from my lungs, twirling me in a circle like I am still five years old. I can't help but laugh as I spin.

He gently places me down on the ground. I'm dizzy, disoriented, happy. "When did you get so tall? I haven't been gone that long! Hey, Ma," he shouts out. "What are you feeding Clare? She looks like a teenager!"

"Welcome home, Luke." Mom briskly passes me and embraces him.

"Ma." The muscles in Luke's arms tense, showing me how tightly he holds her. When they finally let go, Mom pulls his hand to her lips and gives it a kiss. She doesn't glance down to see if I've gotten the stains out of the carpet, leaving me wondering if she knew Luke was coming home today or if she just wanted to keep me busy.

"Come on," she says, leading him toward the couch. "I want to hear about everything. Sit, sit! You too, Clare. Put the cleaning supplies away, then join us. Grab us a few glasses of lemonade while you're up, please." She can't take her eyes off Luke. "So, Luke," she says. "How is everything?"

"Good. It's great to be home." As I pour the lemonade, I take in every note of Luke's deep voice. Trying to bottle it in my ears. It sounds so different in real life than it does over the phone. And since my parents never let Peter and me go with them when they visit, this is the first time I've heard it in person in close to four years.

I'm back in the living room with three lemonades as fast as I can.

"Tell us about your job," Mom says.

Luke's smile droops for a second. Then he tries to pull it back up. "It didn't work out. There was another guy there, interviewing the same time as me. He'd been through a similar training program. And, you know. His record was clean. But the boss said that he's gonna have a bunch of openings in about six months on some big high-rise they're building." He grabs his lemonade and takes a long, slow drink.

"That sounds very promising," Mom says, looking to me and nodding, but I know what she's thinking. It's really hard to get a job out of prison. And when he has one, he does so much better. Is clean for longer. Stays out for longer. What is he going to do with himself for the next six months? What if he doesn't find another job immediately?

As she takes a drink, an awkward moment of silence descends on the room.

"How long are you staying?" I ask.

"Well, that depends. Ma, do you think I could hang for a while? You know, just until I can get a job and some money saved? My PO says he's got some other leads for me."

Suddenly I'm twelve years old again. We are all sitting on the couch just like we are now, Luke saying the same sentence. And even though I can't remember, I'm sure he has said it every time he's been released.

"Of course," Mom says. "You know you're always welcome here. This is your home. And, come to think of it, I have a few chores I can pay you to do. The house needs painting. And the attic is a disaster. I can't pay much, but it'll be something."

"Thanks." Luke reaches out and squeezes Mom's shoulder.

"But." My mother pulls out her serious voice. "If you want to stay here, there are a few rules that you're going to have to follow. I want you home by midnight, every night. No booze or drugs. I tell you which friends you can bring to the house. And you can stay here long-term only *if* you get a job."

"Okay, okay. You got it, Ma." Luke's voice is as serious as hers. Then, smiling, he stands up and kisses her forehead. "I'm not gonna disappoint anyone this time."

I almost flinch when he says that. I really, really want to believe it. But it feels like he has jinxed his chances by letting those words escape his mouth.

"Hey, Squeaks, wanna go for a walk?"

I look to Mom. She's beaming. "Okay, but be back by dinner." I wish I could make her smile like that—all teeth and bright eyes—by just walking into the room.

It's still raining, but the thunderstorms have passed. Luke and I walk close together under our umbrellas. He smells like the road, probably a few days since a shower, his body odor barely covered by a spicy deodorant.

There's a nervous silence, like both of us are scared of offending the other by saying the wrong thing. Asking him about prison is impossible, although I wonder a lot about it. Since I was never allowed to visit him there, I have only movies and the Internet to refer to. I hope that the meals were okay, there was a lot to read, and good TV. I hope it's not as bad as I've been led to believe. Most of all I hope he has never been . . . Stop. I won't even think about that.

"Have you been to Craigen's Hilltop?" he asks.

"No. The only way to get there is through the mayor's

property, and he and his rottweiler aren't so keen on people frolicking through his yard," I say, thinking of the large TRESPASSERS WILL BE SHOT sign.

"I can show you how. No trespassing needed. Completely legal." Luke leaves the road and walks into the bushes. Completely legal, huh? I want to see this. I follow, my jean shorts getting soaked as leaves and branches brush against them. A trail starts, out of nowhere, like it was placed there just for us, and weaves up the hill.

"Man, I missed this place." Luke takes in big breaths and releases happy sighs. Raindrops slow to drips.

"We used to party on this hillside all the time," he says. "In high school I'd hide booze in these bushes. Hang on a sec." He pulls aside the branches of a huge juniper bush and presents a canning jar, half-full of clear liquid. "Wow! Still here. I can't believe it. I used to pour vodka in jars like this, out of Ma's stash, then fill her bottle with water. You know she and Pop don't drink the stuff, and they never have people over. I don't even know why they even keep it." He opens up the jar. Sniffs it.

"Wheeeew. That's some strong drink," he says, grimacing. "I wonder if Ma's vodka is still all water."

"Not all of it," I joke.

"My li'l sis isn't drinking out of Ma's cabinet, is she?" He pokes me in the side.

"No, I don't have to resort to that. I have Peter." Now that Luke's not promising anything, we're getting back into our brother-sister rhythm.

"Well, then, here's to Peter." Luke holds up the jar in a toast, then swigs the age-old vodka. He coughs. "You got any water, Squeaks? This stuff's terrible."

He dramatically twirls and grabs at his throat, and I laugh. The rock in my stomach is breaking down.

"We'll leave this right here." He closes the jar and slides it back under the bush. "It'll be like an experiment. See how long it can stay here, and how much stronger it gets. No swiping, okay?" He laughs.

"Yeah, after that reaction the thing I want to do is drink that poison."

We continue our hike. I can see him as a teenager meeting his friends here. Pulling jars of different liquors out of the bushes, getting drunk in the woods. I'm trying to imagine who he fit in with, who partied up here. Just Luke and a couple of friends, or the whole school, including a different generation of Cranberry Hill girls?

Then we're at the crest. I'm in awe. Who knew our crappy little town had a magical trail that led to this? A green valley, almost glowing against the gray sky, with trickles of water running down the mountainside to a stream far down below.

"You should see it in the winter with all the snow."

"Can we hike down there?" I say.

"Nah. Not from here. Don't get too close to the edge, Squeakers," Luke warns. "That'd be a bad fall down."

He's right. Maybe this is why we don't drink here. That and the hike.

"I can't believe this is here. Pretty amazing," I say.

"This town has a lot of shit in it, but there are some good surprises, too. I'll have to show you a few more. Later. Now we'd better get home. Ma'll be waiting," Luke says. "What do you think she made for dinner? All I can think about is her beef Stroganoff."

"I'm sure that's what she made." It's Luke's favorite. There is no doubt in my mind that my mother practically ran to the kitchen to start on it as soon as we left.

Back on the road, Luke is stopped by a shout.

"What's up, old buddy?" It's his friend that I saw in the woods. Ugh.

"Just got out." They do a three-part handshake that ends in a fist bump. I stand to the side. Silently watching. Silently wishing. Please, Luke, don't get involved with him again.

"Party tonight. You should come," the guy tells Luke. "I've got a good hookup in town now."

"Nah, Dan. Not tonight. Family time," Luke answers. Dan's eyes creep over me.

"You can bring your sister." His mouth is in a wide, ugly grin.

"Don't even think about it," Luke warns.

"Okay, okay." Dan backs up, holding his hands high. "Have fun with the fam, Luke. And come by sometime; I have something that you might be interested in."

"Sounds good. See ya soon." Three-part handshake again. I want to say, "What are you doing, Luke? Whatever Dan has, it can't be good. Don't do something that will put you in jail again."

Instead I fume silently for the rest of the walk home.

. . .

The smells of fried onions, garlic, and meat, and something sweet—maybe brown sugar and peaches—have floated through the house all the way to the street. It wraps Luke and me in the feeling of home. We race to the door.

Dad flings it open to greet Luke with a hug.

"Just in time!" Mom shouts as we enter. "Wash up and come eat!"

I catch Peter's eye as we walk through the living room. He looks at Luke cautiously and gives a stiff "Hey."

Luke grabs him and crushes him into a hug. "What? No love for your brother?" he asks as Peter wrestles his way out of his arms and heads toward the dining room.

Mom has added a chair on my side of the table, crowding my seat closer to Dad's. When Luke and I sit down, my shoulder brushes with his upper arm, causing a brief moment of the two of us shifting a bit apart, finally finding a comfortable spot.

My parents lead the conversation. Questions for Luke, Peter, me, each other. They don't allow the discussion to sag or turn awkward. Even Peter starts to loosen up by the end, joking a little and affording a couple of laughs. As I look around the table at my whole family, together, smiling, thoroughly enjoying each bite of dinner, complete with a peach pie for dessert, I have only one thought. Grab your camera, Mom. You'll want to scrapbook this. It's what perfect looks like.

Chapter 18:

Floating

THEN: Age Eleven

It was sweltering—the thermometer said it was one hundred degrees. All I could think about was the icy-cold lake, but Mom insisted I was too young to go by myself. "You could drown. Besides, you are not supposed to be at the lake without an adult until you're at least thirteen."

My friends had all left for family vacations, Peter wasn't home, and Luke was at the job he'd had for the past three months. So I lay on the cool kitchen tiles, feeling the breeze of the fan and listening to it hum, turning to speak into it occasionally, my robot voice my only entertainment. Until the front door burst open.

Smelling of sawdust, baloney sandwiches, and beer, Luke was home from work early!

"Get Bike-a-saurus, Squeaker," he said. "I've worked hard today, and the lake's gonna feel great."

Luke pedaled his bike fast. I pedaled faster. In minutes we were there. Kids were everywhere, splashing and screaming, and from the picnic benches their moms' craned their heads to see who had just arrived. Skeleton joined them, leaning in to hear the chitchat, slapping sunscreen onto his white bones, looking concerned.

"Last one in is a rotten egg!" Luke ran for the water.

I was always the rotten egg.

Watching me wade my way to him, Luke asked, "When are you gonna learn how to swim right?"

"When are you going to teach me?" My feet sunk into the soft bottom.

"Right now," Luke said. "By the end of this summer, I expect you to be racing the boys and beating 'em."

I didn't care about beating the boys. I just wanted to be able to go into the deep end with my friends. Drea tried to teach me, but after three failed lessons with me not even managing to float, I was pronounced hopeless.

"First you need to trust the water to hold you, Squeaks." Luke lay on the water like a raft was underneath him. "See." He popped back up to standing.

"Okay, now lie back." His hands held me up. "And relax. You'll float. I promise. And even if you don't, I've got you."

My arms and legs felt stiff. I held my breath, tight, in case I sunk.

"You're not relaxed."

"I can't. I'm going to drown." I was scared the water would pull me down.

"I won't let you drown. Stop holding your breath. You can't relax if you aren't breathing. Close your eyes. Do you hear that? Frogs. Remember us winning the Frog-Jumping Contest?" I could hear them croaking even with my ears underwater, and the more I thought about them, the less I felt like I would be pulled down.

"Notice anything different? Anything missing?"

Luke's hands. They weren't on my back anymore! My butt instantly plunged deep underwater, pulling my legs, arms, and head with it.

I didn't get a breath.

Slimy lake weeds drifted like little fingers against my thighs. Grabbing at me. Trying to keep me underwater.

I'm sure I screamed.

My feet found the bottom. I pushed up.

There they were again: Luke's hands looped under my armpits. He stood me up on both feet.

"Clare? You okay?" Luke hunkered over me, pushing hair from my eyes.

I was coughing so hard, I thought my heart might fly out and land onshore.

"Get it out, Clare. Get the water out." He smacked my back, hard.

"Why"—*cough*—"did"—*cough, cough*—"you let go?" I sputtered, gasping, pushing him away.

"Because. You were doing it! All by yourself. Just floating along without me." Luke smiled wide. "You can float!"

I could? I could. Wow. I'd been floating. All by myself.

"Hey, next time, don't try to sit up. It doesn't work that way. Ready to try again? By the time I'm done teaching you, you'll be fast like a shark! Best swimmer of all time!" He raised one of my arms high above my head.

Then I was back on the water with Luke's hands securely below me, looking up at the sky and listening to the frogs, I felt his hands slip away. And this time I didn't sink.

Chapter 19:

Hex

NOW

I pedal across town on Bike-a-saurus. Maybe I should ask for a real bike for Christmas this year. If this thing wasn't way too small for me and the rust patches weren't turning the green paint into some kind of toxic camouflage, it might actually be enjoyable to ride the mile and a half to the lake. But it doesn't matter—I will be driving to work in just six more days.

When I arrive at the lake, I'm surprised to see a car in the lot. Mandy's. At seven forty-five a.m., I'm usually the only one there, except the week when Ryan showed up early to paddle. Why would Mandy be here this early?

She's got her camera on a tripod and, with the lake in the background, has set up some bikini photo shoot for herself. She's leaning across a large rock, her head back, long red hair grazing the sand, her mouth open in a stupid fake laugh. She runs behind the lens, pushes buttons before taking another pose, crawling like a cheetah toward the camera, twisting her face into some sort of sexy growl. She runs back. Pushes buttons, readjusts. This time she's close to the camera, her lips in a pout. Could she possibly be more egocentric?

I toss my bag down, strip to my bathing suit, and dive into the cold water. Why do I have to share *my* quiet time in *my* lake with Mandy?

After my first lap I notice the camera has turned and the lens is now on me. What the hell is she doing? Probably taking pictures for her dartboard or to burn in some private popular-girl voodoo ceremony. I can't keep swimming knowing she's taking pictures, so I dive underwater and stay under for as long as possible. Popping up next to my bag, I jump out and wrap my towel around myself before she can snap another photo. I grab my stuff and disappear behind the Snack Shack. Part of me wants to confront her and demand that she erase the photos. But what good would that do? She won't erase them. It'd just be another argument with Mandy. Another confrontation. Another bout of her and the Cranberry Hill girls talking, pointing, glaring at me. I'd rather just hide.

By eight thirty a.m. I'm in my lifeguard chair, watching Mandy, who's still snapping pictures of anyone and everyone. If she weren't so positively evil, I might be curious enough to ask why.

Drea should be here at some point today. She doesn't even know that Luke is home yet. None of my friends do. At least I don't think they do. But, then again, word travels fast around here.

Around eleven a.m. my friends start to show up, plopping down on the grass next to the lifeguard stand. First Drea. "He's back? What happened to his job and staying with a friend?" Then Omar. "You *finished* all your AP English assignments. And the history ones too! Man, I am sooo jealous!" Then Chase. And Skye. "Why is Mandy going cuckoo crazy with the camera? It's like she suddenly has a goal other than shopping." And Lala. "I have this new boy. I know it's early, but it might be serious." And then Luke.

Luke. Followed closely by Skeleton in sunglasses, matching his swagger, step by step. Why did he have to come here?

Luke takes a seat in the middle of my group of friends, removing his black T-shirt to reveal his defined muscles and tattooed arms, the Virgin Mary on his left, a long cobra wrapped around his right, both all blue with wavy freehand lines. His arms and chest ripple as he tosses his shirt to the side. My brother, the incredible hulk, just released from prison. I feel awful, but I can't help thinking it: Could he look more stereotypical? Skeleton shrugs, flexes, and points to his humerus, is disappointed when the bone doesn't bulge.

"Clare, do you have sunscreen?" Luke asks. "I don't wanna burn." My heart drops. He's planning to stay for a while. I mean, I want to see him. I'm happy he's home. But there are so many people around to stare at us, even the kids, their little curious minds trying to figure out why all attention has zeroed in on Luke and me. Reluctantly I open my bag and hand the sunscreen down to him.

My friends are uncomfortable. Their normal banter is replaced by self-conscious stand-alone comments. They even start talking about the weather.

"God, it's hot." Chase.

"Must be close to a hundred." Skye.

"Man, I am sweaty." Omar.

Leave, Luke. Go home. No. Wait. I want him to be here, but only if he can blend in. Only if no one is looking at him like—well, like he's a criminal.

Instead of Luke leaving, my friends decide to take off. Chase and Skye lead the exit. After only five minutes of Luke and the stares, Chase says, "Tennis match?"

Followed by Skye's, "Anyone else in?"

Omar immediately replies, "I would love to have my butt kicked."

And Lala says, "Sure. If you can teach me how to hold a racket."

Which leaves Drea, and me, and Luke. And, of course, Skeleton. Luke lies back on the grass. Skeleton relaxes next to him.

We're quiet for a few moments. The silence makes the glares feel so much heavier that I have to try to start a conversation. "So how's the job hunt going?" I ask Luke.

"There's a construction site on Orange Avenue. I talked to the general contractor, and he said to show up tomorrow morning. They need some extra hands pouring the foundation. I've done that a few times before."

"So it's a new site?" I say, getting a little hopeful. "Maybe they'll have other jobs for you to do."

"I prove something tomorrow, I might be in for the whole build." Luke closes his eyes.

It was weird tiptoeing past Luke sleeping this morning. Impossible trying to crunch my cereal quietly. Mom offered Peter's bottom bunk bed, but Luke insisted on the couch. "I'm easy, Ma. Not here to make anyone uncomfortable. Besides, I like how the living room feels open. Bunk beds are too . . . cramped." It made me realize that he'd slept on a bunk bed in his cell. It'll take a bit, getting used to him being here, always around, but I'd rather have him sleep on the couch than feel like home reminds him of prison. If he likes how open the living room feels, he must love napping out here in the sun. I instantly feel guilty that I wished he hadn't come here.

It *is* really hot today. I wipe sweat off with a towel, then reapply sunscreen. After I finish rubbing it in, I step down off the lifeguard chair and stick my feet into the water in a desperate attempt to cool off. Wisps of hair that refused to go into my ponytail stick to my neck. Drea gives up and jumps into the lake, takes a dive just past the buoy that marks the deep end and swims out toward the island. As I watch her tread water, too far away to talk to, I know it's not the heat that has driven her away from me.

I plunge my hand into the icy water, rub and drip it across my neck. It feels so good.

My body can't take it anymore. I scan the lake to make sure everyone is safe, then quickly jump into the water, dunking my whole head. It is instantly satisfying. My temperature drops a few degrees.

As I jump back up onto the lifeguard stand, I spy Mandy lying belly-down like a snake in the grass, twenty feet away and armed with a zoom camera, snapping shots again in our direction. I want to grab her stupid camera and throw it into the deepest part of the lake.

Luke wakes up forty-five minutes later. He pulls his shirt back on, looks at the watch on his arm. I recognize it as my dad's. He must be borrowing it. I think. I hope.

"Gotta go, Squeaks," he says, stretching his arms up to the sky. "Home for a bit. Then I'm meeting a friend. See ya." At the word "friend" I can't help but tense up, thinking of Dan in the woods. Is that who he's going to see?

Drea reappears as soon as Luke and Skeleton leave. We banter about her college tour, all the planning that has gone into it. The supercheesy tourist stuff she can't wait to see as they drive from one school to the next. But I'm having a hard time concentrating on what she's saying. I can't stop looking around, catching people's eyes before they quickly look away. Am I imagining it? Or is everyone *still* staring at me?

When my shift is up, instead of staying for my built-in hour, I choose to go home. Far away from curious eyes and Mandy's lens. Even far away from Drea.

Riding Bike-a-saurus Hex home, I'm pushing the pedals as hard as I can, trying to create some kind of breeze that will wash the weird uncomfortable feelings of the day away, when I hear a *beep, beep* behind me.

I feel like a complete idiot for several reasons. One— because when the horn honked, I jumped. Not a little jump, a big jump. Like a murderer had lunged out from behind a tree with an axe.

Two—because my knees graze the handlebars when I

pedal, and my legs are locked in bent position. A clown on a three-year-old's bike possibly looks more graceful than I do.

And three—because the person honking at me is Ryan.

"Hey, you're back!" I say between breaths.

"Just got home today. Need a lift?" He's amused.

"Okay." We both laugh at my current mode of transportation.

"Should I even ask why you are riding this thing?" he asks as he throws my bike into the back of his truck.

"I'm still grounded." I'm red. Bright red. I can feel it, almost see it beaming from my cheeks. We jump into the cab, and he starts to drive.

"Your parents must be really strict," he says. Ryan smells like summer: sunblock, sweat, and some kind of cologne. I lean back against the seat, breathe in deep, and start to relax. He looks even better with a tan and his messy hair full of sun highlights.

"How was Venice?" I ask, allowing myself to admit I *really* missed our mornings on the lake together.

"It was pretty awesome. A good warm-up for Seven Sisters."

"How long are you home for?" I ask him.

"Three days, and then I take off again for Mexico. This is your place on the left?" Are we really almost to my house?

"Yep," I say. Whether it's an advantage or not, everyone in a small town knows where everyone else lives.

He gets out of the truck and hands me Bike-a-saurus.

Mrs. Brachett peeks out her window. A second later she is in her yard, trimming a bush that she just trimmed yesterday. Might as well figure that she's going to give a full report of this conversation to Mom. Luckily, rides home from work are approved, even when grounded.

"I think I like the rust stains the best. How 'bout you, Clare?"

"The streamer barely holding on to the handlebars," I say. Ryan's hand grazes mine; his body leans in close. Is he flirting? A quick vision of Mandy's face pops into my head. I am just friends with Ryan. Friends. As in, I am not stealing him from Mandy because we are just friends.

His thumb brushes against my ear as he tucks back a stray hair.

If I were brave, daring, or Lala, I'd lean in for a kiss. But I'm not. I'm plain-scared Clare. And besides, I'm not the type of girl to kiss a guy who has a girlfriend. That's tacky. And slutty. And stealing. Besides. Ryan shouldn't be flirting with me if he is with Mandy. That's tacky. And slutty. And cheating.

I take a step back, just as I hear a throat clear behind me.

It's Luke.

"Hey, Clare." He crosses his arms, looking Ryan from head to toe. Luke has at least two inches on Ryan. Maybe three. "Who's your friend?"

As I introduce the two of them, I see Ryan shift from one leg to the other, his eyes alert but lacking that glare of judgment I see in most people when *they* see Luke.

"You know my little sis is one of the sweetest, smartest girls alive," Luke says.

"You're totally right. And you left out 'athletic.' If I get her out in the ocean, she's going to rip." Ryan's hazel eyes light up.

"Oh, yeah? Teaching her to surf?" Luke asks.

"If she'll let me," Ryan says. "You surf?"

"No, I don't trust the ocean. Too much you can't see, know what I mean?" Luke says. "Clare is *the* most important thing in the world to me. You take her out in the ocean, you make sure she's safe. She gets hurt in any way, I will hold *you* responsible."

Skeleton jumps from the trees above. He starts to circle the three of us. With his big toe bone he draws a stick figure of Ryan in the dirt, then stomps on it.

I watch Ryan's tan face go pale.

This needs to stop. I need words. The right words.

"Ugh. Luke," I protest. "You sound worse than Mom and Dad. You must be getting old." I force out a laugh that thankfully sounds more natural than I expected.

"Ouch," Luke says, uncrossing his arms and letting them drop to his side. "Alright. I've got to get my old ass to my buddy's house. Clare, let Mom know I'll be back by dinner. Ryan, don't get eaten by a shark." He looks next door. Rolling his eyes, he says, "Mrs. Brachett, tell my parents I say hi when you report to them." Her eyelids turn to slits as her lips pucker. Then she goes back to pretending to trim.

"I'd better jet too," Ryan says. "Luke." He gives a nod. "Clare, see ya later."

As I watch Luke walk away in one direction, Ryan drive in the other, I feel a moment of fury at Luke. Still, it seems like Luke's comment didn't do too much damage. Then I remember the way Ryan looked at me, how his thumb felt brushing the hair behind my ear. Maybe he was flirting. Maybe he wasn't. Either way, I wish he were single, so my only concern would be if he likes me or not, instead of worrying, worrying, worrying that he might be a jerk who cheats. And, worse, that I might be a person who steals.

The next night, Luke comes home from work around six p.m. with cement crusted along the tips of his fingers, under his nails. He worked today. "But only today," he tells us dejectedly. "We finished pouring the foundation. But the boss has enough workers until they get into finishing work. Painting and stuff. He says to come back in a month to check in on things." Luke picks at the cement under his nails. "He didn't have any other job leads. It's gonna be tough finding something here." He sits down on the couch and scrapes at the cement on his hands, letting the gray flakes fall to the carpet. "But I'll find something." He smiles up at Mom and me, our brows equally furrowed. "Don't worry."

"A mother," Mom says, leaning forward as she plants a kiss on his forehead, "never worries too much about her children." Then she surprises me, putting her hand on my shoulder and placing her lips to my forehead too.

There's a knock on the door.

"That's for me. I'm grabbing dinner with a friend,"

Luke says, hopping off the couch. Mom and I both crane our necks to see who it is. Through the glass we can make out the unmistakably skeletal outline of Dan. I am positive that Mom's heart drops as quickly as mine does.

Chapter 20:

Two Stories, One Truth

THEN: Age Eleven

Mr. Jerkland was pounding on the front door.

"My DVD player is missing!" he exclaimed angrily as Mom opened it.

"I don't know what that has to do with us," she said, her body blocking the entrance. Scrubbing the front windows with an old rag, my hand slowed as I listened.

"My kitchen window is smashed in and my DVD player is stolen! And guess what? Mrs. Brachett saw one of your good-for-nothing boys sneaking back inside your house with my DVD player in his hands." His beard shook with each word. I stopped scrubbing.

"Mr. Kirkland! This is ridiculous. Ever since that misunderstanding about that silly statue, you've been blaming my son for everything! That was over three years ago!" Mom started to close the door. "We are done here."

Jerkland put his foot squarely against the door, blocking her from slamming it.

"Misunderstanding!" he said, his arms flying. "Your son stole my duck statue and gave it to you as a Mother's Day present!"

Luke had told us he'd bought the duck at a garden store and that it had cost twenty dollars. Peter and I had each given him five dollars to pitch in for the gift. Mom had returned the duck to Mr. Kirkland. Luke had forgotten to give us our money back.

"I will not be yelled at in my own home." Mom pushed on the door with both hands. Jerkland's foot held it open.

"Then step outside." His lips disappeared under his mustache.

Mom's mouth dropped open. Speechless.

"Now you listen here," Jerkland said. "I don't want to deal with a police report over this, but I will if I have to! I'm getting an estimate to have the window fixed tomorrow. You'll be receiving the bill. And the one for a new DVD player if it's not returned immediately." He pulled his foot out of the door, turned, and marched away.

"Well, I never!" Mom yelled. Then, looking up, she realized I was there. "Are you eavesdropping? Get back to work, young lady."

My hand started spinning in quick circles. I wanted to make the windows shine so much that Mom forgot all about Mr. Kirkland.

When I was done, I grabbed Mom's hand and pulled her to the entryway.

"Ta-da!" I said, pointing to the spotless windows.

"Very nice, Clare Bear," Mom said. I beamed, until she added, "Do you think you can make your room windows look like that?"

I sighed. More work.

"Do I have to?" I asked.

"Idle hands . . ."

"I know, I know." I really didn't want to clean more windows. Then I had an idea. "Wait, Mom! What if I knit something instead?"

"Okay for today," she agreed. "Tomorrow clean your room windows."

I had to eavesdrop again that night when Luke got home. Drea and I had made guesses on what we thought had happened. Drea thought Peter was guilty but changed her mind when I told her he had a strong alibi. He had been camping all week with friends in Arizona. I was sure Mr. Kirkland and Mrs. Brachett had some sort of secret plan to get cash and a new DVD player. With my ear pressed against the crack of my door, I listened to the whole conversation.

"Ma! It wasn't me," Luke said. "I swear!"

"Mrs. Brachett said it was either you or Peter. And considering how much trouble you've gotten into, I thought I'd start with you," Mom said.

"You're trusting Mrs. Brachett as an eyewitness? She's practically blind."

"She does have some vision problems," Mom conceded.

"Come on, Ma. You know I'm working a good job. I don't need to take a worthless DVD player for cash. I'm clean, and I'm not about to screw things up again. I didn't do it," he said. "You believe me, right?"

Mom sighed. Paused. "Yes, I suppose."

A few days later Mr. Jerkland showed up at our door. Mom handed him cash. Did that mean she didn't believe Luke? Or she didn't want police asking questions? Was she afraid that Luke could go to jail again, even if he really hadn't stolen the DVD player?

The answers to those questions really didn't matter. I was glad she paid Mr. Kirkland. Glad that the police weren't going to get involved. Because that meant that Luke could be with us for longer. Even if it was just a little bit longer. It was worth it.

Chapter 21:

Family Dinner

NOW

As we gather around the dinner table, all I can think is, Four more days. Four more days of Mom's hard labor. Four more days and I get my cell phone back and I can watch TV and I can use the computer and I can drive. I want to burn Bike-a-saurus at the end of it all to celebrate.

"You'll never guess what I picked up today," Dad tells us, pulling his chair to the table. "Anyone?"

Silence.

"Raccoon. A poor shot didn't kill it. So the animal dragged itself under a porch to die in peace. Then along comes little Kimmie Walker, playing house out in her yard. She got her blankets all hung up under the porch before turning to find herself face-to-face with this half-dead raccoon. When I got there, she was still screaming and carrying on. That Walker family spoils her, if you ask me. It was no big deal. There was blood, but she couldn't even see the hole in the belly where the shot went in. The raccoon hissed at me when I walked up. Of course I had to go and put it out of its misery." He shoves a forkful of red meatballs into his mouth. Chews loudly.

"Dad! That's disgusting!" Now I can't even look at my

own plate. Outside, the sky has turned from light blue to thunderstorm gray. A few raindrops hit the window. "Can't you think of anything else to talk about at dinner?"

Before he can answer, Mom cuts in, "I have news. Clare, Luke, what do you think about the three of us going to Tennessee to visit Grandma in two weeks? We'll be staying there till mid-August."

"What?" I drop my fork. I want to see Granny, but not now. In four days I won't be grounded anymore. I can actually hang out with my friends, not just at the lake. Movies. Bowling. A trip to the beach.

"That's great, Ma," Luke says. "But I'll have to check in with my PO to make sure it's okay."

"I'm sure it'll be fine. He called earlier, and we had a nice chat. He says you'll need to apply for a travel pass. But considering your grandmother's age, he doesn't think it'll be a problem. And, Luke, good news. Grandma's fixing up the farmhouse and Papa's workshop in the barn. She was going to hire a construction company, but I told her that you were looking for work, so she agreed to hire you at the same rate." Granny's fine with Luke coming to her house? Mom must have promised that he's 100 percent sober.

"Thanks, Ma." Luke is grinning so wide, I can tell he is honestly excited about the trip. But I'm not.

"I can't go. I have work," I tell my mom, trying to keep the wavy feeling out of my voice. "Remember, college fund?" This is awful. I need to work. I need the money. Mom can't force me to go with her to Tennessee.

"Granny will have plenty of work for you, too, Clare.

And she will pay you, if you work hard." Mom taps her nails against the table. "Anyway, I called Lucille and gave her your two weeks' notice today."

"YOU QUIT MY JOB FOR ME?" I stand up.

"No shouting at the dinner table." Dad stops munching on his salad to butt in. He needs to shut up. No one quit his job for him. No one is forcing him to go to Tennessee.

"What about work being important?" I point at Mom. "You said I couldn't go to tour colleges because work was so important, but I can be shipped off to Tennessee! I can't believe this!"

"Family is more important than anything. And this is best for the whole family. It's not always about you, Clare." Mom is using her forced-calm voice, but I know I am wearing her down, because of the vein that is now popping out of her forehead.

"Why do I have to go? Why doesn't Dad or Peter have to go?"

"I've got to keep my job." Peter shrugs. "You know how many people in this town would kill to work at Pizza Heaven."

Smart-ass.

"I've already used my vacation time, Clare Bear." Dad pierces a meatball with his fork. "Sit down and eat," he orders.

But I can't sit down. I think of something else. "I thought you couldn't afford to even buy one ticket to go see Granny. Now suddenly you can afford three? Where are you getting the money from?" I am shouting.

"That's enough out of you, young lady." Mom drops her fork midtwirl. "I am well aware of our financial situation. I do not need a child telling me how to manage our money. Granny needs our help. You are going. No ifs, ands, or buts." She steadies her voice. "Sit down and calm down."

"We'll do something fun, Squeakers. Promise." Luke gives my arm a gentle tug, trying to get me to sit.

It's *Luke's* fault. It's *his* fault I have to go to Granny's. His fault because he's hanging around with Dan. His fault because he can't get a job. Mom set this up to help *him* out.

I yank my arm away from him.

"Aww, Squeaks, we'll work it out. Have some of Ma's spaghetti. It's fantastic." The red mess of noodles hangs from Luke fork. All I can think of is raccoon intestines. What's wrong with this family?

My chest is tight.

"I'm not going." I move away from the table. Toward the door. The kitchen is getting smaller, everything closer. Too close.

"Get back here and finish dinner now!" Mom shouts as I slam the back door hard.

Outside. Breathe the wet air in, feel my lungs expand. Run and grab Bike-a-saurus, pedal away as fast as I can, eyeing my battery-deprived car.

My heart falls. There's no way I'm not going to be severely grounded until the school year starts. Not that it matters. I'll be stuck in Tennessee anyway.

My summer is ruined.

Chapter 22:
April Fools

THEN: Age Twelve

Ruined. My room was ruined. Everything emptied out of drawers. Sheets torn off the bed, stained pink. The scent of Kool-Aid filling the room. My lamp crashed against the wall, shade sideways. Books pulled off shelves. My stuffed animals in naughty positions on the floor.

And a note. *April Fools!*

Peter.

When Luke walked in, I was crying.

"Squeakers? What happened in here?" He wrapped his arms around me.

I handed him the note, Luke bellowed "PETER!" and the chase began.

They ran around the house, weaving through bathrooms, hopping over random shoes, knocking over Mom's miniature saint statues. Finally after racing through the living room, Peter exited through the back door.

"Lock the doors!" Luke yelled. And I did.

Peter was standing just outside the slider. Luke joined me, and we stood side by side, looking at Peter through the glass.

"How you gonna get in now?" Luke taunted. "If you apologize to Squeaks and promise to clean her room, we'll let you in."

"Screw you," Peter yelled. "I don't need to come in. Later."

"Fine," Luke yelled back. "Eye for an eye. I'll be in your room, fucking it up three times as bad as Clare's."

That got Peter's attention.

"Unlock the door!" Peter suddenly started banging on the glass with both fists, his face turning from blotchy to full red. "Clare! Unlock the door! Unlock it now!" *BANG, BANG, BANG.*

"Come on, Squeaks. We have work to do," Luke said as he steered me toward Peter's room.

CRASH!

We turned. The glass had cracked, with two spiderwebs suspended where Peter's fists had just been.

He was frozen. Staring at the glass, frozen.

"Come on, Clare," Luke said. "Let's trash his room." He pulled at my arm. I shook him off. Didn't he realize what we had done?

"Mom's gonna kill us," Peter moaned. He rubbed his fist, wincing in pain.

"Squeaks, c'mon." Luke pulled at my arm.

I shook my head. Looked down at his grip, felt his fingers dig in before releasing.

"I'll have all the fun, then." Fun? He wasn't sorry that Peter had gotten hurt? He wasn't sorry that the glass was broken? He wasn't sorry that we were all going to be in big, big trouble?

I unlocked the door, brought an ice pack to Peter, the only ways I could think to help.

As punishment Luke and I had to dig holes for Mom's garden, ten hours each, to pay Mom and Dad for the new pane of glass.

While digging holes, I started thinking of my friends and their families. We never talked about it, but I assumed that all brothers fought like mine and everyone knew *someone* in jail. I said it over and over until I really believed it, even when Skeleton dropped his shovel and laughed at me.

Chapter 23:

Drunk

NOW

Drea lives too far away. I need a friend fast.

I knock on the door. Praying for Omar to answer. Surprisingly, he does.

"Come on in," Omar says as he opens the door, "newly non-grounded person."

"I ran away," I say. "Crap, I am such a little kid." And then I'm crying. Omar looks horrified. I'm embarrassed. Maybe this wasn't the best place to go.

"Okay, um, here. Sit. You probably need some water or something. Or not. . . . Why are you soaked?"

"I had to bike over here because—because my car still doesn't have a battery." I'm bawling now. Stop, stupid tears, stop.

"Oh, yeah. I forgot," Omar says, patting my back like someone would pat a puppy. "Come on, smile. It sucks to be you, but if you think about it, from like a satellite away, it's pretty funny. Your dad took the battery out of your car and left it out for a whole month. Funny. Huh?"

"Oh, yeah, funny." I hiccup. "My family is—is frickin' hilarious." I try to let a wild fake laugh escape my lips, but it sounds more like a dying animal. "Mom . . . She is making me go—" And I sob again. "Tennessee. For the rest of summer." Omar is moving his mouth and looking at me like he's trying to translate. I cover my face with my hands. It's better to give in to the sobs and stop trying to talk.

"Let's call Chase and Skye and go over to Drea's. You're already going to be in major trouble for leaving the house. You might as well make it worth it." Omar squeezes my hand. "It's gonna be okay, Clare."

We tuck Bike-a-saurus into his backyard so Mom and Dad won't see it if they sweep the neighborhood. Then Omar's texting, pulling the make-Clare-feel-better troops together.

In his car I put my head back and close my eyes. I should go home, or at least call so my parents know I'm okay.

Or not. Screw them. Maybe they'll appreciate me a little more if they think I'm in a shallow grave in the middle of the woods.

Drea meets me at her door, enfolds me in a hug, steers me to her bedroom.

"Let's start with basic creature comforts. You're soaked. Put this on." She hands me sweatpants and a T-shirt. "Do you need a hot shower first?"

"No, this is okay. It's great, even." And I'm crying again.

She gives me another hug.

"How about food? Did you eat dinner?"

I shake my head.

"I have a box of mac 'n' cheese with your name on it." Drea's sweats are the kind of soft that feels like a warm hug. "Meet me in the kitchen."

I didn't think I was hungry. I'm pretty surprised the noodles taste so good. Skeleton chews slowly and nods his head. What is he doing here? Why won't he stop following me?

"Alright, Clare." Drea says. "What happened?"

"My mom just ruined the rest of my summer by announcing that I have to go to Tennessee with her." I start out pretty calm. "You want to know why? Because Luke. He can't get a job. He can't. Because the only job he can get is construction and stuff like tarring roads and roofs. And our crappy town has only one construction site. Just one. So he's screwed. No one else will hire him. It doesn't matter that he works harder than anyone else I know. And he is trying. But no one wants to give him a chance. Then there's that Dan creep. He's got to be on meth. Just look at him. Fucking Dan shows up last night. And I know what's going to happen. I know . . ." I can't say it. I won't believe it. "Luke swears he's sorry and won't do anything to end up in jail again. He's screwed up before, but he's a good person. And you know what I don't get?" I can feel the sobs pushing the inside of my heart. I swallow them and keep going. "Mom loves him more than me. Luke walks through the door, and Mom is a different person. She's *happy*. She's welcoming him right back into the family. Like he's never done anything wrong. Like he was away fighting a war instead of in prison. Everyone in town hates him.

ANNA SHINODA

And they hate me, too, because of him. I know it. I'm not stupid. Even you can't stand being around him."

Drea winces.

"Clare, I'm sorry—"

"No, I get it." I cut her off and continue to babble. "And—and—and at dinner." I pause, trying to catch my words. "Dinner was a mess. I don't understand. I'm so good. I've got good grades. And I *had* a good job. And maybe I break their rules once in a while, but I never hurt anyone. I don't get it." I'm sobbing. I don't know what I'm saying and where it's all coming from. Stop talking. Stop talking.

Drea grabs my hands. "Your parents are crazy." She forces me to look her in the eyes. "I mean it, Clare. They are crazy. Do you know how many times my mom says she wishes she could adopt you?"

My chest is heaving. Through my tear-blurred eyes photos splattered in Drea's kitchen start to come into focus. Drea, her Mom, and me camping. Me and Drea dressed up for homecoming. Photos of us from elementary school, holding up awards for attendance.

Drea's mom is the best. I wish she were home tonight.

"You got it all out?" Drea says as she hands me a tissue. I nod, wiping my face; it's not all out, but I'm going to pretend it is. "C'mon. It's your night, Miss Clare. Everyone's waiting in the living room for you. What do you want to do?"

Skeleton is leaning toward the pictures. He's sipping his brandy and looking nostalgic. He turns to me and points to his almost empty glass.

"I think I want to drink," I say.

"Are you sure?" she asks. Skeleton gives an over-exaggerated nod.

"Positive."

"Promise you'll be a happy drunk?" Drea says.

"Promise."

She opens the never-locked liquor cabinet.

"What would you like?"

"Brandy," I say. Skeleton raises his glass, winks an eye socket.

"Brandy?"

"It's a friend of mine's favorite drink." I smile. My face still feels puffy, but the urge to cry has passed. Drea is right. It's my night out. I'm going to have a great time.

"Clare," Omar says. He bounces the quarter off the coffee table. It lands perfectly in my drink. I take a swallow and feel the brandy slowly traveling down my esophagus, leaving a hot trail.

"Clare!" Drea says, bouncing the quarter. It lands in my drink.

"Baby doll, Clare!" Lala bounces the quarter and misses. "Aw, well." She shrugs.

"Clare!" Skye misses, too, pulling the brim of her newsboy hat over her eyes in mock embarrassment.

"No wonder our girls' basketball team did so lousy this year," Chase teases, then quickly gives her a kiss on the cheek.

"Clare!" Chase misses.

"And now we know who the weak link is on the guys' team!" Skye teases back, then hands me the quarter.

"If I make it, you all have to drink." Bounce. Splash. "Cheers!"

Somehow that ends the game, and now we're sitting around, drinking, and talking loudly. Lounging on the couch, Skeleton lights his cigar. The smoke fills his mouth, leaking from his nose, ears, and eyes. I try everyone's drinks.

"What's in this? I like it." Chase is drinking a screwdriver, with lots and lots of vodka. Omar's margarita is so tasty, I drink half of it. I like Drea's rum and coke, but not nearly as much as Lala's apple martini. I'm getting a real education tonight.

"Baby doll," Lala says, playing with the star charm on her necklace, "you feeling better?"

"Yes, I am, thank you very much." Wow. Look at me, sounding all formal. I'm like a dignitary. I stand up and bow.

"You sound like you're doing a lot better." Lala chuckles. "But seriously, Clare, you can tell me about your problems anytime. I'm full of good advice."

"Oh, thanks, but I don't think you'd understand my family." I almost turn to Skeleton for confirmation, but I decide I don't want to look crazy.

"What? You don't think my family's got issues? Just because my closet isn't wide open like yours doesn't mean we don't have a skeleton or two locked away."

"You do? What kind? Wait. Did you know mine drinks BRANDY?" I gulp my drink now, wondering if it's getting weaker. I announce, "There's not enough brandy in my brandy."

Everyone laughs. Are they laughing at me? Or are they laughing at Skeleton?

"Okay, fine. You want a skeleton. How's this," Lala says, putting her apple martini down. "My mother's mother was a prostitute. In Vegas." We all laugh. It can't be helped. "I don't think that's *such* a bad thing, but you know my family . . . so religious. Sex is right up there with murder. Alright, who's next?" Lala scans the room and zeroes in on Chase. "Your turn, big man."

"So do you guys remember, like, five years ago, when my sister, Kim, took a year to study abroad?" He leans over to untie, then retie his bright white Nikes.

Skye gives him a shove. "Come on, already. Enough with the fake suspense."

"She actually went to go live in some hippie commune because she wanted to 'get back to nature.'" He raises his fingers in air quotes. "But really it was because she met this guy who 'lives off the land' and has 'no carbon footprint.' Mom and Dad were horrified. She dropped the chance to go to Yale so she could learn to compost her own shit."

The sip Skeleton was taking sprays out of his nose holes and mouth, along with his silent laugh.

"Noooo. You lie. Miss Aerospace Engineer with the 'I Break for Technology' bumper sticker? Come on, Chase," Omar says.

"I'm serious. After her boyfriend dumped her," Chase continues, "my parents came to her rescue. As soon as

MIT would take her, she was back in school with no signs of ever wanting to give up her cell phone—or her toilet—again. Yeah, my parents like to think that secret is deep underground. But I think it's pretty funny. Omar's turn."

"Okay. When I was, like, twelve, I was going through my mom's desk drawer looking for scissors, and I saw a few brochures for . . . a clothing-optional retreat." Omar shrugs. "I don't know if they ever went, but, I mean, maybe."

"Your dad?" Lala grabs Omar's face with both hands. "But all his body hair. And his belly."

Everyone's laughter is really loud. Too loud.

"Shh, shh," I tell them. "We have to be quiet. For my ears."

"Someone is druuuunnnk." Omar puts his margarita down and does a tumble across the room. "Ta-da!"

Tumbling. That's fun. I like to do somersaults. I bend over and put my head to the ground, looking between my legs. The room is strange upside down. And moving. Just a little bit. I try to tuck my neck and roll, but I end up crashing into the side of the end table.

"Hi, kids." Wait. Who's that?

"Oh, shit. Ms. P." Omar looks up.

Drea's mom is standing over me. She shakes her head and sighs. "Dump your drinks, guys, and grab yourselves some water. Drea, in the kitchen."

I don't like the way the room is spinning. Skeleton is sitting on the chair. How is the chair moving?

Stop. Stop spinning. Stop, please, stop. My stomach. Oh, no. This is bad, bad, bad.

I spring up from the floor.

I hate puking. Stop, stop, stop. Drea's here now. She's got my hair. She's rubbing my back.

"Sorry. Sorry. Sorry. Do you still like me?"

"I love you, Miss Clare."

Vomit again.

In the morning I'm snug on Drea's trundle bed. A huge bottle of water and aspirin are on the bedside table.

There's a note from Lala. *Baby doll, I'm covering your morning shift. Try to be there by 2:00. I don't want Lucille going crazy on you.*

I look at the clock. It's noon already. I drink the water and take the aspirin. I lie down again. My head is pounding. I feel like shit.

Do a half walk, half crawl to the living room. Drea's mom is on the couch with Skeleton, an ice pack on his skull.

"Hi, Clare." She pats the cushion next to her. "Have a seat."

Please don't yell at me.

"First of all, I was hoping I'd never have to worry about things like locking up the liquor cabinet because I can't trust Drea and her friends."

I feel like supershit. Ms. P is the best mom on this planet, and I've broken her trust.

"Sorry," I say.

"Well, it's locked now." She shrugs.

"Clare. I love you," she continues. "I know sometimes you have to learn by doing." She sighs. "But you have to be more careful. We were lucky you were here, with friends. We were lucky that the worst thing that happened is you got sick and have a hangover. You are worth too much to do this to yourself." She pauses, then adds, "I called your parents last night after we talked."

"We talked?" I remember her coming home, me throwing up.

"Yes, we talked. I told your parents that you were very emotional. After all, Luke being home is a big deal for everyone in your family."

"Are they going to kill me?" I ask. "Did you tell them I was drunk?"

"No, they aren't going to kill you. And I didn't tell them you were drunk. I wanted to check in with you when you were sober first, then decide if they need to know."

"Ummm, I can't remember everything that happened last night," I admit. This is so embarrassing.

"Well, you told me a lot about your feelings about Luke being in prison all these years. Things you are afraid of. Bad memories of things that you've seen him do." She takes my hands in hers. "You told me a lot that I didn't know. I wish things could be different for you. I'm here. You can talk to me about anything, anytime."

"Thanks." What *exactly* did I tell her last night? "I'm sorry."

Pound, pound, pound. I never realized how loud her grandfather clock ticked.

"If you want to be responsible, and make me happy, you can clean the bathroom before you leave," she says.

"Got it." I'm glad to have something to do to make up for being a huge ass last night.

"But first, Drea's in the kitchen putting together a greasy power breakfast for you. Go eat; you'll feel better," she says.

I head to the kitchen.

"Toast for the woman who was super toasted last night." Drea plops down a plate of bacon, eggs, and toast in front of me.

"I am so sorry. I feel like a complete idiot," I tell her. "Not to mention, I don't remember the heart-to-heart I had with your mom."

"Don't worry about it. Everyone was silly and drunk. You were funny. Except that puking. That was disgusting. But overall you were just funny."

"I feel like shit," I say, moving the food around on my plate and eventually taking a bite out of the thing that looks the safest: toast. It's warm and just the right amount of soft and hard. I take another bite and try the eggs. Not bad. Looks like my stomach might want to eat after all.

"You should; you drank enough last night. And don't worry. I stopped you from drunk-texting anyone. You're safe."

Well, that's one good thing. After finishing as much as I can eat, I grab the bathroom cleaner and head to the war zone.

Disgusting. Apparently I have terrible aim when drunk.

Once the bathroom is clean, I shower, replaying

what I remember over and over. Wishing I could recall even a little bit of what I said to Ms. P.

I am never getting drunk again.

To my surprise Peter is in the living room when I get out. He's holding my work bag, complete with sunblock, sunglasses, hat, and bathing suit.

"Thanks for coming by, Peter," Ms. P says. "I really appreciate it."

"No problem," he replies. Then jokes, "Clare, you owe me big. Let's go."

Neither of us says a word until we're almost to the lake. Then Peter breaks the silence by saying, "I don't know what Ms. P said to our mom, but somehow you aren't grounded anymore." I look over at him. "You still have to go to Tennessee, but you have a couple weeks of freedom first. She must have said something about Luke's last sentence. You know how Mom gets about that. She was probably so embarrassed, she would have agreed to anything."

I nod, hoping that was it.

"Thanks for taking me to work," I say. "Thanks for being a nice brother," I want to say, but I just think it instead.

Chapter 24:

Unpredictable Peter

THEN: Age Twelve

Gazing up at the sky and the pine treetops, I tried to guess how long I'd been floating for. Five minutes? Maybe even more. If there were a world record for floating, I bet I could get it.

Then the water heaved, crashing over me. I sputtered to the surface. Peter had jumped in, practically on top of me. "Clare, you won't ever pass the swim test if all you do is float."

"Shut up, Peter. Leave me alone. I can swim."

"Doggy-paddling doesn't count," he replied. "You'll never get to swim in the deep end that way."

"I said, 'Leave me alone.'" Drea tricked off the diving board and then swam toward the little island, to join Omar on his plastic silver raft.

I was stuck on the shallow side surrounded by water wings, mounds of sand claiming to be castles, babies in "waterproof" diapers. Lucky me.

"I'm not here to make fun of you; I want to teach you." He nodded toward the boogie board he was holding.

I dragged my toes along the bottom, sand and slime.

"Really? No jokes?" I asked. Peter was so unpredictable.

Was he going to be nice to me today? My eyes searched the shore, water, even trees for signs of Peter's friends.

"No jokes. Promise."

"Aren't you on duty?" I glanced toward the lifeguard stand, surprised to see a new girl, copper-toned skin, a huge fake daisy holding her long blond hair back.

"My shift's over." Peter waved at Daisy Hair, then turned back to me. "C'mon. Let me teach you. I've taught all your friends. None of them has drowned yet."

Drea was pulling herself up onto the island. I really wanted to be out there with her.

"Okay." I took the board.

"Kick from your hips. Point your toes. No, not like that. Think more like ballet or something. Better. Keep your knees straight."

I felt like a baby kick, kick, kicking my way around the shallow end. Embarrassing.

"There you go!" Peter shouted after me. "Try a couple more laps—shore to the rope. You need a great kick to be a good swimmer." Peter watched from the side as I did laps, pointing at me as he talked to Daisy Hair. So *that's* why he was being so nice to me.

"You're a quick learner," he announced as I kicked my way to his side.

"What's next?" I handed him the boogie board.

"Arms." Peter put his arms up in the air. "I want you to pretend we are picking apples— Don't roll your eyes. This really works. Pick an apple, put it in your pocket. Yep, like that, but floating on your stomach with your face in the water. Oh, yeah. Don't forget to breathe every couple of apples." He took my arms and showed me. Then as he and the golden girl made small talk, I practiced each stroke.

"Now put it together!" Peter jumped into the water and held me with one hand on my belly, one on my back. Then no hands.

I didn't care if Peter was teaching me just to impress her. The water was now lighter, easier to control.

"You're doing it!" Peter yelled.

Luke would be so proud of me. I wished he were here.

I swam back to Peter. He gave me a high five, and then we celebrated with an ice cream sandwich.

Sometimes Peter could be the best brother in the world.

Chapter 25:

Responsibility

NOW

"You weren't here this morning." Chris is glaring at me, his arms crossed in indignation.

"I know. Lala covered my shift." I grab two more aspirin from my purse, wash them down with nearly an entire bottle of water. My stomach twists. I hope I don't throw up again.

"Not for your shift. For, you know . . . before." He leans close to my ear and whispers the last part of the sentence, "To teach me to swim."

Of course Chris shows up the one morning I don't.

"I wasn't feeling well," I growl. Literally, like an animal.

"You look hungover." My mouth drops. Is it that obvious? I'm about to snap at him to go away and leave me alone, when he lowers his voice so only I can hear, "Don't think you can fool me. I know all about drunks."

Chris knows all about drunks.

I want to be responsible, take my sunglasses off, look him in the eye, and tell him that he can talk to me about anything, that I can help because I know about addicts and what they do when they are out of control. But I don't, because I am aware of how sour my sweat smells, the bad cotton taste in my mouth. I'm aware of my actions last night, how hypocritical it would be to say anything to him. So I stay quiet.

"And Mandy says you quit. So I guess that means you aren't teaching me to swim." Chris pouts.

"I'm going to visit my grandma. She's old and she needs our family to help her." The sun glinting off the lake is burning my eyes. I just want to go home and lie down in a very dark room for many hours.

"But what about me?" His whiny voice makes my head pound even more.

He's not my problem. He's not my responsibility. But still . . .

"I have two weeks. I'll be here. You promise to show?"

"Deal," he says.

As he walks away, I wonder who the alcoholic is in his family. The Jordans have done a very good job keeping that skeleton in the closet.

When I return home that night, I'm braced for yelling, for Mom to scream at me about sharing family information. I sneak in the back door, safely making it to the bathroom without encountering my parents.

The cool shower feels so good; my dark room even better.

At family dinner, all together, Mom sets her lips into a deep frown, saying to me, "We will talk later this evening." Then she drones on about Tennessee and flight options.

Before bed Mom treads into my room and drops my car keys and cell phone onto my desk.

"Here. I hope you're happy," she says. "In the future use a little more discretion when discussing our family with others. I am extremely disappointed in you. Luke is trying to make a fresh start. He needs all of our support, including yours. Airing our dirty laundry to Drea's mother is not supporting your brother and our family. Don't do it again. Ever."

Mom stops at the fish tank, gazing in, watching Melanie's dark body glide back and forth. Her brow wrinkles smooth. "You need to ask Dad and Peter about watching your angels while we're away."

"I'll talk to them tomorrow." I say my first words to Mom since I stormed out last night. "And I'll clean the tank before we leave so hopefully it won't be too gross when we get back."

She nods. "That should be fine. Remind Peter to check the water level and the temperature, too. You're doing a good job caring for these fish. Their colors are so vibrant." I can almost feel the compliment, almost enjoy Mom's words, until she adds, "I'd hate for anything to happen to them." She leaves me with that final positive thought. Thanks, Mom, for giving me one more reason to hate this trip.

My cell phone is dead. I pull the cord from my desk, plug it in, and wait for a sign of life. The screen lights up. I've got some bars. I text Drea: "What's on tonight?"

Drea texts back immediately: "Movie night at Skye's. You free?!?"

After getting Mom's permission, I'm sitting in the driver's seat.

I turn the engine. The car rumbles. Dad put the battery back in. The happiness that floods me actually makes my eyes tear. Two weeks. Two weeks of friends. Of work. Of escape.

Chapter 26:

Haunted Farmhouse

THEN: Age Twelve

Haunted. I was sure Granny and Papa's second floor was haunted. Walking up the steps from the tiny kitchen, an invisible hand reached in to squeeze my heart, every time.

Alone, because I was the youngest and it was bedtime for me.

Lightning flashed every few seconds through the window, helping the single ceiling bulb illuminate the staircase. I stood at the bottom, looking up to the first landing, wondering what was past the corner. If I ran, I'd be past the stairs, in the big room, empty except for two beds and a wardrobe, left over from Mom's childhood. Then I could hide under the covers.

I ran. Up the stairs. The thunder rattled the old windows.

Into the room. Into the bed. Without drapes I could see far across the cornfields, could watch the lightning touch down. Please, please, let the lightning hit the rod and not the farmhouse.

I wished I were home. I wished I played soccer like Peter so I could be at camp this week instead of stuck in Granny and Papa's haunted farmhouse.

With eyes squeezed tight I held my breath and waited for sleep. That was when I heard the creak. The creak of the floorboards. Someone was in the room.

It was a demon, rising into a black form through the floor, coming closer. Clawing its way toward me, pulling itself up with nails sunk deep into the ancient bedpost. Staring straight at me.

Cringing, I forced an eye open. And nearly fainted with relief. It was only Luke.

"Luke?" I whispered. "I'm scared up here all alone."

"Squeaks, what are you afraid of?" He turned on the lights, sat on the edge of my bed. It didn't help much. Yellow patches on the ceiling, discolored and never repainted from past leaks, made eerie designs of twisted faces. The wardrobe loomed massively. Anything could be hiding inside it.

"Everything," I whispered. "I'm afraid of everything."

"I'll protect you," Luke said, hugging me close, "from everything."

With Luke in the room sleep came quickly—until the sound of Skeleton's bones came clanking. In the shadows I could see Luke's empty bed. Could hear the creaks of a door opening and shutting, directly under our room. It must be Luke, I told myself. There are no such things as ghosts. I wanted to fall back to sleep, but my bladder wouldn't let me, no matter how hard I tried to ignore it.

I climbed from my bed, tiptoed down the stairs, pushed the bathroom door open.

Luke didn't see me at first. An empty pen connected his nose to the counter.

"What are you doing?" I asked.

He looked up.

"Shut the door!" he spat. Frozen, I stared at him. "I said get out!" he yelled. He rushed the door, slamming it in my face.

"Clare Bear, go back to bed," Dad's voice said from behind me.

"But, Dad, I—"

"Go on." He gently steered me by my shoulders to the stairs, then headed back to the bathroom.

I sat on the bottom stair and waited my turn. I really had to go. But Dad didn't wait; he flung the bathroom door open.

"What in the hell are you thinking?" he sternly said to Luke. "Bringing this into your grandparents' home! Get out of this house!"

An animal roar from Luke. Then he charged. Right at my father. Dad jumped out of his way.

The hall was full now, with Mom, Granny, and Papa, fresh from bed.

"Get out!" Dad shouted this time. "Get the hell out of this house!" He pushed Luke into the living room. Luke shoved Dad back. Hard. Dad fell, and Luke fled.

While the adults were arguing over what had happened, I snuck off the stairs to the bathroom. As I opened the door, I heard my mom gasp. "Oh, no! Clare!" She pushed past me into the bathroom.

"Mom! I have to go, bad!" I protested.

"In just a minute," she said, grabbing the pen, wiping off the counter, looking under the sink. "Okay. All done. Bathroom, then straight to bed!"

Skeleton and I lay awake for a while, thinking about how it had all started—the pen and counter—knowing it had to be something to do with drugs. I thought about Dad yelling at Luke, and another memory tugged at me, one that started with broken windows. But I shut it down as soon as the trail of red circles appeared.

Papa's rooster was cock-a-doodling, and although I was really tired, I rolled over and looked at Luke's bed. Empty. I tiptoed downstairs. Everyone else was still asleep.

Luke was lying on the couch, dried blood coming from his nose and a crack on his forehead. He was still. I didn't know if he was alive.

I ran to Mom and Dad's room, then tiptoed to Mom's side of the bed and gently touched her arm, careful not to wake up Dad.

"Mom," I whispered. As her eyes fluttered open, I whispered again, "Luke." She pulled on her robe and followed me to the living room. After checking Luke, she nodded.

"He's okay, just sleeping." She paused. "Thank you for getting me, Clare Bear. Why don't you grab yourself a bowl of cereal?" Another pause. "And, Clare, let's keep this between the two of us, okay?"

I nodded.

As I ate my cereal, I peeked into the living room,

catching Mom gently wiping away the blood on Luke's head and face while he slept. Adhering Band-Aids. Lovingly, but at the same time like it was her duty to clean it all up, cover it all up—his cuts, the blood, the truth—before he woke and saw what he looked like. Before Dad and Granny and Papa saw him too.

It didn't matter. Later that day Papa told Luke, "I can't have drug addicts in this house. You come back when you've been sober a year, or you never come back. You hear me, Luke?"

While Luke gathered up his stuff, I watched him, sniffling. It wasn't fair that Papa was just kicking him out. He said Luke was a drug addict. Why didn't Papa offer to give him help instead of making him leave?

Luke gave me a kiss and a big Luke-sized hug. And then he was gone. Again.

Chapter 27:

Nightmare

NOW

Icy blue air.

My screams break though my ears, break though the nightmare.

My eyelids fly open.

My room. The lights are all on. Luke is here.

"Squeaks? You were screaming loud enough to wake the whole town. I came running in! You okay?"

"Nightmare." I swallow hard. My heart is beating so loudly that I swear he can hear it, all the way by the door.

"Damn. You still get nightmares?" Why is Luke still in his jeans? Has he been up all night? What is he hiding behind his back?

"Ugh. All the time." I say.

"Will a little four-fourteen-a.m. snack help?" Luke suggests.

I rub the sweat off my forehead. "Okay."

"Alright, Squeaks. One Luke special coming right up. Meet you in the kitchen."

With all the confusion of the nightmare and Luke being there, I almost don't notice him drop my purse to the floor. Almost.

Chapter 28:

Why Is Luke in Jail, Mom, Dad?

THEN: Age Thirteen

"Luke's been picked up. Again," Mom told Dad as he walked in from work. Her voice was quiet and exhausted, her eyes red.

Did she realize I was sitting right there?

"Damn it." Dad pressed his lips together. "What for?"

"The usual," Mom said. I remembered the last time I'd asked about why he was in jail. The wrong place at the wrong time.

"What is 'the usual'?" I asked, surprising myself and my parents.

"He was in the wrong place at the wrong time," Mom answered quickly.

"But what did they *accuse* him of doing?" I was thirteen. That answer wasn't good enough for me anymore. I knew people didn't keep getting randomly thrown in jail if they didn't do anything wrong.

Mom looked at Dad. He ran his hand over his head, then shrugged, giving my mom permission to tell me that Luke had been caught possessing drugs, but he'd claimed he'd been wearing a friend's coat. They'd also said he'd stolen something. She added,

"Now, Ms. Nosy Pants, didn't I ask you to vacuum your room?"

Turning toward the closet where we kept the vacuum, my ear caught one more important piece of information.

"Do we know what he's facing?"

"His lawyer says with his priors he could be looking at four to six years."

Four to six years? My brain raced. Four years at the very least? In four years I'd be *seventeen* when he got out again! Four years of summers. Four years of Halloweens, Thanksgivings, Christmases, Easters. Four years without my brother.

And four years of Luke being in prison. I swallowed hard. I didn't know what that was like, but I knew it had to be awful.

Watching the dirt disappear in neat little stripes while I listened to the roar of the vacuum, I let my mind go where I rarely allowed it. Luke probably was never in the wrong place at the wrong time. My parents just told me that because I was a little kid. So before, had it been drugs? Theft? Or something different?

And this time . . . What kind of drugs? And if it had been his friend's coat, did his friend go to jail too, or just Luke?

It didn't make sense to me that he'd steal something. Luke had a job. And he got to stay here and eat here, and Mom didn't charge him anything, so why would he steal? Maybe he had a really good reason, like maybe he was trying to help someone who was really poor. Like Robin

Hood did? I told myself to stop being stupid. Robin Hood was just a story, and Luke was going to jail. And a drug habit was expensive.

I imagined all the questions I had being sucked out of the air and into the vacuum. I put the full bag in the trash outside. Left my unanswered questions there too.

Chapter 29:

Christmas in July

NOW

Bing Crosby is crooning. "It's beginning to look a lot like Christmas, everywhere you go."

Which wouldn't be strange, if it were December. But it's July. And I was asleep. Finally sleeping deeply and soundly, like a log, which I always thought was a weird saying, but in some ways a good saying because logs don't have nightmares.

Bing keeps singing. As my eyes open, a tiny tree decorated with lights and little paper ornaments slowly comes into focus.

"With candy canes and silver lanes aglowwwwwwwww," Luke's voice joins Bing's just as he slides into view in front of the tree.

I point out the obvious. "There's a Christmas tree in my room."

"I know. It's great. Ma never throws out anything. The attic's like a fucking junkyard, but I found this, and look, ornaments made by you and me and Peter. You were, like, six years old. Do you remember? Man, I loved making those with you guys—all the glitter and cotton balls and paint. We should make some today." I can barely keep up with Luke. Is he talking fast, or am I thinking slowly?

"But why is there a Christmas tree in here?" I sit up and start to survey the room. Everything else seems normal enough. My fish are still swimming, my duffel bag is waiting for me to fill it with clothes for the trip out to Granny's. My purse is on the floor next to the bed, exactly where I left it once I made sure nothing was missing after I saw Luke drop it. And I'm assuming the two twenties and the ten that I took out of my wallet and stashed in my sock drawer are also still there.

"Because. We're gonna celebrate Christmas. To make up for the last few ones that I missed. So here. Merry Christmas." Luke hands me a small box. Wrapped in gold paper, a red supermarket bow from Mom's ribbon stash stuck on top.

A necklace. Silver locket, no inscription, just an oval of smooth metal.

"Open it."

Inside is a tiny photo of a teenage Luke holding a baby Clare.

"It's you and me, Squeakers, from your first New Year's. Right after Ma brought you home from the hospital. You were like the size of a football." Luke looks so young. "Ma made me wear those dorky red pants. Oh, and you spit up all over me right after we took this picture. Ma said, 'Oh, Clare Bear, why did you do that? I hope we have one good picture.' And we did—this one." Luke is still talking at hyper-speed. I'm afraid to look at his eyes. Afraid they will be red. Afraid to smell his breath. I don't want this moment to be ruined. I'm just going to assume he's excited and happy, and that a substance has nothing to do with this morning.

"So do you like it, the locket, the photo? I'm not so good at this. I mean, I don't have a lot of practice at giving gifts." My heart cracks—how could Luke be afraid that I wouldn't like it?

"It's the best gift. I love it. And how can you say you're not good at giving gifts?" I point to the wooden box. "It's for my treasures. Take a look at what I keep inside."

His fingers run along the smooth edges, delicately lifting the lid. His hand floats down and picks up each letter, one by one. Bing Crosby and his chorus are now singing "I'll Be Home for Christmas"—adding a bittersweet soundtrack to the moment.

"You've kept them? My letters? All of them?" His voice is wavy.

"I kept all of them." I rub my eyes with my pillow, telling them to stop watering.

"If only in my dreams . . ." Bing's voice is going to push me over the crying edge.

Luke clears his throat, finally says, "That's cool, Squeakers. Really."

He gently places the box back on my bookcase. Checks the clock next to my bed. "Wow. I've gotta get to that construction site before we go. Remind them about me for when we get back. I guess Christmas is over till December, huh?"

"Thanks, Luke. This means a lot to me," I say.

"You got it." He gives a wave as he leaves the room.

I open the locket. Squint to get a better look at the photo. Luke's comfortable with holding me, and I'm snug in his arms, sleeping.

I'd love to stay in bed all day, pretending like it's Christmas for real, reading a book in my pj's under the covers with no responsibilities, no worries. But it's July. My last day of work for the summer. Chris's last chance to pass the swim test before I leave. He's showed up for five lessons, and we've made good progress.

Chris smiles and jumps up when he sees me.

There are two ways to get into a freezing, snow-runoff-filled lake. One is tiptoeing in, screaming "It's too cold!" with each step, holding your breath as the water slowly covers inch after inch of skin. The other is jumping in, not knowing which part of you is the coldest. Getting the shock over within a few seconds, convincing your body and mind that the water is not really that cold, starting to move your arms and legs, letting the warm blood pump through your body at the same time that you feel the sun penetrating the water.

"On three." Chris and I hold hands. Our toes curl along the concrete edge. We'll be jumping in waist deep for me, chest deep for Chris.

"One," I say.

"Man, it is going to be so cold!" Chris says.

"Two," I say.

"And three!"

Shock. Brrr. Sun. Not so bad.

I've learned a lot about Chris these past couple of

weeks. He's not the bully that I pegged him for, or the annoying brat of a brother that Mandy can't stand to be around, or the hyper kid that Lucille tries to push away because he doesn't fit quite right in her stupidly perfect little family. The first lessons were impossible. He didn't want to do anything. But once his confidence kicked in, he really started working hard. I start to wonder if Luke was like Chris as a kid—his potential overlooked because he got in trouble. Chris *really* wants to learn, and I am desperate to teach him. Desperate to be the outside force that inspires him to challenge himself.

"Let's get warmed up with your kicks." I toss him a boogie board. "More from the hips than the knees. There you go. Perfect." After he's warmed up, we start the swim test. He jumps from the diving board into the deep end and treads water. Three minutes later he begins his swim to the island, me doing a sidestroke beside him. His crawl is pretty ugly, his breaststroke not much better. He's wasting a ton of energy, but at least he's swimming. Kind of. When we get to the island, he pulls himself out of the water and flops down, exhausted. He just doesn't have the endurance to swim back.

"You did great, Chris," I tell him as he rests. Then my heart drops a little. "I wish I had more time. I think with another week of practice we could tighten up your strokes and you could pass the test for sure."

He shrugs, but I can tell he's disappointed. He agrees to practice while I'm gone, and I demonstrate some more strokes in case he wants to try them before I return.

"Hey, Chris," I say, looking him straight in the eye. "You let me know if there is anything else you need help with, okay? Not just swimming. Anything."

His face scrunches up, like he's deciding whether to tell me something or not. Lucille breaks the moment, yelling from the beach, holding his blue towel up.

"Thanks," Chris says. As we swim toward his mom, I try to convince myself that the trip to Granny's will be over before I know it. There will still be enough summer to finish teaching him to swim. I have to believe that, because I can't just leave Chris on his own.

Chapter 30:

On My Own

THEN: Age Thirteen

Two lessons. That's all I had. One from Luke: learn to float. One from Peter: a basic crawl stroke.

Private lessons were out—too expensive. Dad's idea of teaching me was throwing me into the deep end and yelling, "Sink or swim!" Mom refused to help, using her disgust for the lake water as an excuse.

Drea showed me what I would need to know for the swim test: jump off diving board, tread water, swim to the island and back. I watched other kids, little kids, younger than me by three or four years, pass the test using a number of styles: backstroke, crawl, breast-stroke, sidestroke, even doggy-paddle.

Then I practiced. Drea cheering me on.

In July I passed the swim test. All on my own.

The lifeguard was so impressed with how hard I tried to swim correctly that she gave me a couple of free lessons so I could really learn. At the end of summer she gave me information on junior lifeguards. By applying for financial aid, I was able to do the program for free, CPR class included.

The next summer I was a junior lifeguard. And

I knew that once I turned sixteen, I would pass the test and become an official lifeguard and work my summers at the lake. I made the plan, and I did it. All on my own.

Chapter 31:

Favor

NOW

"Hey, Squeaks, can you do me a favor?" Luke is standing at my bedroom door. Everything I think I need for the next few weeks is packed in two mismatched duffel bags, a backpack, and a purse. Our flight leaves at eight p.m. tonight.

"Depends on how long it takes," I say, stuffing another few skeins of yarn into one of the bags. As a last-minute addition I decide to pack enough yarn to knit a blanket, and a beanie for Ryan. "I'm meeting friends later."

"I just need you to drive me to a few stores so I can return some things." Now I notice the three plastic shopping bags in his hand.

"Where?"

"Bargain Bin, Compute This, and Valerie's."

I look at the clock. Eleven a.m. Okay, there's enough time. "As long as I'm home by two," I say, dropping a large feeder into the aquarium that's supposed to keep my fish alive for a month. I double-check my fish care instructions for Peter. "Let's go."

The forty-five-minute car ride is all small talk. Luke asking questions about school and friends.

We pull into the parking lot of Bargain Bin. Luke opens a small black organizer, looks through it carefully. His fingers slide down each receipt as he looks from his shopping bags to the list of items printed on each slip of paper. He pulls a few receipts out, tosses the organizer onto the floor of the car.

"I'll just be a second. Wait here." It's not an offer; it's an order, and I follow it.

Skeleton looks over my shoulder from the backseat. "What are you doing here?" I mutter at him.

He points at the organizer, open on the passenger seat floor, a few receipts spilling out. I reach over and pick it up. Sliding the receipts back in, I notice the organizer is filled with them from different stores, the ink dark and new.

Skeleton's bony finger tap, taps, taps the top of the receipt. Purchase date: June fifth. Luke was still in prison.

I clamp the organizer shut.

"Maybe I should take a lesson from Luke and try organizing things this way," I say to Skeleton, changing the subject. "I can never find any receipts."

Frustrated, Skeleton throws his arms up at me.

"Big deal. It's not a crime to have an organizer." I return it to the floor. Skeleton pushes me, leaning far over the seat, hits the organizer open so papers fly out.

"Stop!" I yell, hurrying to stuff the receipts back in. There are so many. Too many. Luke couldn't have had time to shop for this much stuff. He couldn't have afforded it either.

As Luke exits the store, I quickly put his organizer back.

"Thanks." Luke slides into the car. "Two more stops, then we're done. We're good on time, right?"

"Two more stops?" Check the clock. A little past noon. There is plenty of time. Skeleton shakes his head. He's right. Whatever Luke is doing with this receipt book doesn't make sense.

And I don't want to be a part of it. "I don't know. I don't want to be late."

Luke's smile drops. "C'mon, Squeaks." He pulls his fingers through his hair. "It's only noon. We have plenty of time. Besides, I need to handle these returns today. We leave tonight."

I agree to drive to the next store. Luke exits the car. Skeleton shakes my shoulders.

"Leave me alone." I turn on the radio and close my eyes as I sing along to words I don't quite know.

One last stop. Ignoring Skeleton as best I can.

"Alright. All done." Luke jumps into the car. "One o'clock. You should be home with time to spare."

He tries to start up a conversation, but I fake an excited "I *love* this song!" and turn the music as loud as I can stand it. Maybe nothing that weird is going on. Maybe I'm overreacting. Maybe not. But I know one thing: I don't want to think about it anymore. He's my brother and I love him. And that is all that matters. That has to be all that matters.

Chapter 32:

Broken Bones

THEN: Age Thirteen

When Mom got to the hospital, she was worried only for a minute. Once she realized I wasn't going to die, she demanded, "Explain yourself, young lady."

It was, of course, all Peter's fault.

I'd been lying on the grass next to Drea, in my favorite bikini, my hair still wet from my last laps across the lake, listening to my iPod—well, I should say Peter's iPod.

"Hey, buttface!" Then there was Peter, standing over me, chewing sunflower seeds with an open mouth, his pack of friends chewing and spitting behind him.

"I didn't say you could borrow that." He spit a shell on me, which landed in the pool of sweat on my stomach. I scowled, brushing it off.

"Yes, you did." Well, at least he had before.

"That was yesterday, assmunch," he said.

"You weren't home this morning," I said.

"I'm taking it back." He sent another shell flying in my direction.

"Stop spitting on me!" I stood up, standing on my tiptoes, trying to make my eyes even with his.

"Ooooh. So tough," he taunted.

"You aren't even going to use it. You work this afternoon, pizza boy. *If* you are still employed." The music was a key part of my perfect day. I planned to fight for it.

"It's mine and I'm taking it back." He stooped to grab the iPod. Drea nabbed it first and handed it to me as I ran past her. It was so smooth, I bet people thought we'd planned it.

"Bitch!" Peter yelled behind me.

I ran. Straight across the grass, jumping over classmates sleeping on towels, running through picnics and barbecues. People yelled, "Hey! Watch it!" I caught a glimpse of Skeleton running beside me, picking up a soda from one picnic, a chicken leg off the barbecue of another, reminding everyone, including me, that Peter and I were Luke's brother and sister.

Peter was getting closer, closer.

I turned. Started running down the slope. In one move Peter snatched his iPod from my hand and shoved my back. I saw the brick stairs. There was no other way to land.

Everyone around us heard the snap.

My jagged forearm bone stuck through the flesh. There was too much blood. Too much of my blood. The last thing I heard was Drea screaming for help. Then I must have decided that passing out would be the best plan.

I was in an ambulance. Then the hospital. Surgery. A metal plate and some screws. Stitches on my arm, under a cast. Stitches on my forehead. Words like "shattered pieces" used to describe my forearm.

Mom, stroking my hair, said, "You are lucky it's only a broken arm and that you're going to be okay." Then, suddenly angry, she crossed her arms. "Do you realize how expensive this is going to be? Why can't you leave your brother's things alone?" When I didn't say a word, she pried, "Explain yourself, young lady."

I couldn't see Skeleton, but I could hear his bones *clink*, *clink*, *clink*ing together.

Peter stood behind Mom, red puffy eyes, his face anguished. When she left the room for coffee, he sat on the edge of my bed. "Sorry, Clare. Sorry. I didn't mean to," he said. "I didn't mean to. Sorry."

Chapter 33:

My Own Eyes

NOW

Granny's barn reaches up to the sky, rickety and holey, ready to be put to its final rest. Eye-level weeds engulf the land around, showing the top of Papa's rusted tractor. Why would she want the barn fixed? We should tear it down.

"Let's put anything burnable here," Mom says as she hurls a busted-up tire to mark the spot, "which I hope will be most everything. Then we can torch the whole thing."

"What?" I exclaim. Air pollution, anyone? "We can't burn all this junk."

Mom glares. "Yes, we can. Tennessee law permits it. As far as the old cars and stuff go, maybe we can get a tow truck to come out here and remove them in exchange for parts. I'll be inside calling around, keeping Granny company."

I'm planning to turn and complain to Luke that we have to work in a hundred-degree weather and 90 percent humidity. But he's already hard at it, grazing the weeds down low with the weed whacker. He marches through the sea of tall grass as if he knows there is nothing to fear, no snakes hiding, no red anthills, no rats or mice.

"Hey, Squeaks"—Luke turns off the machine for a moment—"here's the plan: I'm gonna whack everything down. You throw it all in the burn pile. Be careful. Peter stepped on a hive one summer. He looked like a puffer fish." Luke laughs at the memory.

"What about snakes? And rats?" I ask, eyeballing the weeds warily.

"Just keep your eyes open. I don't want you getting hurt." Luke starts up the motor again. "AND IF YOU DO, SCREAM LOUD SO I CAN HEAR YOU!"

Like that makes me feel any better. But I scoop up a bunch of weeds, grateful that Mom forced me to wear long sleeves, long pants, and gloves. Armful by armful our burn pile becomes a mountain. We find rotten boards, a rusted hook, ruined tires, and a sack of old marbles, dirty and scuffed but still whole. Luke puts down the weeder to help me finish cleaning up his trail. The sun is already low. My back burns when I stand upright, and my arms itch despite the sleeves.

"Nice pile, Squeaks. You as tired as I am?" Luke lugs a last few massive armloads of trash to the mountain, and we are done for the day.

After dinner he announces that he's going to go shoot pool.

Granny looks up from a half-eaten slice of berry pie.

"Going to Albert's? You should bring Clare. You've earned some fun," Granny says. "Now go on. I'll do these dishes."

I'm so tired, I can barely hold up my fork, but at least I get to go to the pool hall with Luke instead of doing the dishes and playing Chinese checkers.

We enter Albert's from the back, passing stinking Dumpsters and green splinters of glass. It's dark inside, with four pool tables lit like little shrines across the room. Neon signs—BUDWEISER, PABST BLUE RIBBON, HEINEKEN, CORONA, MGD, GUINNESS—and a few strings of chili pepper lights around the bar provide the only other illumination. Luke picks a table and goes to grab us drinks. There are only eight other people here, including the bartender.

I pull out my cell phone and check. Finally! Service. I've got nothing at Granny's house.

"At pool hall w/Luke," I text Drea. "3 normal ppl. Rest are winners. Think: Night of the Living Dead (1968 version)."

Luke chats with the bartender, whose shiny bald head reflects a green glow from the Heineken sign behind him. I can't hear anything they are saying over some old rock song blaring from a jukebox in the corner. A scrawny woman with brown roots two inches deep into a long mess of orange hair sidles up to Luke. Leans against the bar.

"Woman hitting on Luke. Questioning when her last bath was." No response from Drea. I'm bummed. I should let her know I can't text from Granny's. I type, and also send the same texts to Omar. He texts back, "Don't let zombies eat yr brains."

Shiny Head puts the drinks down in front of Luke, but Luke stays to talk to the woman for a few more minutes before she goes back to the group of her three zombie friends shooting a game one table over from us.

Finally Luke brings over my Coke and his Coors, then hands me a cue stick. We play pool. Or maybe I should say I try to play pool and Luke demolishes me every time. He attempts to teach me how, claiming that since I got an A in geometry it should help, but if my aim is on, the speed that I hit the ball is off. Lack of practice trumps my mathematical experience. But it's fun. Nice to be out with Luke, without Skeleton, without the heavy stares we get back at home. I'm relaxed here, even starting to enjoy the tacky décor and the jumble of songs I don't recognize.

Luke grabs another Coors for himself and more Coke for me. The caffeine is starting to kick in and I'm not so dead tired anymore. The woman with orange hair joins Luke at the bar again. She says something. They laugh. Then Luke gives a wave to the other zombies with greasy hair and sunken cheeks. They raise their glasses to him. Why couldn't he be making friends with the three normal-looking people throwing darts in the corner?

Albert's closes. As I ease Papa's truck from the pool hall, Luke's new friends huddle together by the Dumpster. I swear I see cash exchange hands. I look over to Luke in the passenger seat, his eyes closed. Mom brought him here to get him away from Dan, to get him working. Maybe it doesn't matter. Maybe Luke knows where to find the Dans, regardless of what city or town he's in. But for the moment Luke is here, with me, heading back to Granny's house. A few beers deep, but that's all.

"I think you'll be more helpful cleaning the house," Mom announces after watching me work the second day. "You really haven't gotten much done out here." Wow. Thanks, Mom. That's really nice of you. Way to make your daughter—who, by the way, is practically getting sunstroke out here—feel motivated.

At least I get to be inside, where it's a couple degrees cooler. That afternoon we get mail from Dad. Luke's driver's license has arrived. After dinner Luke heads to the Big Boot Saloon, leaving me, under-twenty-one Clare, at home, playing a mean game of Chinese checkers against Granny and Mom. Mom wins. Granny comes in second. I lose, twice in a row, before heading to my room to work on Ryan's beanie, until I'm so tired that I can't keep my eyes open. I hear Luke tiptoe through our room to find his bed at around one a.m.

He's up the next morning brewing coffee in the kitchen even before I'm aware. Mom's got a new job for him today. I watch out the window as he blasts the peeling paint off the barn with a power sander rented from the hardware store. By the time he comes in that night, he's coated with dust like a shake-and-bake chicken. A hot shower puts him in good spirits. He stays in, beating all of us at Chinese checkers.

• • •

After a few days I have Granny's routine down. It's three in the afternoon. Granny's taking her nap, Mom's out talking to Realtors, and I am scrubbing a toilet, wondering if there is enough chicken to make dinner for everyone tonight. This is pathetic; I'm like a 1950s housewife. Omar and Chase would have enough material to make jokes to last our entire senior year.

I rinse the toilet brush, throw it under the sink, rip off my rubber cleaning gloves, and head toward the kitchen.

Luke is there, holding Granny's coffee can with one hand, pulling bills out with the other.

"Luke?" I feel Skeleton walk into the room. Feel him standing behind me.

"Hey. Clare. Um, Squeakers. Need anything from the store? Granny asked me to get flour."

I bought flour two days ago. I open the cabinet and point to the large sack, so full it might burst.

"She must be confused; I just bought some," I tell him. Skeleton picks up the deflated bag of sugar next to the flour and shakes it. I give Luke the benefit of the doubt. "Maybe she meant sugar. Looks like we're almost out."

Luke readily agrees. "Okay. I can get sugar. Anything else?"

"Chicken for dinner tonight. And, Luke"—I point to the coffee can—"don't take cash from there. That's Granny's emergency fund." I open the drawer next to the sink and grab a ten-dollar bill, leaving a five. Chicken will be about five or six dollars, the sugar around two. I hold out the bill.

He drops the money back into the can, taking the ten from my hand. As he grabs the truck keys from the hook next to the door, he says, "I think the truck needs gas too," and he takes the last five dollars from the drawer.

We filled up the tank yesterday, together, on our way back from the hardware store. I bite my lip.

As the old truck sputters down the dirt road, I open Granny's coffee can. Only $137.00 is left. There was $607.00 when Mom and I counted it the first day we got here. I wish Granny had put the money in a bank, where it would have been safe, instead of in this stupid coffee can. I close my eyes so I don't have to look at Skeleton anymore, hoping he'll be gone when I open them.

"Maybe Granny really did tell him to get groceries," I say out loud to Skeleton, my eyes still clamped shut. "Maybe she's been taking money from the can herself. Maybe he didn't steal the money."

Maybe he did.

Probably he did.

Should I tell Granny? No, not Granny. What about Mom? The one thing we've agreed on is loving Luke regardless of what he's done. Giving him second chances. Trusting him. I think about telling her, just to get her advice. But I decide I can't. She'll tell me I'm mistaken. Or worse, she'll find a way to blame me. Making the missing money somehow my responsibility, my fault it's gone. I decide to keep my mouth shut.

• • •

We wait for Luke to come home. He always takes good care of his tools, putting them away when he's done working for the day. His toolbox sits open next to the barn until the sun sets. It's nearly time to eat, so I make pasta instead of chicken. Luke misses dinner.

Mom goes to bed, but Granny and I stay up, our knitting needles clicking in syncopated time. We talk about our projects—her blanket for a friend's great-granddaughter, my beanies—talking around the subject we are both thinking about: Luke. Finally, around eleven p.m., Granny stands up.

"I'm going to hit the hay," she announces. "You probably don't want to wait up for him, Clare dear."

"Just a little while longer—" I start.

"Clare." Granny lowers herself back next to me. "I spent many nights on that couch waiting for your grandfather. Your brother is going to struggle with those alcohol demons. Maybe he'll end up sober. Maybe after he does something that he'll regret forever. And maybe he won't. But I can tell you one thing: Sitting on that couch waiting is just a waste of time."

"Granny?" My jaw has dropped down in surprise. "I didn't know Papa . . ."

"It's nothing to talk about. By the time you were born, he was done with all that. Heck, I haven't even cooked with wine for over thirty years." She gives my knee a pat, then uses the armrest to help herself stand up. "Now go on up to bed. Looking at the door won't bring him home any faster."

At the bottom of the stairs, I take a breath, hold it for a few seconds before letting it go. It's stupid. I know it's stupid. Still, climbing these stairs alone gives me the creeps. I'm the Cowardly Lion. I do believe in spooks. I do believe in spooks. I wish I could magically appear in the bedroom. But I can't, so I hold my breath and run up the stairs as fast as my legs can go.

I stay up late, lying in bed, pretending to read and listening, listening, listening. Granny is right. Worrying is not going to bring Luke home any faster. I think of her and maybe even my mom, sitting on the couch together, acting like they were playing Chinese checkers, but really waiting for Papa to come back from the bar. I try to imagine what he was like when he drank. Angry? Careless? Silly? Scary? An involuntary shiver makes me pull the covers up as I think of Granny saying, "Maybe he'll end up sober. Maybe after he does something that he'll regret forever."

I don't want to think of Papa any differently than I always have. His deep voice humming old prayer hymns as he took junk and melted it down to create something new. His leathery hands pulling a brush down a cow's back. His frame, so thick and tall that it made the tractor look small. And in the late evenings, him sitting on the front porch, smoking a cigarette and staring up at the stars, naming off constellations to me. I can't think of him any other way. Just like I want to remember only the good things Luke does.

Luke. This is partially my fault. If I'd told him we didn't need any groceries, maybe he'd be here in his bed right now.

Late that night I wake up hearing the truck loudly bouncing up the driveway. From the second-story window I see Luke fall from the driver's side, sugar bag in hand. He trips on the three little stairs leading to the back door. Holding the house key, his hand moves back and forth, up and down in little circles. After several stabs the key slides into the lock. He's so fucking wasted. I'm tempted to run downstairs and yell at him. But images of broken windows and a trail of blood make me pause. I turn on my nightstand light and grab my book, letting the words push away my thoughts. When I'm too tired to read another line, I lie on my back, eyes focused on the door.

He doesn't come up to our room. Somehow I eventually fall back asleep.

In the morning I find Luke flopped on the couch. Still fully dressed, shoes on and all. Snoring heavily. The smell of urine, beer, and something sour fills the living room.

The bag of sugar is on the kitchen counter. Along with one dollar change. Only one dollar. And no chicken. Checking the truck, I'm relieved to find that at least the tank is almost full. When I go back to the living room, Mom and Granny and Skeleton stand near the couch, looking cautiously over, the way someone would look over a cliff.

Granny says, "We need to pray for him."

Skeleton shoves Luke.

"Should I wake him?" I want to help. I let him take the money. I even gave it to him. I should have sent him out to the barn to work again, said we didn't need anything. But. I wanted to believe him. I wanted him to come back with a full tank of gas and sugar and chicken and change, all before dinner. I wanted him to show me that he wasn't going to screw up.

"Don't," Mom warns. "Let him sleep it off."

He needs to get up. To prove that he isn't going to do this again. Not to us again. I reach down to shake his shoulder.

Mom catches my arm. Says sternly, "Clare. Luke is intoxicated. Don't wake him. It's dangerous." Then she changes the subject. "You've been doing a good job in here taking care of Granny, but I could use your help painting the barn today."

The paint glides on, thick like honey but as smooth as oil. Luke did a good job blasting the wood evenly. Working with the direction of the sun, we paint the shaded side, moving along to another when it gets too sunny, west to east.

Granny makes sandwiches and brings them to us when the church bells chime noon. We silently chomp in the shade, sitting on grass and ignoring the beast still sleeping on the couch, just as we left him that morning.

At the end of the day, I gather trash to add to the pile. Mom leans down, the sun at her back, sinking, sinking into the surrounding fields. She lights the pile in one little corner, her hand, surprisingly, trembling.

"All this junk," she whispers. "My father used every little thing until it rotted or rusted . . . and even then he wouldn't get rid of it, because he saw promise in turning it into something else." Her tiny flame bursts across the newspaper, to a plank of wood, quickly taking over the whole pile.

A pair of hands rests on my shoulders. Luke's hands.

Mom silently looks at him, her jaw set, her eyes dull with exhaustion.

"Ma, Squeaks. Granny and me just finished making dinner. Come inside and eat. I'll watch the fire."

Mom simply nods and heads for the back door, her footsteps slow and steady.

"Luke, can we talk?" I want an explanation. An excuse.

"What about, Squeaks?" What about? Like he doesn't know.

"We were all worried about you this morning," I start.

"Oh, yeah. That. Sorry. I got carried away last night. I was in the store and ran into one of the guys from the bar and he invited me out to party. I just lost track, that's all." Luke wraps his arm around me and constricts. "Don't worry about me."

"But I can't help it. The way you were sleeping, like you wouldn't wake up." My mind imagines drug-induced comas. Him vomiting in his sleep and choking on it.

"I'm fine, Clare. Don't worry about me." He folds his arms over his chest.

"But I do."

"Don't." His voice is suddenly edgy.

"Hey, you know, maybe you should stay with us

tonight. Not go out and see your friends." A suggestion. Just a suggestion.

"Maybe *you* should leave me alone." He turns and lights a cigarette, drawing in a deep breath, letting the smoke out slowly, controlled. His eyes have gone hard. Hard and glassy, bloodshot from the night before.

"I love you," I say. Please hear me, Luke. Please.

Silence.

I leave him alone with the fire.

He's gone before we finish dinner.

Chapter 34:

Compassion Will Cure Him

THEN: Age Fourteen

At the end of my eighth-grade school year, my honors English class took a field trip to see the musical *Les Misérables*. Selling candy bars gave us each a ticket and the school bus ride down to the theater.

Early in the play—was it the first or second scene?—the main character was released from prison, his sentence for stealing bread so his family could eat. Everyone in the audience felt sorry for him—sorry that his family was starving, sorry that he had to resort to stealing, sorry that he had to serve a prison sentence. I could feel the audience's pity. It wasn't fair. Should stealing bread if your children are starving be considered a crime?

Out of prison he found sanctuary with a clergy member, who took him in, fed and cared for him. In the middle of the night, the main character decided to steal from the kind man. He was caught, but when the police brought him back to the bishop, the bishop not only did not press charges; he gave him the stolen goods, as well as additional items.

From there the main character changed course,

became the unlikely hero. Compassion saved him.

I left the play running those scenes over and over in my mind, thinking, Maybe all Luke needs is more compassion. Maybe I can provide the compassion that will cure him.

Chapter 35:

Good Things Await in Tennessee?

NOW

Compassion will cure him. That thought rolls over me as I sit in the pew while the priest drones on about the prodigal son and forgiveness. It's one of Mom's favorite gospels. Maybe because it justifies all the chances she gives Luke. The parable ends with the welcome home for the son who squandered all of his inheritance. But what I want to know is what happens later. After the feast is over. Does he spend the rest of his life working hard and staying out of trouble? Does his father's compassion cure him? Or has his father given him his trust only to find that his son can't change? I look at Luke. He blends right in with the church crowd, in his khakis and collared shirt. Looking at him, no one would be able to tell that he's been out nearly all night almost every night. I don't know where he goes, and I wish I didn't care. At least he's up every morning with the rest of us, ready to work.

I shift uncomfortably. Three more days and we'll be on our way home. Then what? We'll just be taking Luke back to Dan.

. . .

From the backseat of the truck, I see the barn from a distance. Damn, it looks good. It stands straight and tall, no trash or weeds to obstruct the view, the new coat of paint making it shine in the sun. I know up close how rickety it still is, how it creaks when the wind blows and how none of us dared go into the certain-death hayloft. But now at least someone might be willing to work on it some more. Give it another chance.

For a second I feel happy. Proud of the work that Luke and Mom and I did together—something good. But then Luke says something that rips it all away.

"So hey, Squeaks. I've decided to stay in Tennessee."

"What?" He's not coming home with us? "Why?"

"I made some job connections in Chattanooga. This guy I met has a brother who lives near there, so I'm gonna crash on his couch," Luke says. "They're even looking for a welder. And I took those metal classes, so maybe they'll hire me. I'll bet there's some good pay for that too."

My emotions are splitting in a million different directions. He's leaving us again? Without us, there will be no one to check in with. Nothing to keep him from drinking, using, falling even deeper into old habits.

Then there's the other part of me, a selfish part. The part that's a little relieved. Glad that when we left California, he was still on his best behavior; he hadn't done anything to start gossip. Or at least, if he had, he hadn't gotten caught.

"Hey, I'll be home for Thanksgiving, and Christmas," Luke says. "And we'll keep in touch. Don't worry."

. . .

The next day Mom and I drop Luke off at the bus stop.

"I wish Peter and your father were here," Mom says as she hugs Luke. "Wish I'd gotten one more family photo before we left. I guess I just didn't expect you to end up staying here."

"I'll be back before you know it," he says. Then, "I love you guys." Luke hugs the breath out of me. "I'll be good. I promise. I'll write or call once I get settled."

I hold him as tight as I can for as long as I can, trying to let every sense take in Luke—how his arms feel around my back, his smell, the sound of his voice, the way his eyes are glowing with hope. I hold back a sob and convince myself this is not the last time I'll be seeing him.

"Hey, Squeaks, don't cry," Luke says as he lets me go. "Thanksgiving. I promise."

Chapter 36:

Luxury

When I was fourteen, the women's council decided to do family photos for the church directory after Christmas mass, the theory being that it would be a great success, since almost everyone had attended service that morning, looking so nice in their holiday best.

Mom, Dad, Peter, and I waited in a long line out the front of the church door in the freezing cold while a photographer arranged each family in front of the poinsettias around the alter. "Okay, line up. Look toward me. Smile. One. Two. Three. And thank you. Next."

The Jordan family was in front of us, complete with both sets of Mandy's grandparents, visiting from New York and Florida.

"Isn't it wonderful to have the whole family together for Christmas?" Lucille gushed to Mom.

"Yes, you're very fortunate," Mom politely replied.

I couldn't tell if Lucille was blind or just being a bitch. I wanted to say, "What whole family? I don't see my oldest brother here. Go be merry with your whole family somewhere else."

We waited in line silently, an uncomfortable tension rising as we listened to Lucille drone on and on about having a full house and how wonderful this family photo would be as a treasure.

Our picture appeared in the mail on the same day we got letters from Luke.

Mom sighed irritably. "Why do they insist Luke write the name of the prison and his number on the return address? It's an embarrassment!"

I raised my eyebrows. Luke in prison was no secret, so how could that be an embarrassment? I knew she really meant that she didn't like the reminder. That without that prison number, she could pretend he was just off somewhere else, living a normal life.

"Do you want me to frame this?" I asked Mom, holding up our new Christmas family photo in one hand, the old framed one in the other.

Her face distorted a little. The old photo was from three years before. I was eleven, with braces, and my haircut looked suspiciously like a mullet. It would have been nice to have an updated family picture in our living room. Even if Luke wasn't in it.

"I don't think so," Mom said, crinkling her nose at me. "It's not really a family photo." Then, her voice lighter, she added "Here's yours" as she tossed me a letter from Luke.

It didn't matter to me that Luke was in jail because he'd been found guilty of stealing. I was excited to hear from him.

Dear Squeakers,

Thanks for your letter and the care package. I can't tell you how much I needed that stuff. Clean T-shirts, boxers, and socks are a luxury here.

This time of year is so hard for me. I just want to be home with you guys. It's lonely. All I can think about is snow, crackling fires, Ma's cooking, and the Christmas tree with our special ornaments. All I can think about is everything I'm missing.

What I did was wrong. I know that, and I'm paying for it.

Don't ever do anything that will land you in jail. It's miserable here, worse than you can imagine.

I promise that when I get out of here, I will never ever make any more mistakes like that. I will get a good job. I will buy a house. I will find someone really nice to have a family with.

Everyone has abandoned me except you, Ma, and Pop. I don't know what I'd do without you. Don't give up on me. Please. Your letters mean more to me than you will ever know. Keep writing.

Love,
Luke

After reading it, I grabbed on even harder to the idea that my letters were making a difference. That they had some sort of power not only to help Luke get through his prison sentence but also to change him forever. A fear crept inside me that if I didn't continue to support him, all hope for him to lead a normal life would be gone.

Chapter 37:

Homecoming, Part Two

NOW

Shit. Shit. Shit. Shit. Shit.

Dad called from the house.

Said that the police had asked to search my car.

Then there was Mom, sitting me down on Granny's couch, grabbing both my hands and questioning me, over and over: Was there something she should know? Had I done *anything* illegal? Anything at all? I told her no, but I know she doesn't believe me.

Dad is at the airport with the police when we land in LA. They're wondering if I might be able to answer some questions for them.

So now I am in the police station, sitting upright in a hard chair next to my mother—who has to be present because I am under eighteen—waiting, waiting, waiting to find out what questions they have. Skeleton is sitting in the corner, legs crossed, reading a trashy tabloid. He's been here before.

The man who comes in to interrogate me looks like a nice guy. He probably has a nice family, with well-behaved kids, who are possibly playing tag in their backyard, waiting for their hard-working dad to get home.

He says that he just wants to talk to me a little bit, that I'm not under arrest, but it's still policy to let me know my Miranda rights. It doesn't feel at all like they portray it on TV. His voice is relaxed and he rattles them off in a tone of voice like he might be offering me something to eat. When he gets to the part about a lawyer, he pauses and looks up at me, saying that if I didn't do anything wrong, I don't need a lawyer. I didn't do anything wrong. I think. So I shouldn't need a lawyer, right? But *do* I need one? If I ask for one, I'll look guilty, right? But if I don't, could I end up doing or saying something that will get me in trouble?

He asks if I understand everything, and I say yes. Then he says it's time for me to answer some questions. I look to Mom. Wondering if she'll cut in and ask for a lawyer, but she just nods. Maybe she does believe me.

But maybe, maybe I was in the wrong place at the wrong time.

Wrong place, wrong time. My heart starts to pound. Wrong place, wrong time. My vision blurs for a second, and all I can see is Skeleton, pointing at the receipts on my car floor. My eyes focus as the detective starts talking again.

He says he knows I am a good student. He knows I have plans to go to college. He knows that I've never ditched school, never gotten a ticket, and that I volunteer sometimes as a lifeguard at the kids camp that the school organizes. He says he also knows what kind of car

I drive, and that on one particular day I drove to three different stores with my brother Luke.

He asks me if I remember that day.

I say yes.

Wrong place, wrong place, wrong place.

He'd like for me to write down everything I remember about that day in my own words; he says that details are important. Where will this lead? What if I do or say something wrong?

Trying to remember every detail, I pick up the black pen and write: *On July 19th my brother Luke asked me to drive him to a few stores so he could return items. He had three different bags, one from each store. He pulled out a receipt from his organizer at each store and returned the items. I then drove him home.*

The interrogator looks at what I wrote and shakes his head. Maybe he can help me remember some of the details. Maybe we can figure this out a little better, together.

He asks about Luke's organizer. I say that it is black, and small.

He asks why my fingerprints were on the organizer. I say because I picked it up when Luke was in the stores. I wonder how the police have it. Did Luke leave it in my car?

He asks why I touched it. I say, because it fell on the floor of the car and the receipts fell out, so I wanted to put them back in for him.

He asks what items Luke returned. I say I don't know.

He asks why I don't know what items Luke was returning. I say they were all in bags, and I didn't see inside the bags.

He asks if I remember what time we were gone. I say I remember I had to be back by two, so earlier in the day. I think we left the house around eleven.

He asks a.m. or p.m. I say a.m.

He asks if there was anything I noticed about the organizer. I say just that it was black and had receipts in it.

He asks if I looked closely at the receipts. I say I glanced at a few of them.

He asks if there was anything I noticed about the receipts. I say I noticed that they were all very crisp, very new.

I pause, thinking about Skeleton pointing at the receipts. They were *fake*? No! I need to think about this more. But—why else would he question me about the receipts?

The interrogator notices my pause. He asks why I paused. I say because I am thinking.

I want Mom to cut in. To say something that will slow the questions down. Give me more time to be allowed to think. But she just sits silently next to me, rubbing at her thumbnail, and I know she's not really here. Mentally she's at home, buffing a stain off one of her ornaments. I wish Dad were here. Maybe he would say something. Probably. I'm sure that's why Mom asked him to wait outside.

The interrogator asks again about the receipts.

I say they were from different stores, with different items; they were dated recently. I don't dare say that one I looked at was dated from when Luke was in prison.

He asks how long I looked at the receipts for. I say just a few seconds.

He asks what I thought. I say I thought that there were a lot of receipts and that Luke has a great way of organizing his files.

He asks why the organizer was in my car. I say I don't know.

He asks if Luke left the organizer in my car. I say I don't know.

He asks if Luke told me what he was returning. I think, They've already asked me this. Are they trying to trick me into messing up? Into saying something new, something different? Maybe I should have asked for a lawyer. I say no, I don't know what Luke was returning.

He asks if Luke has ever wanted me to drive him anywhere else before. I say yes, to the store so he could buy snacks and cigarettes, to the pool hall, to the lake a few times.

He asks if Luke ever returned anything else when I was driving. I say no, not that I can remember.

He asks me if this is my car in this photo. I say yes.

He asks if this is me in my car in this photo. I say yes.

He asks if this is Luke getting out of my car. I say yes.

He asks me if I knew Luke had printed fake receipts. I say no.

I think, Oh, crap. They *were* fake receipts. It was a scam. It was a scam. And I *was* in the wrong place at the wrong time. I could go to jail. I could go to jail. I'm an—what's the word? Accessory. I'm an accessory to a crime. Am I? If I didn't know?

How could Luke do this to me?

Little splotches of green and yellow appear in front of my eyes as the room tilts. I close my eyes and tell myself to concentrate. When I open them again, I am looking straight into the interrogator's dark brown eyes.

He asks me if I knew that Luke was returning stolen goods. I say no.

I think, Luke wouldn't do that to me. Luke wouldn't make me an accessory to his crime.

The interrogator asks me if it was my idea to make the receipts and return stolen goods. I say no, I didn't know he was doing that. I thought he was returning items he'd bought.

I think, Mom, please say something. Please make this stop. But she just sits there, rubbing her damn fingernail.

He asks me if when I looked in the organizer, I realized Luke had stolen items and was returning them with fake receipts. I say no, Luke would never ask me to drive him if he were returning stolen goods. Luke wouldn't do that to me.

He asks me if I am sure that Luke would never involve me in an illegal activity.

I pause. And have to answer truthfully. I whisper no. I am not sure. I hear Mom's sharp inhale beside me. She did not like the way I answered that question.

He asks me if Luke confided in me that he had made fake receipts. I say no.

He asks me if I saw Luke with any of his friends that day. I say no.

He asks me if I saw anyone else in the parking lot of Compute This who might have been suspicious. I want to say yes, that the person looked a lot like Luke, so maybe they are mistaking this other person for my brother. But I know I can't lie, even if I thought it would help him. Even if that is what Mom would want me to do. So I say no.

He asks me if Luke has ever asked for my help before. I say yes. I am sure he has, because he is my brother. But never for anything illegal.

He asks me if I am sure. I shake my head.

He asks me to answer yes or no, verbally. I say no. I'm not sure.

He asks me if I know where Luke is. I say I think still in Tennessee, living with a friend. I can't remember the city.

He asks me if I have a phone number or address for this friend. I say no. He said he'd write or call with his new information, but he hasn't yet.

He asks me if I know any information on any of Luke's friends in Tennessee. I say no.

He asks me if I know the names of Luke's friends in Tennessee. I say no.

He asks me if Luke left a cell number, or any phone number at all. I say no.

He asks me if Luke has an address in Tennessee. I know I have answered this already. I say no.

He asks where I last saw Luke. I say when we dropped him off at a bus stop.

He asks where the bus was going. I say I don't know,

because we dropped him off before he bought his ticket. And he didn't say where.

And then I think how weird that was. How strange that we didn't park and walk him to the window. That Mom didn't buy the bus ticket for him. That we didn't sit with him on the bench, waiting for the bus to come. That we just dropped him off and said good-bye on the curb.

Then I realize. Oh, my God.

Mom didn't *want* to know where he was going. She didn't want *me* to know where he was going. Maybe she'd had a call from Dad to warn her, when the police had showed up. Or maybe she'd just guessed he'd be in legal trouble soon.

He asks me what bus station it was. I say I don't remember.

Mom breaks her silence. Offers to write down the name of the station and the time we dropped him off. He hands her a pen and paper. I'm surprised that she would give that information up. But how much help is that, really? We don't know how long he waited at the bus station before leaving. How many transfers he made. He doesn't have a credit card, so it was paid for all with cash. And who is going to remember Luke out of all the passengers taking a bus that day?

The interrogator looks at me and says he thinks I can probably remember a little better now that day I drove Luke to the three stores. And that I am probably ready to rewrite my account of what happened, including looking at the organizer, the stops we made, the approximate times, and anything else I think is important. He tells me I am doing fine, and to take my time.

He is silent while I write a much more detailed account of the day. Mom is silent too. I sign it and date it.

He tells me he'll call if there are any more questions. He gives both Mom and me his card and says I should call him if I remember anything else.

He says that if Luke comes home or calls or writes that I need to call him immediately. That goes for Mom, too. And Dad. And Peter.

He says that he can have me arrested for obstructing a police investigation if I do not call, that they will have no choice but to assume that I was an accessory to this crime if I do not call.

He asks if I understand.

I nod and say yes, I understand.

Safe in the car, my head starts pounding. I'm exhausted. The detective's questions have my mind spinning. The seriousness of it all crashes over me. If they think I helped Luke . . . If they think I knew he was doing something illegal, I could go to jail. Acid rises in my throat, burning my esophagus, then my tonsils. I swallow. Don't vomit. Don't vomit. Don't vomit.

Dad asks, "How did it go, Clare? Everything okay?" I glare at him. Is everything *okay*? Really?

Mom says, "They have her fingerprints on evidence but nothing that will convict her."

"Where did they get her fingerprints to compare?" They continue the conversation as if I'm not in the car, creating a sense of disbelief that this is actually happening to me.

"Remember? They do a fingerprint scan on anyone getting a license now. At least she didn't do anything illegal. I think she's safe. Let's just hope that nothing she said will get Luke in trouble."

I turn my glare toward her but don't say what I'm thinking: Fuck that. If he goes to prison again, it's *his* fault. Luke's making me an accessory to his crime could ruin my *life*.

But Luke wouldn't do that to me. He wouldn't. Besides, the police could be wrong. Maybe it wasn't a receipt scam. Maybe Luke's innocent. My stomach turns, telling my brain that I know better. Luke *is* guilty. And he almost made me an accessory to his crime.

In the wrong place at the wrong time.

Chapter 38:

Reputation

THEN: Age Fourteen

"Tovin, Clare?"

"Here."

"You come from a family with quite a reputation." I had been in high school for less than fifteen minutes, and I already hated it. Skeleton squeezed into the seat with me, knocking my pencil off my desk. As I bent to pick it up, my new teacher continued with roll. When he finished, his eyes traveled around the classroom.

"I am known for being one of the more strict teachers at this school. I can tell you all now that I do not teach people who are slackers, nor do I teach those who cannot follow the rules. If any of you fall into either category, I suggest you save us all a headache. I'll happily transfer you out to another teacher's class, hmm?" His eyes fixed on me.

Choice one: stay in a classroom with a teacher who obviously has preconceived ideas about me, prejudices based on my brothers' actions in his classroom. Choice two: transfer out. Would transferring out make it an admission of guilt? After all, he did tell me to leave *if* I were a slacker or a troublemaker.

Would other teachers look down on me because of who I was related to?

I sat up straighter, blinked back the tears, drained the hot blood from my face. Stayed and proved him wrong. Lucky for me, teachers gossip, and by the end of June, my own reputation of being a smart, hardworking, well-mannered student began to overshadow the others that I had by association.

Chapter 39:

Fault

NOW

Mom barely sets her luggage in her room before heading to her ornaments, now covered in three weeks of dust. I escape immediately to my room to check on my fish. Come on, guys. Make me happy. They've survived the vacation feeder and the power going out in our house twice while I was gone. The tank is a little dirty, but the water level is good, the temperature is right, and the fish look bright and healthy. Peter did a great job taking care of them. I slide down the wall and sit on the floor in front of the fish tank, trying to let my mind rest as I watch the fish glide.

There is a knock as the door opens. That's usually Mom's move, but this time it's Peter.

"Hey," he says as he sits on the floor next to me. "Drea's called about three times in the past two hours. She says she's been calling and texting your cell phone all day."

I pull my phone out of my pocket. I didn't even remember to turn it on when the plane landed.

"You should at least call her to say you are home and alive," he says, picking at a piece of white fuzz on the carpet. "She's stupid worried."

"I can't talk to Drea about this." I groan. "What am I going to say? That my idiot brother I'm always so quick to defend made me an accessory to theft?"

"Clare, thirty seconds after the police arrived, the whole fucking neighborhood was up in our business. They all saw your car being searched. Sure, they're all assuming it has something to do with Luke, but they know it was *your* car."

I bury my face in my hands. "What am I going to do?"

"If it were me, I'd clear it up once, to my close friends. They know you, right, so they know you wouldn't be involved. Screw anyone else. They can think whatever they want." He pauses, looking from the fuzz to my eyes. "You okay? After the police?"

"Not really," I say. "It was brutal. I don't want to talk about it. And I'm not really allowed to talk about it anyway."

After we sit for a second or two in silence, the house phone rings.

"Drea, I bet," says Peter, pushing himself up from the floor. I shake my head at him. "Fine. I'll tell her you're home and alive."

He leaves, shutting the door behind him. Part of me wishes he had pressed me to talk. Part of me wants to dump every thought I have swirling around my head about Luke. Maybe Peter would have some good advice. Who else will understand like Peter?

I drag myself over to my bed.

Dad has thrown a pile of mail onto the middle of my mattress. Most of it is college junk mail: packets and brochures from universities, bragging about their scholastics, their campus life, their setting, their sports. The rest are postcards. I flip the first one over, see Drea's scribbly handwriting: *Hey, Clare! Can you believe they still make these things? How could I pass up a postcard with a cat wearing a cowboy hat!! Best $1.50 I've ever spent.* The other postcards feature Drea's college rating system on the back—*hot guys: 10, scenic: 3, dorms: 4.5.* The normalcy of it is jarring. My life is spinning so out of control. Was it only two months ago when I was most worried about asking Mom's permission for the college trip?

I turn on my cell phone. Ten missed calls and eight text messages from Drea. Missed calls from Omar, Chase, and Skye. Nothing from Luke.

It's not like I expected anything. Not really. He probably knows he's in trouble. Knows he dragged me into this. I'm so pissed at him right now. So why do I desperately want to hear from him?

It's better this way. As soon as he calls, as soon as he writes, as soon as he shows up, I have to call the detective. I *have* to.

The next morning Mom pops her head into my room early. "Clare. Phone for you."

"I don't want to talk to anyone." My voice is scratchy.

"You will take the call. I already told Chris Jordan you're here."

I sit up in bed. He must be calling for more lessons.

"Hi, Chris!" I can't believe how happy I am. "How's the swimming going? I'm back home now, so we can do another lesson. What works for you?" Fantastic. I can't wait to teach Chris again. And it'll help take my mind off . . . everything.

"Ummm . . . hi, Clare. Actually, I'm calling to say that my mom won't let me take swimming lessons from you anymore." His voice is sad and low.

His mom won't let him take lessons from me.

It doesn't matter that I was able to convince him to try. That I'm a certified lifeguard. That there probably isn't anyone better in our town to teach him.

"Oh," I say. "I'm sorry to hear that. Is she sure? Maybe I should try talking to her."

"Yeah, she's sure," he says.

"Okay. I understand."

"Clare." Lucille's voice suddenly replaces Chris's. "While we have you on the phone. In light of recent events it'd be best if you don't reapply for lifeguard, or even cover any of our lifeguard's shifts. I'm sure you understand why. Well, then, good-bye."

They hang up before I have a chance to even ask a question, or try to convince Lucille to change her mind.

This is Luke's fault. It's *all* Luke's fault. Wait in the car, he told me. Like staying in the car would protect me from any of this. He made me his getaway driver! And me . . . How could *I* be so stupid? How could I have trusted him? Why the hell didn't I stop and think before I agreed to drive him? I could go to jail. And even if I don't, *everyone* thinks that I was in on it. Maybe even my friends. Maybe even Drea. I've already lost my job. What's next? I'll have to work three times as hard at school to prove I'm not cheating. I'll be watched every time I go to the grocery store or the gas station. No one will hire me. How could he do this to me? How could he be so stupid? So selfish?

I start to scream. Out of control. I'm going fucking crazy. I throw myself onto my bed and let my pillow muffle my screams until my voice dies.

Chapter 40:

Class Discussion

THEN: Age Sixteen

"In keeping with our unit on social issues of contemporary society, today we are going to discuss our prison system," Mr. Clark, my US history teacher, said. My head snapped up. If I had known this was on the syllabus, I would have stayed home. Omar sent a caring glance from his seat next to me and reached over to squeeze my hand when the lights were turned off. I sunk down as deep as I could in my chair.

A spotlight appeared, zooming around the room, then settling on Skeleton, in a top hat with a cane. He began to tap-dance. *Tap, tap, tappy tap.* From one side of the TV to the next. Using his cane, he pointed at the screen: violent criminals in orange, looking insane and not one bit sorry for all they'd done.

Tappy tap, tap. He pointed at weapons carved out of toothbrushes, sharpened to makeshift blades.

Tap. Tap. Tap. A fat, balding officer gave us the virtual tour, saying, "Three meals. A library. An hour of exercise out in the yard. People can send them televisions for their rooms, magazines."

Skeleton twirled. Stopped and pointed. Criminals,

talking about splitting into gangs. About how every day is a day of war. About how they have to avoid being someone's bitch.

Stomach acid rose, my throat burned.

Don't think about Luke. He's not like any of these people. Don't think about gang wars and rape. Don't think about makeshift weapons. Don't think about how Luke could fit into that.

Tappy tap, tap. The grand finale. Skeleton twirled, twisted, tapped down my aisle. Transferred the spotlight from his glaring white bones to my blood-drained face, just as Mr. Clark flipped off the TV.

I felt like all eyes were on me.

"We have about fifteen minutes left," Mr. Clark said, "so let's discuss. Do our prisons serve their purpose?" He scanned the room. "Yes, Mandy?"

"Three meals a day, an hour of exercise, TV, magazines, a warm and dry place to sleep. Doesn't sound like a bad deal, especially for someone who can't keep a job to earn those things on their own."

Not a bad deal, Mandy? From watching a stupid twenty-minute video, you think you know enough about prison to deem it not a bad deal?

She looked over to me, giving me a smug smile before she continued, "Look at Clare's brother, Luke. He's obviously not learning his lesson. How many times has he been in and out of prison, Clare?" With this, Skeleton stood on Clare's desk, clapping his hands in a circle. Bravo.

There was a collective gasp from everyone in the room. I stopped breathing.

"But what about programs that can actually help them integrate back into society?" Omar said quickly, rescuing me, steering the conversation away from what Mandy had said, before Mr. Clark could even react. "This video didn't go over things like job training or drug rehabilitation or mental health programs. If we invested money in those types of programs, maybe we'd see fewer repeat offenders."

"And spend more tax dollars, *our* hard-earned money?" Mandy retorted. "No way. They deserve only bread and water. Maybe then they wouldn't want to go back."

By "they" she meant Luke. Luke deserved only bread and water. My hands balled into fists under my desk. I wanted to punch her pretty little button nose into her head.

"We are talking about *humans* here, Mandy," Omar angrily retorted. "Not stray rabid dogs."

Mr. Clark cleared his throat. "Okay. Interesting points from each of you." Pausing, scanning the room, he asked, "Does anyone else have anything to add?"

Nothing to add. No one wanted to discuss this. Especially not me.

"Okay. Let's talk homework," Mr. Clark told us. "Write an essay on your thoughts about our prison system, based on the video and on what you'll be reading in our government book tonight, pages 259 to 314."

And then the bell. Which I hoped would release some of my discomfort. But instead I felt *everyone* glancing my way. I could only hope that something dramatic would happen to take the attention off me. But there was no girl fight with one biting the other, or someone getting caught smoking weed, or a major earthquake. Just everyone's persistent eyes following me, and the loud clank of Skeleton's bones.

The next day I expected the rumors and whispers to continue at school. My savior came in the form of one gorgeous new student. His name was Ryan Delgado. His messy hair, hazel eyes, and perfectly crooked nose gave the girls all something else to talk about.

Chapter 41:

Uncomfortable Routine

NOW

There are two weeks left of summer, and I am practically hiding, staying in my house away from eyes and questions. Skeleton is everywhere. Whenever I leave home: whisper, whisper, whisper. I know everyone is putting random facts together mixed with gossip, coming up with a story: that Luke and I are thieves, that I was the getaway driver, that we ran off to Tennessee to evade the law, that my parents are hiding Luke somewhere and not telling the police. Our whole family: criminals. I never want to go back to school. But at the same time I miss the distraction while studying history, English, science, and even math. The only thing that makes me feel okay is sliding stitch after stitch to create baby blankets, listening to my needles *click* as I watch my fish swim.

After two days of my successfully avoiding everyone, Drea busts into my room, saying, "You can't hide in here forever. And seriously, you need to tell me what happened. There's a crazy rumor going around that you and Luke stole some shit together and you were arrested."

I tell her I didn't steal anything, that I have never done anything illegal besides drinking with her, speeding, and making a rolling stop instead of a complete one. She's hurt and angry that I haven't taken her calls or sent a text. She wants more information, more details on what happened. She wants to be able to defend me. She needs me to tell her something more.

It's too tiring to deal with this conversation. I wish she'd just leave, but I know she won't. So I tell her I was just driving Luke around as a favor. If he did anything illegal— Ha! I used the word "if." I'm still trying to defend him. If he did anything illegal, I didn't know anything about it.

I don't tell her Luke used me. He used me for my car. And I don't tell her how angry and sad and frustrated and confused I am.

Hiding behind the excuse that I can't talk while police are still investigating, I let her change the topic to her trip, Lala's latest, the scholarship Omar was just awarded. I let her talk to me like everything is normal. At least it makes *her* feel better. After about thirty minutes I make up some job that I need to do for my mom, so Drea will leave.

Back to my knitting. I finish the last row of another baby blanket. Usually as soon as I have one finished, I take it to Loving Hearts immediately. I have two ready. But I'm afraid. What if Peggy somehow knows? She couldn't. The shelter is forty-five minutes out of town. Still. I can't drop them off now. I can't risk seeing her disappointed in me.

I fold up the blanket, gently giving it a little hug before sliding it under my bed. In the next moment I am casting on another 132 stitches. This blanket won't go anywhere either. I'm just knitting now to hear the needles *click*.

School is back in session. My friends and I sit in the shade of the spruce trees in the quad, chowing on our lunches, listening to the sounds of Ryan tapping his bongo drum and his friend Gary playing an acoustic guitar, surrounded by Cranberry Hill's finest. A flyer for their upcoming performance at Luv-a-Latte sits on the grass next to me.

I expected stares when the year started, and the first day was a little rough, but now no one seems to be saying anything about me. Not even my friends. Drea must have talked to them. They haven't asked anything, and I'm not providing any extra information. Even Lala, who usually can't get enough of gossip, hasn't brought it up once.

"Can you believe the amount of homework we have? It's only a week in. They're killing me already!" Omar's eyebrows rise, almost cartoonlike.

There's a collective grumble from Drea, Chase, Skye, and Lala, and they continue to banter about school and deadlines. I chime in with an obligatory complaint.

I'm actually glad for the extra homework, for the excuse to avoid any situations where people might bring Luke up, to avoid seeing Ryan and Gary playing at the coffeehouse, where Mandy might feel the need to show off to her Cranberry girls by asking ridiculous questions. I'm glad to stay at home and escape into essays. But I'd never actually say that out loud.

. . .

Toward the end of September a tube of Mandy's lipstick goes missing from her purse during AP French, the only class we have together. When she starts squealing, every eye in the room—even Skye's—*even Skye's!*—goes to me. Never mind that I rarely wear lipstick, especially not the deep lavender shade that has disappeared. When the teacher insists that Mandy dump the whole contents of her purse out before we send out the bloodhounds, she pulls the lining out as extra proof. Skeleton points out a small hole, just big enough for a lipstick tube to escape through. The lavender shade is found between the lining and the shell. Mandy begins to rant about how cheaply made the purse is, interrupted by our teacher saying, *"En français, s'il vous plaît!"*

Skye won't look at me, her porcelain skin turning a deep shade of red. She thought I was guilty. Maybe not on the surface, but somewhere inside she did. She's my friend. She *knows* me. She still thought it was possible that I'd stolen the lipstick.

Instead of going to Chase's for a movie that night, I go home to my room.

It was hard enough to feel normal before, hoping at least my friends thought I was innocent. Now, knowing Skye isn't sure . . . Will my friends slowly desert me too, one by one?

Autumn winds chill the apple tree outside my room window. Its heavy fruit bends the branches, making it easy for me to pick the apples.

We prepare them for apple pie, applesauce, apple jelly. Peter, Dad, and I help Mom cut and core. Almost as a family. Almost. Mom cans and stores like the world is going to end and we will survive because of our basement filled with apple products.

The police still haven't found Luke. They haven't questioned me again. Luke hasn't called; he hasn't written. In a way it's strangely relieving. I'm starting to feel like maybe my life could go back to the way it was before. I even applied for four jobs in town, hoping that someone is ready to give me another chance.

But I'm also starting to wonder if Luke will stay missing forever. Would that be better than knowing he's in prison? He's probably out there somewhere. With a safe place to sleep at night. Maybe he even has a job. Friends. A girlfriend. But he could be dead. He could be *dead*, and I wouldn't even know it. I imagine Luke facedown in an alley somewhere. Overdose? Gunshot wound? Stabbing? It seems dramatic and unreal, but even so, possible.

I want Luke to be found, even if it means his going back to prison, so at least I know where he is and that he's alive.

For the first time since I got home from Granny's, I take Luke's locket out and look at the picture, wanting life to be like before he got into trouble for the very first time. I fasten it around my neck but snatch it off in seconds. It's too heavy, and the chain irritates my skin.

I put the locket into Luke's wooden box. Lock it up and put it on a high shelf in the closet.

October 25. Beanie Day. I pull out all of the hats I've been making for the past year, fold them up, and put them into my backpack. All except one: Ryan's. I haven't talked to him since before I left for Granny's. Whatever friendship we had this summer is gone. I toss his beanie back into the box.

As I get to school, everyone is wearing their favorite hats, except for my friends. They are waiting for me.

"Do you smell what's in the air, Clare?" Omar says, taking in a big whiff as we meet up in the quad. "Wood burning in a fireplace, that weird smell of wet, dead leaves, and your mom's applesauce. Yes, smell it. Take it in. It's the smell of fall. It's the smell of the no-hat rule dying until spring."

Chase rubs his hands together. "Bare head no longer. Tomorrow, Yankees cap. Today, beanie."

"So . . ." Omar turns to me. "What do you have for us this year?"

"Nothing," I joke. But my friends don't laugh. Skye and Drea exchange a knowing glance. The air around us grows even chillier. Do they think that I've been so out of it I would forget? "I'm joking, guys," I say as I open my backpack and start pulling them out, presenting them one by one.

"Yankees blue and white! Nice, Clare," Chase says, pulling his on.

Skye's green eyes pop even more as she pulls the

white cable-knit onto her head, her braids cascading down her shoulders on either side.

"You have outdone yourself this year," Drea says, her fingers running over the beads.

And I'm relieved that the slouchy style I chose for Omar fits perfectly over his big mess of curls, unlike the too-small one that I knitted last year. Finally I pull on my own ocean-green one with three stripes knitted from the same tan yarn I used to make Drea's.

My friends are all chatting and complimenting me. Everyone is so happy. And I'm feeling pretty good too.

Until Skye says something to Drea about Gary's sexy grooves and they both crack up. When I ask them what happened, Drea tries to explain, but she's laughing too hard, so Skye steps in, then admits, "I'm not doing the story justice. I mean, it was funny then. But now . . . Maybe he'll do it again at Luv-a-Latte tonight. You should come."

For a second I consider it. Then I think about Ryan, playing on his bongos, and Mandy, floating around the room like she's the hostess. And it doesn't help that I applied for a job there and, like the other three places, they didn't even call me back. I get too nervous that Mandy will ask me about Luke or that no one will say anything to me but everyone will talk *about* me.

"I have this big calculus test on Friday," I mutter as my excuse.

Drea sighs. As she pushes her books into her bag, I can see a corner of the beanie I knitted her last year. My best friend knows me best, and she brought a backup in case I flaked.

"I'll pick you up at six thirty," Drea says to Skye. I can actually feel the distance between me and my friends getting wider. And yet I can't convince myself that it will feel okay to go out, even if it means losing my friends.

Until Halloween.

"We can't let this opportunity pass," Chase announces to us. "We may never trick-or-treat again. Until we're old and have kids."

"Weren't we too old last year?" Skye asks, her head on his shoulder. "And the year before? And the year before that?"

"But they still gave us candy," Omar reminds her. "Lots and lots of delicious, beautiful candy."

"I'm in," says Drea. "I frickin' love Almond Joy. Especially free Almond Joy."

"Makes no difference to me. I have a date. I'll meet you at the party," Lala says with a shrug.

"Clare?" Omar asks. Everyone looks at me. If I don't go, it will be more time spent apart from them, more inside jokes that I won't understand. I may not be able to have the safety of my room, my bed, my knitting needles, and my fish tank, but I will have a costume to hide under.

"Okay," I say. "I'm in."

I watch in the mirror as my face disappears under strips of rags. I am a mummy, no longer Clare Tovin. Skeleton stays at home, sitting in his chair, reading a book. Except for my friends, no one will know who I am.

Mom and Dad take a few pictures and then follow me to my car. As I toss my overnight bag into the backseat, they tell me again to keep my cell phone with me at all times and to make sure that we are back at Drea's no later than midnight.

At Drea's we all pile into the back of Chase's truck. One mummy, one vampire, one makeshift superhero, a baby, Stanley the Squirrel.

There are no whispers tonight, no Skeleton, just adults grumbling, "Aren't you a bit old to be trick-or-treating?"

Just after ten I leave a message for my parents. We're done and I'm dead tired, so I'll see them in the morning. Our pillowcases filled with candy, we head up to the campgrounds for the next half of Halloween.

Everyone is huddled in close to the bonfire, grateful for the warmth. My wrappings keep me anonymous; the layers of white thermals under them keep me warm. It feels good. Almost normal.

"Little Ho Peep." Omar's furry Stanley the Squirrel elbow jabs me as Mandy runs from her car, pulling Ryan with her.

"It's freezing out here. Get me another drink, quick! Pretty please with cherries on top?" She pushes her way to the front of the circle with her shepherd's hook, while Ryan walks over to the keg, which happens to be next to me.

"Nice sheep costume," I say, hoping it sounds as ironic as I mean it to be.

"Oh. Mandy's idea." He puts a hoof in the air, gesturing to Mandy's bloomered butt, swaying dangerously close to the fire. "Who's in there? Wait. . . . I know those eyes, that voice. . . . Clare."

"Yep." Here I go again with the "yep"s.

"Hey! How did the rest of your summer go? I mean, I left for Mexico, and you just disappeared. Didn't see you again at the lake, even once."

"I went to my grandma's in Tennessee and painted a barn," I say, trying to make the end of my summer sound as normal as possible. Not that it matters. I'm sure he's heard the rumors. "And spent the last few weeks finishing up my summer AP assignments. Not much time for swimming." The last words almost hurt coming out of my mouth.

He sneaks a look out of the corner of his eye: Little Ho Peep is turning around. Of course, she sees only a mummy talking to her sheepish boyfriend.

"I gotta go get this drink to Mandy," Ryan says, almost an apology in his tone. "Um, but, real quick, Clare. I don't think you had anything to do with the whole stealing junk. So just don't lump me with those people, okay? You don't have to avoid me." He pauses. "I mean, I'm pretty sure that I've actually watched you turn and walk the other way when I've seen you in the hall. That's not cool."

I'm so shocked, if this were a cartoon, my mummy rags would fling to the sides, unraveling and wrapping back up. I'm silent. Ryan starts walking away.

"Ryan!"

He turns back.

"Thanks." I'm thinking of saying, "You have no idea

what that means to me." But I don't. Because I realize that maybe he does. It's possible.

"No problem." He raises his cup of beer to me, joins Mandy by the fireside.

I'm surrounded by friends, enjoying the bonfire, drinking a few beers. Despite the cold it's a warm scene. The only thing that gives me the chills is the forest beyond the campsite, the path where I ran into Luke's friend Dan, and the darkness that provides a place for things to hide.

Ryan walks past our spruce tree during lunch the next day at school. He stops to say hello, flashing his bright smile. It feels good, having another ally. I can do this. I don't have to lock myself in my room, waiting for the rumors to dissipate. Maybe I can even find the courage to deliver the blankets to Loving Hearts.

"It's Friday night. . . . Who's in for the movies?" Chase asks after Ryan leaves.

If I try really hard, I can break my uncomfortable routine. And make it at least a little more comfortable again.

"Sure," I say. "Comedy sound good?"

Chapter 42:

Warmth

THEN: Age Sixteen

The January winds were blowing gusts so cold that they made my eyes water. Mom and I hurried from the entrance of MegaMarket to our car. A woman was making her way across the parking lot, head down into the wind. As we passed her, I heard the wails and turned. A tiny baby in her arms, tucked down as well as possible into the woman's worn coat. The baby had no hat, no jacket, no blanket.

As I helped Mom load the trunk of the car, I watched them cross the street, then enter Loving Hearts Homeless Shelter.

Even though she disappeared, I carried her with me. I saw her when I closed my eyes. I heard her baby in every creak of our floors. And I felt the cold wind as I sat in my room, knitting a green blanket I had intended for myself.

When the blanket was done, I pulled up a website that had baby beanies and bootie patterns, and was able to make a matching set. I pulled out leftover yarns and knitted together a small panda bear.

I headed to Loving Hearts. Outside the door I

waited. What if they didn't want the blanket? What if they knew that Luke Tovin was my brother and he was a thief, and they'd rather have nothing to do with my family? I told myself to stop it. Being scared to make a donation was ridiculous. A cold wind whipped around me. It was time to go inside.

The bell chimed as I pushed the door open.

"Can I help you?" a woman Mom's age said warmly as she looked up from her computer.

"Hi. Um. I made this," I said, pulling the blanket, hat, booties, and bear out of a canvas bag. "There was a woman that I saw about two weeks ago, in the parking lot across the street. She had a baby but no blanket. And I saw her come in here."

"This is lovely!" The woman exclaimed, running her fingers across the stitches. "My name's Peggy. What's yours?"

"Clare," I said, glad that we were just doing first names. "Is the woman with the baby here?"

"Yes, she is. And many women like her," Peggy said. "Would you like a tour?"

As we walked through the shelter, she explained that Loving Hearts was a temporary place for women and children to live and eat while the mothers looked for work, saved money, and eventually moved into a place of their own. The tour ended in the living room. Peggy nodded toward a woman holding a baby on the couch.

"This is for you." I handed her my gift.

Her eyes watered as she wrapped her baby in the

blanket. "Thank you so much," she whispered. "Amelia looks beautiful in it."

It felt better than swimming. Better than getting 100 percent on a test. Better than Luke coming home. Better than Mom saying she was proud of me.

I wanted to keep that feeling all to myself. I didn't want to have to share it with anyone. I didn't want Skeleton to ever ruin it for me.

Chapter 43:

Fork

NOW

It's the day before Thanksgiving, and I'm standing in the kitchen with Mom, rolling dough out, lost in thought about my college applications, the last one finished and submitted online yesterday. UCLA and UC Berkeley went out first. Then just a week ago I decided to apply to Drea's dream school, Pepperdine, and another on her list, Long Beach State. Maybe we'll end up at the same school. Oh. And Mom and Dad made sure that I sent an application to the shithole local college that they want me to attend. As far as they're concerned, it's the only application I sent out. Dad blindly signed each financial aid form that I handed to him. Now the waiting begins. Acceptance or rejections expected to land on my doorstep sometime in March or April.

"Nice job, Clare," Mom says, feeling the dough with her fingers. "I'm impressed."

I smile, turning and tumbling in the compliment.

The front door suddenly swings open. My mother and I both turn toward it and stare.

It's Luke.

His eyes are sunken. He is thin, dirty. My nostrils burn as he nears us.

I freeze, my fingers curling around the counter edge. Why is he here? He can't be here. Then a thought crashes into me so hard, I feel dizzy.

I'm supposed to call the police.

"Ma! Squeakers!" Luke calls out. "I'm home. Just like I promised. I hitched all the way here, just for Thanksgiving."

Mom puts down the wooden spoon she was just using to stir the pie filling. She steps from around the counter, taking Luke into her arms. How can she hug him?

"Hitchhiked? All the way from Tennessee?" It's my voice? It's my voice, responding to him. Asking him a question. Trying to find normal.

"Yeah, that's really the only way I get around," Luke says. "I'm gonna leave after Thanksgiving, cuz I need to go back to my girl Chastity. She's really great. She cares a lot about me. I wanted to bring her, but she's got this little girl, and no way could we hitch with her, you know. But I'm here now. Like I promised." Luke scratches his face, pinches his nostrils, scratches his arms.

"Luke, you must be exhausted. Why don't you take a nice hot shower? There are clean towels in the bathroom, and I'll find some of your old clothes for you to change into." Mom steps back, her face uncontrollably grimacing from his odor. She attempts a smile to hide it. "You'll be ready just in time for dinner."

"Okay," he says, walking to the bathroom.

When the door closes, Mom and I face each other.

"Sit down, before you fall and hurt yourself." Mom pulls a chair behind me. Plop. I'm sitting.

"We need to call," I say. But I'm not moving toward the phone. Mom's not moving toward the phone.

"We will, Clare. After he's had a shower and something to eat. You don't worry about that. I'll take care of it."

I can't ignore that Luke is in the house. I can't pretend that we are going to have a lovely homecoming dinner for my brother. I'm not risking the rest of my life.

I breathe in deeply, exhale slowly. I understand that Luke will be arrested when the police get here. I have to do what is right for me.

I pick up the phone, start to dial the detective's phone number I've memorized.

"What are you doing?" Mom asks sharply, pulling the phone from my hand. "It's the day before Thanksgiving. Are you really going to put your brother in jail just before a holiday?"

I stare at her.

"But we have to call," I say.

"You don't need to worry about this. I told you that I will take care of it. End of story. Do I make myself clear?"

I nod. She's not going to let me call. She'd sooner smash all our phones with a sledgehammer.

But Mom will take care of it. Mom will. She'll call after he's had a shower and a meal. Or maybe she'll hide him here until the day after Thanksgiving, so she can have her perfect holiday. Then she'll call. She'll do what we have to do legally. She won't choose letting him be free over me going to jail, right? She'll choose me. She *has* to choose me. I haven't done anything wrong.

She hands me a glass of water.

"Drink," she tells me. "You're as white as a ghost."

I sip the water slowly and look at the wall.

"Maybe you can help me," she says, this time softly, "and put the pie crust dough into the pans."

I nod.

"Do you remember how to make the lattice top after you add the filling?"

I nod again, letting my fingers press the dough.

"Now, I need to get those clothes for your brother. I can trust you, right?" she asks.

I nod. She leaves the room.

Luke is in the bathroom. Mom is in the attic. I can call now. I have to call now. I look at the phone. But my hands won't pick it up.

Pick it up! Pick up the damn phone and dial! The police will arrest you, too, if you don't.

My hands won't listen. After everything Luke has done. After everything he's cost me.

Instead my fingers, on autopilot, have prepared the bottom of both crusts, poured in the filling, and are now making the strips to make the lattice top.

Luke and Mom join me in the kitchen as Peter walks in through the back door. "Peter, come say hello to your brother," Mom calls out. And Peter stops, mid-stride, staring at Luke. "And don't go off to your room. I need you to set the table."

"I'll do it, Ma," Luke says, his huge pupils surrounded by blood vessels, red and swollen.

"How about you all set the table together. Dinner should be ready in fifteen minutes." Mom closes the oven, places the mitts on the counter. She smiles at the three of us. Peter gapes at me, and I know what he is thinking—how can she be acting like Luke has just come home from a day at work instead of months on the lam?

Maybe she's just faking it. Just acting normal for Luke. Pretending.

"I'm going to go wash up for dinner," she announces as she leaves the room.

Peter and I look at the phone. He shakes his head and drops himself down in a chair.

I abandon my pies, wash my hands, and pull the plates out of the cabinet. Turn around to see Luke heaving Peter out of his chair.

"Get up and help," Luke says, his hands digging under Peter's armpits.

"Okay, let go. I'm up." Peter hits Luke's hands off him. "Fuck off."

"No. You fuck off, you little shit. Have a little respect for your mother and help us set the table like she asked." Peter glares at him, so Luke leans close to his face. "Don't make me say it again."

"Stop. Just stop," I say. Look at Peter. Look at the phone. Hand Luke the plates and reach into the cabinet for glasses.

"I don't know why you are always helping him, Clare. Call," Peter says quietly into my ear while taking the glasses out of my hands before setting them on the table.

"What was that?" Luke snaps from the table.

"Nothing," Peter and I say at the same time.

"Luke, can you get the forks and spoons? I don't think we'll need knives tonight," I say. Large bubbles break the surface of the stew, splattering broth onto the stovetop. I give it a quick stir, turn the heat slightly down. Then grab the bowl of salad out of the refrigerator. Peter sets the last glass down and turns just as I'm about to put the bowl on the table; he crashes into me. The salad flies into the air, falls to the floor. The bowl shatters into a million pieces on my bare feet.

"Fuck." Peter pushes past me, holding out his shirt covered in dressing.

"Did you just hit her?" Luke asks, his voice angry loud.

"No. I— We just bumped into each other." Peter stops midway to the bathroom, looking at his shirt, then looking up. Looking in the past for the chronological order of events.

I stand completely still in the shards of glass, my eyes down at the pieces stuck in my feet. Looking at the red droplets pooling.

Broken glass, broken bones, broken trust, broken home, broken family, broken heart, broken, broken, broken, broken.

Skeleton puts his hand on my shoulder, backbones curving forward, posture limp and sad. He's done. He's had enough too.

Each muscle is tensing up, tensing up. My heart, my lungs. I can't breathe.

It's a whimper. A slow whimper that comes out first. I can't do it anymore. I can't do blood and broken glass and broken bones. I can't do sleepless nights, and fights and whispers. I can't not cry.

Peter turns, he sees my feet, sees the blood. "Oh, shit."

Luke runs to me, the five forks in hand.

"Are you okay, Squeaks? Are you okay?" But Luke doesn't wait for an answer. "You shit. You little fucking shit!" Luke heads toward Peter, huge strides. He's left me standing in the glass.

Peter laughs. An uncontrollable laugh with hints and hiccups of fear.

"It was an accident! I didn't see she was cut." His facial muscles spasm as he tries to placate, tries to smile. "Look. Clare needs help. Get her some Band-Aids. I'll clean up the glass."

"I warned you to stop hurting Clare. You broke her arm. I told you to never lay a hand on her again. Remember?" Luke is getting closer to Peter. "You know what you are? You're a fucking loser and a bully. Taking out all your shit on a girl who is four years younger than you."

Luke drops all the forks to the ground. All except one. His fist tightly wound around it. Peter steps back. His face drained of color.

"Come on, Luke. Don't get upset. I'm sorry. Okay? Clare, I'm sorry." Peter looks to me. No, Peter! Don't take your eyes off Luke.

The fork goes into Peter's arm. Luke pushes it hard, letting go as it breaks the flesh.

Stew boils and pops, glass crunches under my feet. I'm walking? I lean forward to look at Peter's arm. I'm curious. I'm not horrified? I don't scream. I don't run out of the house for help or for safety. Silent, intrigued. I wipe my tears to see the fork sticking out of Peter's arm, straight out into the air, as if it were in a piece of steak. Little blood comes out. Italian dressing and simmering stew in the air. It's a comfort scent; it doesn't make sense with what I'm seeing. With that smell there should be a family sitting around the table, laughing, passing dishes, sharing. Not a fork hanging out of my brother's arm, and a girl cocking her head to the side, leaning in closer and closer, like a scientist instead of a sister.

"What is going on here?" Mom yells as she rushes into the room.

"Ma." Luke is calm? Talking to her like this is all okay, all normal. "It was an accident. A mistake. He hit Clare. He hit Clare, and then the fork I had . . . slipped."

There are bloody footprints on the floor. Mine. Peter's eyes wide and hurt, tears filling the bottom lids. He is looking past me, past Luke, past the walls, and past the sky beyond the house. Mom looks from one of us to the other. It's like she is trying to decide which side she'll take.

We hear sirens. Police sirens. Mom called. She must have.

"It was an *accident*." Luke's face is blank. Isn't he supposed to be crying and shouting? "You don't want me to go to prison for an accident. Tell her, Clare. Tell her it was an accident." Luke smiles at me. He smiles at me?

My voice is broken.

"Tell her, Clare!" Luke insists. Now anger is there. He's angry at me?

The fork is in Peter's arm. Peter, stone, rock. Peter has both his eyes closed, but tears stream out anyway. No one pulls the fork out.

"You know what, fuck all of you!" Luke snarls. "You don't love me. That's why I'm this way." Luke runs out the back door. Runs as the sirens get louder.

Later that night, while Mom finishes the apple pies, Dad sets me up in Peter's room, on the lower bunk. I'm afraid to be alone. I have my pillow, my blanket, my cell phone. Hoping I can trick my mind into thinking I am safe and letting me sleep deeply, no dreams, no nightmares, only uninterrupted nothingness. It's not likely, but with Peter so close, maybe it's possible?

I'm not sure why we all weren't arrested for not calling the police when Luke showed up. It turns out Mrs. Brachett was the one who saw Luke arrive, was the one who called. Mom didn't. She didn't choose me.

When the detective arrived at the hospital, he asked me why I hadn't called. I told him the only real reason I could think of, because Mom had said she'd take care of it. My parents were pulled aside. The only thing I know they said was "No, we aren't interested in pressing charges. And Peter will not be pressing charges either."

Peter climbs up to the top bunk.

"You all good down there?" he asks.

"Sure," I say.

"How're the feet?"

I wince. Six stitches total: four on the right foot, two on the left. Countless cuts too shallow to sew. "They hurt. Probably about as good as your arm."

"Ha."

"Do you think they found him? Do you think he's back in jail?"

Peter is quiet for a moment.

"No. He always calls Mom first thing. We would have heard from him by now."

So he's still out there.

"Peter?"

"Yeah."

"He won't come back tonight, will he? Or for Thanksgiving?"

"No. He wouldn't risk getting caught. Just go to sleep and don't worry about it."

"I'm not worried," I lie.

"I guess that makes sense, since he's always so nice to you, little Squeakers." Peter's voice has turned edgy. This is not the way I want this conversation to go. Turn it around, Clare.

"He's nice to you sometimes. Like when he used to play catch with you."

"He broke my nose with the ball when I was ten."

"But didn't you miss it?"

"Nobody throws a ball that hard when they are just playing catch."

Okay. Good point.

"C'mon, Clare. Don't forget all the other ways he's hurt us. He's always taking something." Always? "He stole my camera second-to-last time he was out." True. "He's written checks to himself from Dad's checkbook." True. "He stole our piggy banks. Who steals from little kids?" True. "And, you know, he made you an accessory to theft." True, true, true, true. He steals. He steals because he needs money. Addicts need money. But it's not like he's *really* hurting people.

I think of the fork dangling from Peter's arm, and I have to ask, "Do you think he's hurt other people? I mean, physically?"

"I *know* he's hurt other people. Thieves don't get locked up in a maximum-security prison for four years."

"What?" I sit up and bang my head on the bunk above me. Nobody had told me that Luke was in maximum security. Oh, my God. *Maximum* security?

Maybe this morning I'd have thought that there was no way it was true. But watching him stab Peter . . . It could be true.

"*Maximum security*, Clare," Peter spits out. "The place for rapists, murderers—serious, serious criminals. That's where he was." He pauses, then adds, "Sorry. I thought you had figured it out." I blink in the dark. I hadn't. Everyone had told me, little blind Clare, that my favorite brother was in prison for theft, no big deal, nothing major.

My stomach churns. Maybe it's the pain medication. Probably not.

"Do you know what he did, to get put in there?" I ask, even though I am pretty sure I don't want to know.

"I don't keep track. I'm just happy when he's locked up, scared when he's not." His voice breaks. "Can't we stop talking about this? Stop talking and go to sleep? He'll stay away, for now. He won't come back, because the police might be watching our house."

I wish that Peter's room had no windows, and a lock on the inside of the door. But it doesn't.

And I finally realize what I'm afraid of.

I'm afraid of Luke.

I am afraid of my own brother.

The clarity of the thought takes me by surprise. I am afraid of Luke. I never feel safe in my own house, my own room, my own bed. Never. Because of Luke. It's the most awful truth, one I've never wanted to admit.

I lie on my back, looking from Peter's window to Peter's door. Waiting for Luke to smash in, a weapon in hand. A fork, a knife, Mom's cheap candlesticks. Maybe even her angel ornament has sharp enough wings. An escape plan forms in my mind. I keep imagining it until I am certain it will work. Slowly that blends with my half-asleep dreams.

Icy blue air.

Stairs, stairs, and more stairs. Old and splintering. My bare feet sting as they hit each one. Tall figures under thin black cloaks rise from the shadows and close in toward me. I run to the top. The stairs end where a door had been. Only hinges now. Silver metal covered in red rust. A room. Large and open with no furniture. A baby girl in the corner. On the floor crying. Floorboards groan. I'm running toward her to protect her. My arms swoop her up. But the shadows are near to me now, wrapping me in silence. The baby girl isn't crying. She is soft and innocent and important to me. She is dead. Trying to run, to protect myself, I trip. Fall to my knees, land on something sharp. My legs won't work. I can't run from the shadows. I scream.

"Clare, Clare, Clare! Wake up, Clare!" Peter's face. Peter's room. Peter's door. I am on the floor, looking at Peter's door. Shaking and shallow breaths. Is my throat closed completely?

"You were having a nightmare." Peter takes my hands. "See. You're awake now. I'm here." He reaches over, clicks on his desk lamp. Blood is coming from my right knee. My left knee is turning blue. The bunk bed is on the other side of the room.

"Do you want to talk about it?" Peter examines my knees.

"No." I hate that no one understands how real my nightmares feel. Why try to explain them? "I wish it were morning. This is so stupid. I'm seventeen years old. I'm not supposed to be afraid of the dark." I look down. "And why in the hell is my knee bleeding?"

Peter looks around the room. "That." He points at his hockey skates, lying on the floor, blade-side up. "I should have cleaned up before we went to sleep. I'm sorry. I forgot." He shoves everything into his closet.

"I'll be back in five seconds. Are you okay alone?"

"Sure. I'll be okay." But I'm not. Concentrating on

the posters of Peter's all-time favorite athletes, I stay frozen to the spot where I woke up. Studying the faces of Michael Jordan, Wayne Gretzky, Lionel Messi, Alex Ovechkin, Pelé, and Kobe Bryant, I try to think of something other than one of my brothers stabbing the other with a fork, and my nightmare. But I can *only* think of one of my brothers stabbing the other with a fork, and my nightmare.

Peter returns with two glasses of water. An ice pack. Hydrogen peroxide and Band-Aids. I gulp my water and hold the ice to one knee as he cleans the other.

"The cut isn't bad at all. It looked worse with the blood. Only two Band-Aids," Peter says. I look at my bandaged feet and my knees.

"Maybe I'll fall and accidentally slit my wrists next." I try to make a joke.

Peter shakes his head, forces out a "Ha." Then adds, "Don't even joke about that shit, Clare."

I shrug.

"Do you want to try to sleep again?" Peter asks. The answer is no. I never want to sleep again. I look at the window. The clock. It won't be light for a whole two more hours. "We can leave the light on, okay, Clare?"

He leans against the base of his desk, his eyelids fluttering as he tries to keep them open. I can't ask him to stay awake with me.

"Okay," I say. "I need to read something. Something nice to get my mind off of . . . everything."

"*Sports Illustrated*?" Peter suggests. I don't play sports, except when I'm recruited by Chase or Skye so they can practice. I don't get sports. Reading about sports is exactly what I want to do right now.

Back in the bottom bunk I tuck the covers around me. Peter lays his pillows on the floor next to the bed.

"No, Peter. It's okay. You don't need to do that."

"I can use a rolled-up sweatshirt. I'll sleep better knowing you have something there in case you fall out again." Two nightmares in one night. I can't handle that.

In the morning Peter's desk lamp is still on. *Sports Illustrated* is lying across my chest. My body is sore all over, but I have made it to daylight nightmare-free.

Wondering where Peter is, I slowly roll out of the bed, stretching my arms as I stand up and limp to the window. I pull the shade up, letting the gray light of a cloudy sky fill the room. Placing one hand on the glass, my fingertips feel the cold air leaking through. It could snow today.

Gazing out on Peter's view—our front path that leads to the parking area where all our cars sit—I start sifting through my memories. Through all of those spinning pieces of the jigsaw puzzle of my past.

Looking out at the front path, I can still feel how my heart quickened when I saw the broken front window, the trail of blood.

I allow myself to remember. I allow myself to follow the droplets and turn the corner.

Chapter 44:

Perfect Circles

THEN: Age Eleven

Dad was standing next to the couch. Tall, straight, strong. But his face was pale and blotchy red, veins strongly pounding beneath the thin surface. A mix of anger and fear. I stepped backward.

"GET OUT!" Dad shouted, pointing at the back door.

"Leave me alone! Let me go to sleep." Luke leaned against the couch, running his bloody fingers down his face, showing us the red under his lower eyelids.

Dad grabbed Luke by the shirt, pulled him close.

"I said, GET OUT!" Dad pushed him toward the door. Luke stumbled, slammed into the wall. I shut my eyes tight. Was this really Luke? Was it really my dad?

Luke's face morphed and mutated. He showed his teeth and his blood-filled eyes. Ugly.

Then he attacked. He attacked Dad, fists and hands and fingers clawing. They wrestled like two dogs, faces reddening as their breath ran low. Luke pinned Dad to the floor, his knees on his chest. His fingers around Dad's neck. Red spatters and smears on their faces, arms, shirts, teeth. There was so much blood. So much blood.

Dad coughed. Spurted. Gurgled. Luke didn't let go.

Skeleton wrapped his fingers around my eyes, but I pushed them away, running to the middle of the room.

"STOP! STOP! STOP! STOP! STOP!" My screams froze the room, froze the scene for one tiny moment. Luke's hands dropped from Dad's neck.

I expected something more to happen. Did I break the spell? Dad moaned as Luke stood up. Fumbling, Dad grabbed the phone off the end table.

With his eyes on Luke, Dad said in a raw voice, "Go. Now. Don't make me call the police."

Luke stumbled, stretching out a bloodied hand. He pushed me to the side, leaving a handprint of red squarely on my chest, more complete than the ink prints in our baby books.

Then the sounds of the front door slamming. Of Luke leaving the house. Where did he go, red with blood?

"Clare, be a big helper. Get old towels in cold water, bandages, hydrogen peroxide, and ice packs. Go on now." Dad's voice was so weak.

I ran to get everything.

The old towels soaked the red covering Dad. As they cleaned his skin, they revealed slivers of cuts, some deep and long. Ice pressed on his nose and eyes and neck to keep the swelling and bruising away.

"This mess," Dad said faintly, "is going to be harder to clean up than a roadkill skunk." He sputtered a fake laugh, looking out of the corner of his swollen eyes to me. I could tell it was for my benefit. I couldn't join him.

"Clare, you know we need to keep some things just in the family, right?"

I nodded.

"Anyone asks . . . I fell down a hill while I was working."

I nodded again.

I carefully picked up pieces of glass, scrubbed stains of red, placed thrown objects back. Imagined the house was not mine, the brother was not mine, the father was not mine, the Skeleton was not mine. Allowed this memory to cloud over, eclipsed by all the good memories of Luke being kind and gentle and loving, giving myself permission to forget what Luke was capable of doing.

Chapter 45:

Thanksgiving

NOW

I back away from Peter's window, letting the memory completely finish, down to the slow process of watching Dad's face morph—blacks, purples, blues, greens, yellows—finally back to skin tones, even the scars eventually fading. Once the house looked normal again and Dad's face looked normal again, I could make myself forget. I could pick and choose the memories of Luke that I wanted to keep, playing over and over and over only the good ones.

But as I look at my bandaged feet and think of Peter's arm, I realize: It has done nothing for me to filter memories and leave that one out. In fact, maybe if I had allowed myself to remember what Luke was capable of doing, I would have been more cautious. Maybe Peter and I wouldn't have gotten hurt yesterday.

I limp my way to the living room and lie on the couch for most of the day, mindlessly watching balloon after balloon float down the Macy's parade route. Then I watch hours of football with Peter, until dinner is ready.

One twenty-pound turkey, four family members. Mom sets the table for five, stands back and sighs, then puts the other place setting back in the cabinet. Sitting down, all together, the room feels full. Especially with Skeleton clunking around the table, dancing by the cabinet, pointing at our family portrait and counting on his bony fingers. Four, not five. He wraps one long arm around Peter.

We all pretend to ignore him. Peter wears long sleeves, concealing the holes in his arm. My bandaged feet are under the table. Saying aloud we are thankful for food and shelter and the love of friends, and of family. No one says they are thankful for safety. Skeleton sits down on the counter, between the apple and pumpkin pies, and watches us eat.

As soon as I've taken the last bite of the last piece of pie, I hobble to my room. I'm still scared to be alone, but Peter is going out with friends tonight, and there is no way that I'm going to resort to sleeping on the floor in my parents' room. I guess I could call Drea, but then I'd have to explain my bandaged feet. I just don't want to talk about it.

The light outside my window illuminates our backyard. I watch as fat snowflakes begin to fall from the sky, kissing the branches of our apple tree before dissolving. It's so beautiful, so peaceful. My eyes blur, and I imagine the yard in the summer, my mother happily sitting under the tree, clapping as Luke and I chase my frog. I want to jump into that memory, live there forever. Forget everything else about Luke.

No more, I resolve. No more floating back into my good memories. No more avoiding the truth.

I double-check to make sure the window is shut and locked, before pulling the curtain closed and crawling under my covers. My bedside lamp is still on, and I plan to sleep with it on for the rest of my life if I need to.

Chapter 46:
Let Me Introduce You
to a New Family Skeleton

NOW

The snow continues to fall, on and off for the next five days. The roads are icy enough to cancel school Monday and Tuesday. Wednesday morning the sun is shining and my feet have healed well enough for me to go to school and be able to walk somewhat normally. It's nice to be back in class, surrounded by my friends. It's comforting to know that even with my world at home flipped upside down, there will always be a steady stream of lectures and assignments, the security of bells keeping me on schedule. There's an avalanche of extra homework in my AP classes to keep us to date on our syllabuses. I'm extra busy for the month of December, barely having time to help Mom decorate the house.

Finally, the Saturday before Christmas, I have a morning free to patrol the mall for gifts. One day of shopping. That's all I have time for.

I fight the urge to buy something for Luke. If he shows up at the house for Christmas, I *will* call the detective immediately. No shower. No food. No nothing. Skeleton walks beside me, nodding his head at every thought. Even he agrees.

But. What if he shows up sober? Sober and happy and sweet?

I catch myself stroking a black sweater that I know Luke would love. I picture him wearing it. Skeleton tries it on. It fits just right. I shove it back onto the pile. No. I will not buy him anything. If he shows, I will call the police. Even if he's sober.

After I buy my last gift—a new pair of slippers for Mom—I make one more stop before I go home. Yesterday an envelope appeared in the mail, containing a congratulatory letter and a five-hundred-dollar check. One of the essays I wrote this summer for a scholarship was picked as the winner. I'm figuring what I have in my account: $9,125 plus the additional $500 that I will be depositing today makes a total of $9,625. It seems like a lot of money, but I know it won't even get me through the first year of school, especially if I live on campus, which I plan to do. Considering no one will hire me in my crap town, I'm relying on scholarships now, a good job wherever I move to later.

"Hi, Sue," I greet our teller, one of two in our town's only banking establishment.

"Making a deposit today?" she asks as she takes my check and deposit slip. "Okay. Five hundred into your savings. Did you want any cash back?"

"Not today."

She stamps the check and initials a few spots before sliding it into a drawer. Then she hands me my receipt.

"Here you go."

I glance at it. Seeing the total grow always feels good.

But this time I do a double take. This can't be right.

"Sue?" I point at the slip. "I'm confused. I had $9,125 in my account. It's showing only $520. It should be $9,625."

"Well, that's because your mother came by earlier today and withdrew everything but the twenty dollars we require to keep the account open." Her eyes, framed by fake lashes, blink twice.

"But . . ." I can feel panic entering my chest, squeezing my heart and lungs. "But . . . this is *my* account. I didn't authorize her to withdraw any money."

"Honey, until you are eighteen, your mother is the joint holder of the account and, therefore, may withdraw money at any time."

Remain calm, Clare. Stop and think. Be smart right now, not emotional.

"Can I help you with anything else today?"

"Yes, actually. I think I would like to withdraw the remaining money in the account." I force myself to smile. "All of it. Including the twenty dollars that is needed to keep the account open."

"Okay. Let's see. You're going to have to fill out a few forms." Her false eyelashes flip up and down as she looks from her computer to me, pushing papers under the bulletproof glass. "And I'm going to have to verify the funds on this five-hundred-dollar check in order to give you cash. It's from one of our affiliate banks, so it shouldn't take but five or ten minutes."

I fill out the forms to the sound of Sue's fingers tapping on the keyboard, then of her chatting on the phone for a moment or two before she asks to verify funds. As hard as I try to write with a steady hand, the forms are barely legible when I give them back. I need to get home. I need to find my money.

"All verified. Here you are. Five hundred and twenty dollars. Are hundreds okay?"

"Yes. Thank you." I try to walk out at a normal pace.

I drive the few blocks home carefully, thinking, thinking. If I confront my mother, I will never see my money again.

Quiet as I can be, I tiptoe into the house. Where would she put it? I instantly think of the fire safe. I find the key. Silently, quickly. Open, look. Nothing there but my parent's checkbooks and Mom's only necklace with a diamond. Close, lock, key back.

Why did she take my money? What if she spent it already? What would she spend it on?

Wait. Find the money first. Ask why later.

Where else? Her purse. I look around the room. It's not in here. Where could it be? Her bedroom? Her closet? I wouldn't even know where to look.

Kitchen. That's where she sorts the mail. Maybe in there.

I push the door open, freeze.

Mom greets me with, "They arrested your brother this morning." She says it like any other mom would say, "We're out of milk."

It takes me off guard.

"For the receipt thing?" Oh, shit. I'm going to have to testify against him.

"Well, yes, they did have a warrant for that." She pauses.

"And?" I ask.

"Well, not that I believe a bit of it, but this twenty-something girl is claiming that she picked him up when he was hitchhiking and then he stole her car when she stopped to get gas." Mom pauses. "Not that I believe it. I mean, really. What respectable person picks up hitch-hikers these days?"

Skeleton nods as Mom steps toward me.

"Clare." Mom's fingers close in on my shoulder. "It would be a shame for Luke to spend Christmas in a holding cell, waiting for the trial, don't you think?" She doesn't wait for my response. "I know how much you love him, and I knew that you would want to help him, so I withdrew some money from your savings account today."

Bail. This is about needing bail so Luke will be home for Christmas! She wants me to sacrifice all my hard work, all the time I spent working at the library, as a tutor, as a lifeguard. Ten hours a week during the school year since I was twelve years old. Thirty-three hours a week all summer and a half lifeguarding. So that Luke can be home for Christmas. I pry her talons off my shoulder. She must be sick. Ill. Mentally ill. There is no other explanation. I take a few steps back.

"Do you know how bail works?" Mom asks, in a voice that she uses for small children. "Let me explain. Luke is going to be tried sometime in February, or maybe early March. If we post bail, from now until that time the judge allows Luke to be free, to be with his family or friends. What they require is that a certain amount of money is held by the court. If he shows up on his court date, we get the money back. It's that easy. And the bail bonds company takes a little percentage of the amount of bail for their services."

"But what if he doesn't show up? I've been saving that money my whole life," I say. "For college. I need it." Where the hell is my money?

"But you won't be giving it away permanently. It's just a loan, until Luke's trial date," she says. "We can't afford it without your help."

"What happens if he doesn't show for the trial?" I ask again.

"We don't worry about that, because Luke will show for his trial date. He always has."

"Just so I completely understand how it works, what happens if he doesn't show?" She's not going to say. "If you don't tell me, I'll just look it up online."

"Nothing comes back." Her lips thin out, and the vein begins to show in her forehead. Has she already posted bail?

I have to stall for time. "Okay. I'll think about it," I say. I need to find the cash now—if it is here—and let her think I'm considering. Where would she put it? Then I see the strap of her purse, pinched in the pantry door.

"The decision's been made, Clare," she tells me. "I have the money and I'm going to use it for Luke's bail."

She said "going to use it." So it should still be here. Remain calm. Let her think she's won.

"Okay," I say. "I guess you've made the decision for me."

She smiles.

Miraculously, she goes into the bathroom. It may be my only chance.

Open the pantry. There is Mom's poorly hidden purse.

Inside is an envelope, filled with hundreds. There is a receipt. My account number is on the bottom. The relief is overwhelming. I stuff the envelope under my shirt. The guilt is overwhelming. It's my money. Why do I feel like I'm stealing?

Mom's purse drops back into place. I grab my keys and drive to Drea's as snow begins to fall once again.

"Your mom's seriously crazy, but I can't believe this." Drea's fingers are shaking as we count the money. With the cash I just withdrew, it totals $9,625. It's all there.

I shake my head. I can't stop crying.

"Will you hide the money here? Just until I can figure out what to do?" I'm still crying, but at least my brain is working.

A mischievous grin crawls across Drea's face. "I've always wanted to slit open the bottom of the mattress and hide a big wad of cash there."

"Do you think that's the safest place? I mean, if they do it in a movie, doesn't everyone know about it?" I ask.

"Who would think of looking for almost ten thousand dollars in *my* mattress? Otherwise we can tuck some here and some there. As long as we don't hide it so well that we can't find it again."

The next half hour is spent splitting and hiding the cash, feeling more like criminals hiding our illegally acquired loot than two high school students putting away my college savings.

"Thanks, Drea," I say, leaving her house and preparing to go into battle.

No one seems to notice I was gone. Mom is in the kitchen, fixing dinner. My heartbeat slows—the confrontation can be put off for now. I find Peter in his room, wrapping gifts.

I hold up my shopping bags. "It'd be handy if we had more than one pair of scissors in this house."

After a few minutes of cutting and taping, chopping through Santa's face and lining it up with reindeer, I get the courage to talk to Peter.

"So . . . I'm not in here just to wrap gifts," I say.

"What's up?" He doesn't look up from the tag he's writing.

"They arrested Luke today," I say.

"Yeah, I know. I overheard Mom talking on the phone to Dad," Peter says, looking at the pile of ribbons.

"Mom wants me to give up my college savings for Luke's bail." Now I have his attention. I continue, "She actually went to the bank today and took all the money out of my account."

"Is that legal?" he asks.

"Apparently it is, since I'm under eighteen and she had to sign on to the account originally. But I found the money in her purse and took it back. She doesn't know yet." I look him in the eye. "She's going to kill me when she finds out."

"Wow. Mom's stealing from her own kid's savings account. It's a new low, even for our family."

"Crazy, right? Mom says she needs my money since she doesn't have enough. But she says I'll get it back when he shows for the trial. Do you think he will?" I ask.

"I don't know. Maybe. Probably not." Peter looks down, starts to tie gold ribbon around a package. Gives up and slaps a premade bow onto the top.

"I don't know why they'd need that much money," I say, "He stole a car. Bail couldn't be that much, could it?"

Peter clicks the top of his pen, looking up, his jaw clenching.

"Clare, he didn't just steal a car. He . . . raped someone."

"What?" My stomach acid rises. Luke couldn't have done that.

"I don't have any details. Just what I overheard. The charges are grand theft auto and something to do with sexual assault." Peter's jaw muscles tighten and release.

"Luke has made some bad decisions in the past, and I know he's violent when he's wasted. But I don't think he'd do that. That's a whole different level of fucked up than what he is," I say as Peter clicks the pen as fast as his thumb will move up and down. *Click, click, click, click, click, click, click.* Finally he stops.

"Clare, I've been seeing a therapist at school. It's . . . helpful. Good, actually. And you should do it too." He looks back down, flipping a box along the wrapping-paper roll.

"Why?" What, I'm crazy now? And so is Peter? Why therapy?

"For a lot of reasons. You know we don't have the best parents. And Luke—Luke is . . . Can I tell you something? Something only my therapist knows, so you need to keep it a secret forever. No telling Mom or Dad. Or Drea. Or anyone." I want to walk out of his room. Nothing that he is planning to say can be anything I want to hear.

"Okay." My stomach turns.

"Promise?"

"Promise."

"Not ANYONE."

"Okay, I promise. Not anyone."

Peter takes a big breath in, looks back at his wrapped gift, winds a piece of ribbon around a finger. "I was twelve. Dad was at work that day. And Mom took you with her Christmas shopping. She told Luke that he was responsible for me, and we were just here at the house watching TV, but then his friend Heather— Do you remember Heather? The girl with long black hair and blue eyes who used to come over sometimes? You were eight and you used to always tease Luke—'Luke and Heather sitting in a tree—'"

"I was hoping they'd get married," I interrupt. "She was so nice. And she didn't seem to care that Luke had been in jail a few times."

"Yeah. I liked Heather too." He gives a half smile. I want him to stay on this part of the story. Just remembering Luke and a friend, a girl we all liked. Nothing bad. But. Pushing away my worst memory of Luke never helped me. I need to hear what Peter has to say. "Anyway, she called and wanted him to come over. We put on our coats and boots and walked the mile over to her house. I forgot my gloves, so when I got there, my hands were freezing. It's crazy. That detail. How clearly I can remember the cold. We didn't knock, so Heather was still sitting on the couch, chewing her fingernails. Next to her was this guy with gray front teeth and sullen cheeks. I think his name is Dan. I still see him around sometimes."

He stops again. Rolls out another piece of wrapping paper and measures the next box. Cuts the paper jaggedly. For a moment I think he won't tell any more of the story. Then he continues. "Heather jumped up and ran over to us, just gushing over how cute I was and how happy she was that I was there. Her breath had that almost sweet smell that you get when you're drinking. She gave Luke a kiss on the cheek and told him she'd make him a cocktail. As she walked to the kitchen, I remember Luke nudging me, pointing at her butt because it was barely covered by her long-sleeved dress or shirt or whatever it was she was wearing."

His jaw muscles tighten again for a second. It's hard for him to keep talking. Keep telling me this story. It's hard for me to hear each word, because, really, don't I know already where it's leading?

After Peter's jaw relaxes, he continues. "She made me

a hot chocolate—with marshmallows. As soon as we sat down on the couch, Dan tapped Luke on the shoulder and said, 'I got what you need.'

"Luke said 'Shut up' at the same time Heather said, 'Hey. Not in front of the kid.'

"Luke told me to stay on the couch and watch the basketball game, and he headed down the hall to Heather's room with Dan. She stayed with me, ruffling my hair and giggling and drinking and saying how she wished she had a little brother like me. She refilled my hot chocolate each time she got up to make herself another—five times. I remember it was at the beginning of the second quarter when we got there. Knicks versus Heat. By the middle of the third period, she was pretty trashed and Luke hadn't come back. It wasn't bad sitting there, but the Heat was ahead by twenty something, and Heather kept passing out and waking up, and I was bored and I wanted to go home.

"So . . . then Dan came out of the room, woke up Heather, and told us he needed to leave. A minute later Heather said, 'I'd better see what kind of trouble your brother is getting into' and stumbled down the hall. She was really drunk, Clare. . . ."

Peter stops again. The box sits on the wrapping paper. He looks down, as if he's just now realizing that he was in the middle of wrapping a gift. He folds the edge, making it smooth before taping it. Then he looks up at me. "I've thought a lot, Clare, about what I could have done differently that day. I could have told Luke I wanted to go home as soon as I was bored. I could have asked Heather for another hot chocolate, even though I didn't want one. Or maybe if I had gone back for my gloves, we would've gotten there a little bit later and Dan and whatever drugs he had would have been gone. Maybe if one thing had gone differently that day. Know what I mean?"

I nod. We sit in silence for a minute or two. He's done with the story. He can't tell me any more. But he has to. I need to know. "Peter, what happened?"

"I had to pee. So . . ." Peter pauses. My stomach is a rotten apple core. "I walked down the hall to the bathroom. Heather's door was open just a crack. I peeked in. I could see Luke and Heather lying together on the bed, facing each other. Luke was running his hand up her bare leg, and she looked like she was asleep."

Peter pauses again. "I went the bathroom." His eyes are watering. "On the way out I heard Heather saying no. I stopped at the door. I wanted to keep walking, not look in, but then I heard her again." He pauses, swallowing.

"I've never heard anyone's voice so scared before." His voice cracks. "She was begging him to stop. I put my eye up to the crack, Clare." Another pause. "I looked in for only a second. Just a second. But it was long enough to see. He didn't stop, Clare. I know what I saw."

Peter's nose is running, and he wipes the tears before they can stream down his cheeks. "I wonder if I could have tried to stop him. If I burst open the door, or called the police or screamed or anything. If I did anything. But I didn't."

His voice lowers to almost a whisper. "I was so scared. Clare, I was so scared. So I went back to the couch. I sat on the couch and I turned the volume up on the TV until I almost couldn't hear anything anymore. And I stared at the screen, trying to just watch the game. But no matter how loud I put the volume, all I could hear was Heather screaming.

"After a long time Luke came out of the room, all proud of himself. I was terrified. He sat down on the couch and asked who'd won the game. I couldn't answer him. I didn't know. He tried to put his arm around me, and I jerked away. I was trying so hard not to, but when he looked at me, I started to cry.

"Then he got angry. He told me to put on my jacket because we were going home. As he flipped off the TV, I could hear Heather sobbing in the other room. Luke could hear her too.

"Right outside the front door Luke grabbed my shoulders. He got right down in my face and said, 'What's wrong with you?'

"I shook my head. I couldn't speak. He knew, Clare. He knew I saw. And I thought he was going to kill me. He told me that Heather was a slut and liked to scream like that when she was having fun." Peter spits the words out. "And when I cried harder, he grabbed me by the throat and said, 'Don't you spread any lies about your brother!' Clare, he lifted me off the ground and said, 'If you spread lies about me, I will kill you. Understand?'

"I was able to somehow say yes. And that I wouldn't say anything. He dropped me into a snowbank. And he left me there. It was freezing and the sun was setting. Once he was out of sight, I got up and walked home. I cried the whole way.

"I told Mom and Dad that Luke and I got into a fight when we were out walking. He never came home. I was scared for weeks that he'd show up in the middle of the night and kill me. Finally he called from jail . . . and I felt safe.

"Know what's crazy? I don't think he remembers—he was so wasted. Either that or he acts like it never happened." Peter is answering questions before I can think to ask. He takes a deep breath in. Lets it out.

I am underwater suddenly, and I can't find the way to air. My stomach turns hard; my lungs fill with liquid.

Luke is the reason women are afraid to go out at night. Luke is the reason police carry guns. Luke is the reason for guard dogs and security systems and pepper spray. Luke is the bad guy.

"Peter . . . I'm so sorry." What else can I say? There are no tears, because I am forcing them back. My head feels like it's going to explode. All of these years Peter has been carrying around this secret. While Mom and Dad and I have been welcoming Luke home with big hugs and kisses, Peter has been scared to death of what Luke might do to him. No wonder he never told any of us. Why would he? We'd probably all take Luke's side.

Santa's jolly face looks up at me from the wrapping paper. HO, HO, HO. He laughs. I want to vomit all over his stupid rosy-red cheeks.

"Clare," Peter says. "I'm sorry. I know I was really

rough on you, growing up. Even before I saw Luke do that, he was always so violent with me. I just . . . I didn't know what to do with my anger. So I was rough on you. I'm sorry. I've owed you that apology for a long time."

"Thanks," I say, finding a little air in my lungs. "And for telling me. You can trust me. I won't tell your secret." Part of me wishes I didn't know his secret still. "And, I don't know if this needs to be said . . ." My words stumble; I don't want to say anything wrong. . . . "But just so you know, I'm not letting Mom use my college fund for Luke's bail. He can stay in jail."

Peter nods.

"So." Peter breaks the uncomfortable air. "Can I help you wrap your gifts?"

"Sure. Thanks."

He turns on his computer, selects a playlist, and lets the music soften the edge of his truth.

We tie a few bows, tape holiday paper closed. With the gifts all wrapped, I head to my own room. Almost as soon I shut my door, it crashes open.

"Where is it, Clare?" Mom flies at me, teeth bared. "Where is my money?"

I don't give myself time to be intimidated. "It's not yours, and it's not here." I manage to keep my voice monotone and calm, saying exactly what I want to say.

"You will give me that money now. Luke is in a hold-ing cell waiting for his bail. I promised him. Where is the money?"

I bite my lip, but the angry tears come out anyway.

"You can't have it." My voice wavers but I pause and make it as firm as I can. "I saved that money for college."

Dad pokes his head into the battle, still in his work jumpsuit. "What's going on in here?"

Where to start?

"Our selfish little daughter won't help with Luke's bail."

Dad looks from me to Mom. He's going to side with her. He always does.

"Let's talk about it, Clare Bear. This is a great opportunity to do something for your brother," Dad says.

"Dad, I've worked for *years* to save that money." Please, Dad, side with me.

"You'll get it back! As soon as he shows up for his court date," my father says. "Mom and I trust him enough that we are using our savings."

"I saved that money for college." I am a broken record, afraid that if I say anything else, Peter's secret will come out.

"Clare." Mom's tone softens. "Clare, we can't leave him in jail. I . . . I didn't tell you this before, but he's been accused of a sexual crime. Do you know what they do to people who are being held for trial for that? They get beaten up. Raped. Luke is my son. He's your brother. We can't leave him in jail, not when he can be safe at home with us."

She almost convinces me. Even knowing what Luke has done, I don't want him to be hurt. I want to protect him somehow. But the fear of Luke is strong, and that trumps everything else. I force myself to say, "I can't."

My mother's face turns ugly. "You are so selfish, young lady," she hisses. "If Luke gets hurt, it will be all your fault."

I shake my head, repeating to myself, no, no, it's not my fault. It's not.

"He's your brother, Clare," Mom says, her cajoling voice back. "It's Christmas."

"No." I don't have anything more to say.

"Don't bother to ask us for anything ever again." Mom pulls Dad out the door and slams it behind them.

I stay frozen to the spot where I'm standing. Trying to process it all. To make sense of it all. Luke is a thief. An addict. An alcoholic. A sexual predator. Only a month ago he attacked Peter. And years ago he almost strangled Dad. And yet they still choose him over me. They still choose *him*. In its own way it's almost worse than hearing Peter's secret. Mom thinks Luke is innocent. She doesn't know what Luke did to Heather. But she can't deny what he's done to us. She loves Luke more, and she'll always choose him.

Chapter 47:

Christmas

NOW

The next morning Mom is up early, clicking away on a website that sells and ships approved items to inmates. "I'm working on a care package for your brother," she says. "And tomorrow I'm going to mail out his Christmas card. Do you have your letter ready for him?"

"I won't be sending him a letter," I mumble.

Mom crinkles her brow. "You always send him a letter with our Christmas card."

"I have homework to do and scholarships to apply for," I say, grabbing books off the kitchen table.

"He's your brother, Clare. The least you could do is take five minutes to write him a letter." Skeleton stands behind Mom, jaws flapping open and shut, mirroring her stance, one hand on the hip, the other dramatically thrown in the air. "Especially this time. He would be home with us if you had helped with bail."

"Just because he's my brother doesn't mean I have to write him," I announce, to the surprise of Mom, Skeleton, and myself.

Skeleton spins a card with the nativity scene across the desk, snapping Mom out of shock.

"It's Christmas, Clare! You will write your brother, and that is final!" She shoves the card on top of my books. "Don't bother to come out of your room until you have written something nice."

I take the pen from Mom's hand, put my books down.

What do I write? *Dear Luke, I'm glad you're in jail, because I'm scared of you.* Or *Dear Luke, I don't want to believe you hurt that girl, but I know it's true. How could you have done that?* Or *Dear Luke, I loved and trusted you, and all you are is a sick asshole. Merry Christmas.*

Or maybe I'll just do what everyone else seems to. Pretend nothing is wrong. Know he did something bad and ignore it, because maybe by ignoring it, it will fix itself.

Dear Luke, I write. *Best wishes for a happy, healthy holiday season. Clare.*

I hand her the card, hand her the pen. Push Skeleton out of my path.

In my room I try to work on my homework. But everything around me reminds me of Luke. The desk was his. The bed. The dresser. Even the carpet. Who knows what has happened in *here*? I hate my room.

I bundle up in my down jacket, beanie, scarf, boots, and gloves. I could go to Omar's. He's probably working on the same AP English assignment. But he'll ask how I'm doing. Then I'd have to lie. He doesn't want to hear the truth. None of my friends do.

My feet take me to my apple tree. After wiping off the snow, I plop down into the chair under the tree. It's freezing and my face starts to hurt, but I read through the assigned Yeats poem, making notes for my essay. At least I'm outside, away from my parents and all the reminders of Luke. Even in the cold I'd rather analyze Shakespeare, Brontë, Keats, and Yeats than my family any day.

Christmas morning. Coffee and bacon. Carols are turned up the loudest Mom can get them; even a fire is blazing when I stumble down the hall still in my pj's.

"Merry Christmas! One egg or two?" Mom smiles over the stove, filling up plates. It's unnerving how cheerful she is this morning. After the last three days of angry glares and constant reminders of what a shitty daughter I am, I expected Christmas to be canceled. But the gifts are wrapped, perfectly placed under the tree, and the stockings are all stuffed, items practically spilling out over the top. Skeleton sits smoking a corn-cob pipe by the fire, Santa hat on, wearing a pair of old pajamas with "Luke" embroidered over the pocket. Very funny, Skeleton, very funny.

Mom takes pictures of us sitting around the table. Then takes pictures of us opening gifts, with our photograph smiles painted plainly on our faces. Dad takes pictures of her opening little gifts from each of us, including the new slippers I got her. Then she takes more pictures of us all helping with the cleanup.

Now she has all the photos she needs to prove we are the perfect family. She immediately prints them, frames them, displays them around the house.

Skeleton doesn't show up in even one of the photos.

I go along with everything, smiling when I'm sup-posed to, even though I'm sick of pretending it's all okay. Until the phone rings. Mom runs to get it, and I *know* it's Luke. As soon as she confirms, "Yes, I'll accept the charges," I grab my car keys and bolt. I drive a block away and park, waiting out the call, feeling ashamed and cowardly. I know I can't run away from everything that makes me uncomfortable forever, but it's all I can think to do for now. I'm not ready to talk to Luke. I don't know if I will ever be.

Chapter 48:
Happy Birthday

NOW

My friends pick me up, we go out to dinner, and I celebrate turning eighteen by buying a lottery card. I scratch off the bags of money and find that three of a kind means I win five dollars. Lucky me.

When I get home, there's a gift from Peter, a letter from Luke, and a card from my parents on my bed.

I unwrap Peter's gift first—the Speedo swim watch that I was eyeing over the summer. I can't believe he was paying enough attention to know that I wanted it.

Then Luke's.

Clare,
  Please write. It is so hard in here, and I _need_ your letters. Write back soon, okay? Please.

Love,
Luke

I'm a little surprised he didn't even acknowledge my birthday. Not knowing what to think, I toss his letter to the side and open the card from my parents. It's generic with a kitten on the front, and the only thing in their hand is *Happy Birthday, Clare. Love, Mom and Dad.* And a Post-it note: *You can have your birthday gift when you write a proper letter to Luke.* Apparently Mom is back to hating me. Christmas could still be on. Birthday, not so much.

I don't care about the gift. The truth is, part of me wants to write Luke so bad that it hurts. In two days it'll be New Year's. While the rest of the world is celebrating a fresh start, he's in a holding cell waiting for a trial that will decide his future. I can't help but feel sad for him. Feel how lonely it must be. It's confusing, because at the same time I'm scared. Scared that if he's found innocent, he'll hurt someone again. Maybe that some-one will be me.

The trial should be soon. His preliminary hearing is a week after New Year's. It's out of my hands. But writing him, that's something I could do. I look down at my new watch on my wrist. What would Peter think if I wrote Luke? Peter, who trusted me more than anyone else to hold his secret. Luke may be lonely and sad, but he's awaiting trial for a violent crime that he is capable of doing. I need to remember that.

I ball up my parents' card and Luke's letter and throw them into the fire.

Chapter 49:

Arraignment, Pleas, Pretrial, and Trial

NOW

I'm staring at the bottom of the toilet. No, I do not have the flu. My stomach has wrapped around itself, looped and bound into a large knot. Tomorrow is the pretrial hearing, where they will determine witnesses. Tomorrow I find out if I will have to testify against my brother. My stomach contracts. I expect it to empty out. It loops around itself one more time, leaving me staring at the toilet bowl with the sensation of a dry heave. Ten minutes later I give up, crawl to bed. Facing the ceiling, I try to think of warm, sunny days at the beach, or laughing with Drea. But Skeleton's cigar smoke circles the room, filling my nostrils, reminding me that he is here.

I have to go to school in the morning. Even though my stomach is still in knots and my head pounds from the mere two hours of sleep I was able to get last night. Usually I pick up Drea, but she's sick, so I slowly navigate the icy roads alone. Maybe it will be nice, being in school today. Distracted from what is going on in the courthouse less than an hour's drive away. I have a history essay test that I spent the greater part of last week reviewing for. The prospect of doing well on that looks good.

A bright orange flyer for the winter art show is posted next to my locker. All this week the walls of the cafeteria will be graced with student work, featuring award-winning photography by Mandy Jordan. Really? Award-winning? According to whom? I remember her zoom lens on me and Luke at the lake this summer. My stomach turns again. I check my watch. With fifteen minutes before first period, I can head to the cafeteria to see this award-winning art.

I pass Omar on my way and stop to stab my pencil into the middle of the flyer on the bulletin board, right above Mandy's name.

He looks up and comments, "Award-winning, huh? This I gotta see."

"I'm going there right now. Want to join me?"

"Meet you in five?"

I walk into the empty cafeteria. Mandy's pictures are immediately to the right of the door. A panoramic-style black-and-white photo with all of the Cranberry Hill girls looking very serious and sullen in front of the entrance to the school is the first photo. They are all dressed the same—tight white T-shirts and jeans, their hair slicked back, eyes, cheeks, and lips overly made up. Each holding a roughly drawn letter dropped down lazily between their chest and their thigh to spell out: "Soul Escape." Oh, please. Mandy is attempting to be deep? Can't wait to see what the rest of the photos are going to look like. I'm about to roll my eyes, when I stop myself—the topic might be a stretch, might even be classified as cheesy, but the picture itself isn't bad. She's caught the entrance to the school at just the right angle to make it look like it could be the concrete wall of a prison. And the makeup, though overdone, makes the girls have that creepy kind of soulless pretty that horror films can so perfectly capture.

If this picture is as calculated as it seems, Mandy is not nearly as stupid as I thought. Or as untalented. While her friends played fashion model for her title picture, she set them up as a subject. Their escape, their comfort, is being clones. Alright, then, award-winning Mandy. I hate to admit it, but you've got my attention.

The next picture is of Ryan, tucked inside the barrel of a huge wave. She has saturated the water to look bright turquoise; the white foam almost bleached. It's too much. Too cheery. Too overwhelming. Dreamlike and dangerous. I want to pluck him out of the wave and put him onshore.

Although the words are blurred, a SKYY Vodka bottle is the unmistakable subject of the next photo. The sunlight filtering through the glass creates an eerie blue shadow on the beige-tiled table below. An older lady's hand featuring a huge emerald ring—Lucille's—holds a martini glass, the stem pinched just so between her fingers.

I walk in front of the last two photos. The largest of them all, a 20" x 24", features the lake during a summer morning. I breathe in sharply as I scan the picture, the sun just over the top of the mountain in the background; the tall, knotted trees along the edge; the soft green grass and wispy reeds; and an arm—my arm!—sweeping up through the air, water suspended between my skin and the lake below; the red of my bathing suit barely visible under the surface, a white wake all around me. I'd be a little dot of white and red in the middle of the blue water if the print were only a 3" x 5". Instead, somehow, the lake, the trees, the sun all become just part of the background. Me swimming is the focus.

It's beautiful. Incredible. Award-winning.

Maybe I should be angry that I'm the subject. That swimming, my personal soul escape, has become part of her art project. But looking at the ball of sun in the background, the way my arm is cutting through the surface of the water, I can't feel anger. Instead I can almost feel how good it was to swim in the mornings, how strangely exhilarating and comforting the freezing water can be. The picture leaves me with the deep longing for the one thing that could make me feel better right now, the one thing that I can't have until summer.

One last picture. Considerably smaller at 8" x 10". It's Luke's arm, nuzzled into the deep green grass. The Virgin Mary solemnly stepping on the head of a viper as the warm light from the sun perfectly highlights the muscles in his arms. This one leaves me with a different longing, the longing for things I can never have again: the innocence of believing Luke is really a good person at heart and the hope that he can be different.

Sinking to the floor, I'm thankful that the cafeteria is empty, because suddenly I can't stop crying.

It's Omar's arms that find me and pull me off the floor, his voice trying to make an uncomfortable joke. "Mandy's pictures are so bad they made you cry, huh?" His hands guide me to the restroom, where Skye and Lala are waiting. Skye helps wash and dry my face, applies a layer of her cover-up to conceal my red, blotchy skin.

They don't ask any questions. I don't offer up any information. Besides, if I start talking about Luke or me, or any type of emotion, I'm going to cry again.

I'm still looking a mess, but the first bell rings. Mom will flip if I go home. She'll claim I'm ditching on purpose. And I have that history test today. I have to go to class. As I leave the bathroom, Omar steps forward and puts his huge sunglasses on my face. "Keep them for today. Or for always. Whatever you need."

By lunch I'm feeling okay. The need to cry is gone, and English quotes and history dates are bouncing around in my mind. The freezing air drives us from the quad into the cafeteria. A small crowd is walking past Mandy's pictures, taking a few minutes to stop and look at them.

I see the back of Ryan's head in front of the exhibition. I wonder how he feels to be on display as one of Mandy's subjects. At least no one except my friends will know for sure it's me in the picture of the lake. And who knows Luke's tattoos well enough to know that it's his arm? Ryan, on the other hand, is perfectly recognizable. Did Mandy ask his permission? Show him the picture first? Did he see the whole series before she displayed them on the wall?

He turns and looks directly at me, then heads toward my table. Quickly excusing myself, I grab my backpack, toss my uneaten lunch into the trash, slip on Omar's sunglasses, and practically run to the library.

I don't want to talk to anyone. Not about Luke. Not about my soul escape and the reality I am swimming from. I don't want to talk to Omar, Lala, Skye, Chase, my parents, Peter, or Drea. And I certainly don't want to talk to Ryan.

"Hi, Clare. Set your bag down and have a seat," Dad says as I walk in the door after school. I lower myself to the couch, apprehensively dropping my backpack onto the floor, trying to read my father's face. "Your statements taken during your interrogation will be sufficient," he tells me. "You will not have to appear in court as a witness."

I'm not going to have to appear in court as a witness against Luke? I'm not going to have to appear in court as a witness against Luke! I won't have to sit on the stand, worried that something I say or do might make him have more or less of a sentence. I won't have to see his face while testifying against him.

I allow myself to feel a hint of relief.

"Just so you know, Clare Bear, Luke told his lawyer that if they did want you on the stand as a witness, then he wanted to plead guilty so you wouldn't have to go through that."

"Oh," I say.

"Mom told me at Christmas that you didn't want to write Luke. Maybe now you want to write him a little thank-you or something."

A thank-you? My teeth grind. With enough pressure they will split into a million shards, flying through my cheeks with all the force. I did not get him into trouble. What am I supposed to thank him for? How can my parents not get it?

"So, um, that's it. Unless you had a question or something?" he asks.

I have plenty of questions.

"What about the other charges, the stolen car and sexual assault? Are they all tried at once? Or is that separate? Did he have the preliminary hearing on that already? Is there enough evidence for that trial?"

"Oh. Don't you worry yourself about that, Clare Bear." Dad gives me a weak smile. "How about a hot cocoa to celebrate your not having to appear in court?"

Skeleton does a little dance around the room, taking this opportunity to rattle his bones louder than usual. Don't you know, Dad, that you aren't protecting me by avoiding my questions? Don't you know that Skeletons don't like to be kept in closets?

Chapter 50:

Frozen, Partially

NOW

Mandy's photos haunt me. I return to them again and again.

Some days I zero in on the photo of the martini glass in Lucille's hand, wondering what life is like in the Jordan household. I force myself to not feel sorry for Mandy. Even if we both have a taste of what it's like to live with an addict. But Chris. I miss Chris. I miss watching him improve and grow. I just want to tell him that I understand. Even if I can't promise him it'll turn out okay.

Some days I look at Luke's tattoo. Some days I pretend it isn't there. But I always take in every detail of my lake, swimming in the photo, letting myself feel the water surrounding me.

Then Friday comes; the photos disappear. All I'm left with is winter.

"Clare, are you okay?" Drea's mom plunks down next to me on a bench by the edge of the lake, frozen milky thick.

I shrug. "I haven't been sleeping well." I think about

the night I got so drunk that I couldn't remember what I said to Ms. P. And I think about Luke and wonder what he remembers. If he knows what he has done. If he cares.

"On your walk?" I ask, moving the subject from me. It's cold. The mountains above the lake are bogged in with thick clouds, promising snow.

"Every day. You know, the trail around the lake is a full two miles. Good exercise. And this time of year I don't have to worry about rattlesnakes, either." Drea's mom puts her arm around my shoulder while she pauses. Then, "It's been bad for you lately, huh?"

I chew my tongue, trying not to cry. Nod, feel the warmth of her hug through my jacket. It was too thin a choice for such a cold day. I didn't notice until now.

"The lake's frozen hard this year," she says after a moment of silence. "I always wonder, what happens to the frogs? During winter, when the ground and the water are both frozen." Ms. P looks far to the other side, where reeds stick stubbornly through the cloudy ice. "We always have frogs in the spring. It's a sign of a healthy environment. They're the first to leave and the first to die if the water is toxic."

Frogs wouldn't last long in my house.

"So, enough small talk. I think what you need is a little time out of your house. I was thinking of taking Drea to visit her aunt Tiara who lives in Dana Point. You have a three-day weekend for Presidents' Day coming up. Come with us. I promise a lot of fun and relaxation." She leans in tight, squeezes my arm for extra emphasis. "The ocean, a Jacuzzi, a library where you can sit and read all day if you like. And the food. To die for. My sister makes the best chocolate cream pie. What do you say?" Her face is full of excitement and promise. She really believes that a trip will make me all better. She really believes that she can fix it. Enough that I want to believe it can bring me sanity, help me understand myself, my parents, my brothers.

"Okay." And I think for the hundredth time, Why can't my mom be more like Ms. P?

"For now," she goes on, "I could use some company. It gets lonely in the woods sometimes, walking alone."

Past the guard at the gate, the car sways with each turn, bringing into view a hodgepodge of beach-weathered homes and palm trees reaching to the sky. After driving through the neighborhood, we stop where homes line cliffs like birds on a wire.

The proximity to the ocean doesn't impress me as much as the cameras that surround Drea's aunt's house, watching us get out of the car and unload our bags. I elbow Drea and nod toward one.

"Oh, yeah," she says. "All the houses have a system like that here. Especially since some of these places are empty a lot of the time. Vacation spots."

Will it feel different tonight, sleeping in a house with all this protection? Or will I still lie on the bed, looking to the door, the windows, closing my eyes only when they will no longer stay open?

The sun peers out from behind a cloud, warming my

skin. It's probably no more than sixty-five degrees out here, but it feels hot since we've come from the land of ice and snow.

"Think it's warm enough that I can swim in the ocean?"

"Maybe." Drea throws her bag over her shoulder. "Let's get to the beach while it's still light."

Bags drop in the entry. There are hugs and welcomes. Aunt Tiara aunt locks arms with Ms. P, angles her toward the patio for some coffee and catching up. We're invited to join but opt to change into our bikinis and take the steps down the cliff to the ocean.

We put our toes into the water first.

"No fucking way." Drea pulls her foot out, backs to the dry sand, where she sits with her towel wrapped around her. "I bet the Jacuzzi is nice and warm."

"I'm going for it," I say, plunging in—knee deep, waist deep, then finally diving under waves.

"It's not so bad. Once you get used to it. The lake is hot in comparison!" I yell to Drea even though my teeth chatter. It is freezing.

"Whatever, crazy. You have all the fun." She opens the rag mag that she grabbed from her aunt's counter.

The best way to warm up is to swim. Long strokes out, out to the open ocean. Stop and look back at Drea, becoming ant-size on the beach.

There are so many things I could think of, but all that comes to mind is Luke. The words "sex offender" and "criminal" are strong in my mind, but so are the images of him teaching me to float, his hand supporting my back, keeping me safe. Keeping me from drowning.

I dive under a wave, as deep as the salt water allows. How long can I stay down here? Under the surface, out of the breeze, in a place that tricks me into thinking I am warmer the longer I stay. No wonder people want to believe mermaids exist. Nothing would make me happier than one grabbing my ankle and pulling me deep down until I turn into a mermaid with silky blue locks and a shiny tail. In peace. I'd live in peace.

A bubble of air releases now. Again. I open my eyes and watch the bubbles float to the surface, imagining they each represent a good memory of Luke that I have to let go. Maybe I will let all the air run out, and sink to the bottom, mermaid or not.

It's not a bad idea. I'd be done. No longer having to think, think, think all the time, swinging from anger to fear to depression. It might just be a good idea.

I let another bubble escape.

Then I picture Drea. Waiting on the shore. I picture Drea, dark skin deepening as the sun dips into the ocean. I picture her realizing that her best friend isn't coming to the surface.

I push the water to the side, break into the air.

"What the hell are you doing?" Drea yells, already chest deep by the time I surface.

"Sorry. You know how I get, with swimming. I was just enjoying the ocean," I lie.

Drea swims with strong stokes toward me, saying, "That better be all it was."

. . .

Hot, hot, hot water. Neck deep. My body is tingling, tiny little pinpricks on the skin, shocking my body back up to 98.6 degrees.

"Are you relaxing?" Drea says, one eye open, watching me, the other closed, her head resting on the cement rim of the Jacuzzi.

"Yep." The sun has almost completely set.

"Really? Good, because this trip is all about you relaxing."

"Great," I say.

"You know, Clare"—Drea rolls her head to the side, looking directly at me—"lately you have gotten quite a knack for just using one word around me."

"Sorry," I say. Crap. She's right. When did this one-word thing start?

"Listen. I know what Luke is accused of doing. Talk to me. I won't judge. I just want you to be okay," she says.

When Luke was just a thief, or at least when I thought he was just a thief, it didn't seem so bad. But she won't be able to understand *this*. She wouldn't be able not to judge. How could she? How can anyone else understand, if I can't put it together in my own head?

"Thanks, but I'd rather not talk about it. I'm so tired of even *thinking* about it. I'll be okay."

She looks at me with *You've got to be kidding me* eyes. "I can't fucking believe this," she says, her voice filled with anger and getting louder. "You don't want to talk to me. Fine. But figure out a way to pull yourself out of this shit. Because I can't keep hanging around you if you don't. It's fucking exhausting being your friend right now."

Her words hit me hard. Like she has any type of problem that even comes close to what I've been living through. It would be so easy being Drea. Everyone likes her. She doesn't have any skeletons clanking around her. And I would do anything to trade my mom for her mom. It's fucking exhausting being my friend? It's really fucking exhausting being *me*.

She waits for a response. When I don't give one, she shakes her head and turns away.

The jets pound my back and shoulders, their loud groan drowning out my thoughts. A few minutes later Drea looks back at me.

She's my best friend. She won't judge. She just wants me to be okay. And no, this can't be easy on her, either. It doesn't matter what anyone has said. She has believed me even with the tiny bit of information I've given her. She knows me enough to still be my friend. My best friend. I have to trust her.

"Fine. I'm not okay. At all." I let my eyes pool. "I can't figure anything out. How can Luke be one person? I think he's guilty, Drea. I think he really hurt that girl. And I'm scared he's done it before but this is the first time he got caught. So why does part of me still love him and hope he's innocent?"

Drea's eyes close; painted fingernails tap at her chin. She nods.

"He's always been kind to you, and you've seen the caring side. Of course you have compassion for him," Drea says. "But he's done violent shit. And you have to consider that."

"I think about that all the time. Am I an idiot because some of me loves him and I hope he'll turn around someday?"

"No. Love is a fucked-up emotion. Sometimes I think of good things about my dad, and a little of me still loves him. But I don't forget he left and has never had any interest in us since. As far as Luke turning around—no offense, just my opinion—I would have given up on him a long time ago. You've given him so many chances. Maybe he's just this way, and there is nothing you can do about it. You can't control him. You can't change him." Drea pauses. "As much as I couldn't control or change my dad, you know?"

A breeze rustles the palm tree next to us, making a soft shushing sound. Maybe Drea is right.

"It's not just Luke. It's my parents. Why do they love him more? Why do they put so much energy into him? Why him and not me?" Saltwater tears drip off my face, joining the chlorinated water. Crap. I sound like a five-year-old.

"Are you shitting me?" Drea's eyes are on mine, refusing to let go of contact. "Why *him* and not *you*? You are beautiful. You've got great friends; none of them are criminals. Your grades are so high that colleges are begging you to choose them. You've worked hard to save money, and even harder to get scholarships. Not to mention, you are a fantastic lifeguard. Clare, you have so much going for you. You don't need them. Luke does."

It sounds so simple. Maybe it's true.

I suddenly have a flashback of Mom the day we left Tennessee. Her tiny hands wrapped around mine. Her line of questioning. Did I do anything illegal? Anything at all that she needed to know . . . *before* we left Tennessee. Was she trying to protect me then? Figure out a way that I could run so I wouldn't go to jail? It's a strange thought—comforting and disturbing all at the same time. I push it away, instead focusing on Drea's words—I have so much going for me.

"Thanks," I whisper, feeling a little better now.

"Anytime you need me," Drea says, taking a deep breath in and submerging herself completely.

She pops back out just as a cold breeze blows.

"Mom and Aunt T have a feast planned for tonight. We should go in."

Wrapped in damp towels, we run up the stairs, run from the chill, the creeping darkness, and the increasing wind. We fly through the back door, and the wind slams it shut behind us.

Safe and warm, amazed by how much protection a pane of glass can provide, I look, down to the shore, across a field of grasses forced to the ground with each gust. They bounce back, only to be flattened again a second later. Bent branches of palm trees fling back and forward. The palms rest between gusts, drooped and panting. Even the ocean's waves appear to be pushed back, pushed away from the beach.

The next morning the wind has stopped completely, leaving the grasses standing, the palm branches with their regal arcs, but a couple of juniper trees along the edge of the grass are still bent to the side, their branches reaching toward the ocean, looking old and tired, reshaped their entire lives because of the wind. Bent to the side, permanently.

If Luke and his actions are the wind, what am I? The proud grasses, the regal palms? Or the permanently bent tree?

"Mom, I hope I get into Pepperdine. I really want to live at the beach," Drea says, looking out the back window of the car as if to catch the last glimpse of the ocean before our weekend is over. I look back too, but in the darkness I can see only a black pit.

"Don't I know it," Drea's mom agrees. The cloudy sky starts to sprinkle.

My smile is leaving. Over the weekend we swam and played board games, and watched girl movies where everything was so funny or so dramatic, it made me forget all about my own problems. I slept completely through the night. Not one bad dream. I even fell asleep lying on my stomach. I forgot about home. Forgot about Luke. And Peter. And my parents.

The radio reports snowfall in the mountains. "Only in California," Drea's mom says as she raises her eyebrows and looks at the clock. We have already driven more than an hour; we are going forward.

As we drive up the mountain, the falling rain turns to snow.

Plows have been up and down the highways, making dirty drifts that grow as we rise in altitude. Even with the four-wheel drive engaged, we inch up the road, the snow now falling rapidly. The plow has carved its way down my street, making banks on either side at least three feet tall. Drea's mom cautiously drives down the one-lane ice cave. We stop in front of my house.

"Wow. Looks like nobody has shoveled your walk today, Clare," Ms. P says. "Do you need help getting in? Do you want to come to our house instead?"

Yes. I want to go to your house forever, is what I think, but I say "I'll figure it out."

"Do you have your key?"

"Yep," I say, double-checking. Then I grab my bag, put each strap over a shoulder like a backpack. Leap into the snow, sink to my knees. This is going to be more difficult than I figured.

Looking ahead, I feel awful for having to push through the fresh snow. It's so beautiful. Untouched, smooth, perfect.

"Clare? Is that you?" Mom opens the door. "What are you doing just standing there? You'll freeze. Come inside."

I push through the snow toward my mother, ruining the perfection.

Mom's raging fire has the room perfectly warm. Her chair shows a dip of where her body just was, hot coffee and a newspaper sitting to the side. The scene is cozy, warm. It actually makes me want to grab a book and read with her right next to me, in some sort of comfortable silence.

Peter joins us in the living room, flipping on a

Lakers-Suns game. Mom pulls out her polishing rags and lines them up on her desk. She goes into the kitchen and brings a small bowl of sudsy water back into the living room, places it next to the polishing rags. The room fills with the smell of white vinegar as she splashes some into the mix. Her hands cautiously remove the crystal snowflake from the holder. After dipping it into her cleaning mix, she uses a brush to get the dust out of each crevice. I lean back on the couch next to Peter, trying to ignore Mom.

Dad shuffles in from outside, covered in snow. "I'm lucky I got home tonight. There's no way," he says to Mom, "no way the roads will be clear by tomorrow. I'm sorry." He gives her a little hug, then adds, "I don't think we'll be able to go to the trial."

I had completely forgotten. Completely and totally. In my vacation haze with Drea and Ms. P, my mind had floated away from my reality. Including Luke's trial.

Mom gives a sad little moan. She looks like she might cry. But instead she pulls the crystal snowflake from the water, gently places it on a polishing cloth, and says in a somewhat upbeat voice, "This storm can't last all week. I'm positive we'll be able to make it at least for the verdict." She hangs the snowflake back up, leaving the rest of the ornaments unpolished. She's saving them, just in case.

But the storm does last. Piling snow higher and higher, until we look out the windows and see only a sheet of white. School is canceled day after day.

On Tuesday our Internet, cable, cell phone, and phone service—all of it goes out. Skeleton points to the dead phones and the computer, reminding us that our connection with Luke and his lawyers is completely gone now. I pull out every scrap of leftover yarn I have, knit squares of bright colors until my fingers burn.

On Wednesday the electricity goes out. I watch the temperature in my fish tank drop degree by degree. Making it my new mission to keep my fish alive, I wrap blankets around the glass and add to the tank a Ziploc baggie of hot water I warmed by the fire, and replace it every few hours. It gives me something to do, something to think about other than Luke's trial.

While I'm concentrating on keeping my fish warm, Mom and Dad pack snow in the refrigerator and freezer to keep our food cold. Then they bring out every board game we have, insisting it'll be fun. There is no way we can get any information on Luke's trial; the phones don't come back on despite Mom's obsessively lifting the receiver every fifteen minutes. We don't even know if, one hour away and fifteen degrees warmer, this storm would be bad enough to postpone the trial. Nobody says a word about it, but Mom polishes the silver star by candlelight as I stitch my squares together, slowly forming another blanket. That night we all pull our blankets and pillows into the living room. It's more comfortable to sleep in front of the fire.

On Thursday the water pipes freeze. Mom melts snow in a pot on the fire. We eat hot dogs and marshmallows for dinner for the second night in a row. Skeleton pings

Mom's bell ornament with his finger, making the silver clapper and mallet hit the fragile crystal again and again. Its high-pitched *ding* drives me out of the warm living room into my chilled bedroom. By flashlight I can see that the fish are lethargic but still alive.

On Friday morning Peter and I can't stand to be inside for another second, so we go out to attempt to shovel the front walkway together. We give up within fifteen minutes and sit with our backs against the house, somewhat protected by the eaves above us, watching the snow fall.

"This seriously sucks," Peter says. "If I have to play one more game of Chinese checkers or Monopoly or Life or watch Mom polish another ornament, I'm going to go crazy."

"It'd be really endearing if our family weren't so messed up," I say flatly. "Kind of like camping."

Cold is already creeping under my parka, snow pants, and gloves. But I can't go inside and watch Mom desperately rubbing the glass ball for the second time today.

"I've got to move out this spring," Peter says. "I'm going to go insane if I live with Mom and Dad for another year. I don't care if I blow all the money I've saved for school renting an apartment. Owing student loans can't be that bad. I should have moved out two years ago."

Just as he's talking, the snow actually stops falling. We sit for five minutes, watching the sun slowly melt a hole in the clouds, then pick up our shovels and start making a thin path to the road. The top of the bank comes up to my eyes. I can't help but wonder what Luke is doing right now. What a trial is actually like. What the witnesses said he did. What they look like. What they talk like. Did they tell the truth? Did he have anyone on his side, other than the lawyer? He'll be found guilty, at least of the receipt scandal, so that'll be a sentence. But the sexual assault. If he's innocent and the lawyer can prove that . . .

Peter breaks my thoughts. "My hands are starting to blister. You want to finish this tomorrow? The plows haven't gotten to the road yet, so we are kind of digging a path to nowhere anyway."

I nod, and we head back inside.

Sometime in the middle of the night, the electricity flickers to life, throwing on lights, the heater, and our TV, without signal. Mom runs to check the phone. Dead. She fumbles to plug in her cell phone as the rest of us gather our blankets and head to our own rooms. As the fish tank slowly warms up, my angels start to swim around again. I give them some flakes and add some stuff to the tank that's supposed to help keep them healthy when they're under stress.

The next morning Mom wakes to find no cell service but a dial tone on our landline, and immediately calls Luke's lawyer. When she's done, she turns to face us, her lips thin. Skeleton standing tall behind her.

"Luke has been sentenced. A total—" Her voice breaks. She takes a breath and continues. "A total of twenty-seven years, twenty-four years good behavior, in a maximum-security prison. He was found guilty of everything."

Twenty-seven years? *Twenty-seven years?* I won't see him for twenty-seven years. Not unless I go to visit him in prison. *Twenty-seven years.* That's almost as long as he's been *alive*. He'll be so old when he gets out. Fifty-six years old.

I have to admit that despite everything I knew about Luke, I still had a little quiet whispering type of hope that wanted the jury to find that he's not guilty. For the evidence to *prove* he's not guilty. A hope that his assault on Heather was a onetime occurrence, a horrible mistake he'd never repeat, a mistake that I could maybe, someday, possibly forgive him for. That the thing with the fork was just because he was on something, and he could go to rehab and get better and never let that happen again. It was such a tiny little quiet hope, but Skeleton and I watch it snuff completely out.

Chapter 51:
Thawing

NOW

The weather starts to warm in March, slowly, slowly melting down the huge snow walls. I can logically compartmentalize my emotions about Luke: anger, betrayal, grief, frustration, guilt. The emotions all combine and win over reason every time. At school, surrounded by friends, I'm okay enough. I make sure to do my homework and chores, but aside from that I don't do much. I just let the heavy, heavy sadness hold me down.

Toward the middle of the month, the whole school chatters about how Mandy showed up at a party with some guy she met in her weekend photography class at Pasadena City College. She broke up with Ryan by introducing her new boyfriend to everyone that night.

After school the next day I see Ryan sitting on the hood of my car.

"Hey, Clare," he says, jumping off and shoving his hands into his pockets. "I need to go snowboarding tonight. Half the mountain is lit and open till nine. You in?"

My eyes widen. We've had feet and feet and feet of snow, but not once did it dawn on me that I should leave my room to go up on the mountain. Not once. What the hell is wrong with me?

I could go up with him. Ride the mountain, just for a few hours.

"C'mon, Clare. Please," he says quietly. "I've got to get on a snowboard or a surfboard. I know you get that. And I want to go with someone who's just going to be chill. So come with me."

"Okay," I reluctantly agree.

Being on the snow feels good. It takes a few runs for me to figure it out again, get comfortable enough to link turns easily. Ryan rides fast, taking jumps, going through trees, waiting for me at different points on the side of the mountain. There's barely anyone else around.

We settle on the ancient chairlift that will take us to the top again.

"Have you ridden much this winter?" I ask.

"No, just a few times. I got busy with other things." He gives an unconvincing laugh. "Normally I would have been out every day. Guess I just got derailed." He stops for a second, long enough that I wonder if he'll talk about Mandy, but after a quick shake of his head, his voice lightens as he says, "But it feels awesome to be out here. What about you?"

"I've been spending most of my winter thinking," I say. Above his goggles, I can see his forehead raise a bit. The lift stops halfway up, causing our chair to sway lightly. I suck in a deep breath and admit, "It's my first ride all winter. I guess I've been hiding. Just hiding from everyone. Trying to figure things out. . . ."

"That's good. I mean, you don't want to make my mistake and let someone else figure things out for you," he says.

A clump of snow falls from one of the branches next to our chair and lands with a soft plop in the deep drift below. I love being in the treetops. I love that I can feel the cold creeping into the tips of my fingers and surrounding my toes. And I love feeling that Ryan can somehow understand the complexity of everything that has happened in the last nine months, without me really having to explain anything to him.

"I should have been hiding on the mountain instead of in my room. If the snow is this good tonight, it must have been insane midseason." I readjust the way my board rests on my foot.

"It was." Ryan zips his jacket up a little more. "After one of our really big storms, I went backcountry with a couple of guys that I surf with. They're all really solid—they would dig me out of an avalanche, or dive into a riptide. They know I won't bail on them, I know they won't bail on me." He pauses. Then adds, "It sucks when you think you have that trust with someone and then you find out that you don't."

"And that maybe you never did," I say.

The motor of the lift starts to run, our chair slowly moves forward again.

It's weird how I know so little about Ryan that he's almost a stranger, but at this moment I'm feeling more comfortable with him than any of my friends.

I think of the beanie I knitted for him, shoved deep under my bed, and decide to give it to him tomorrow at school, even though on April first the no-hat policy returns. Maybe he can wear it next winter.

It's better out here, in the cold, under the unnatural fluorescent lights. Sitting next to someone else who feels heartbroken and betrayed. Maybe not exactly like me, but close enough.

Chapter 52:

Sunlight

NOW

It's April.

Happy letters of acceptance arrive from UCLA, Pepperdine, CSULB, and Shithole State. It feels good. Good to be wanted. Good to have options, even after UC Berkeley regrets to inform me that I'm not good enough for their school. My future is becoming a reality. In the fall I will be out of this town, able to start fresh. I imagine meeting new people and the conversations being like talking with Ryan or Peggy. I'll leave Skeleton here. He's not allowed to follow me.

For now I have to deal with the loud clanking of his bones that keep me up all night—he wants me to think about Luke, all the time. No matter how good I feel hanging out with my friends. No matter how hard I study. No matter how many times I try to have a normal conversation with Mom or Dad or Peter, Skeleton is there. And he wants to go to college with me.

The more I try to ignore him, the more he persists. Each night he gets closer and closer to my bed. I hide under the covers, drowning out the clanking with my pillow over my head, until, in the middle of the night, toward the end of April, I wake up to see Skeleton lying in bed next to me. His fingers draw in the air T R U T H.

"Why are you here?" I snap at him.

T R U T H.

"I know the truth. I know everything that I want to know about Luke, okay?" I say. "Can you please just let me sleep?"

He pokes me with his pointer finger.

"What more truth could there possibly be for me to face?" I ask him.

Then a horrifying idea occurs to me: Megan's Law. I've never thought to look for Luke on the sex offender registry. I've never thought to look for the truth there.

I'm trembling and afraid, but I get out of bed and walk to the family room, turning on every light switch as I go. I don't care if Mom or Dad wakes up. I don't care if they yell at me for being out of bed, or burning their money with the illumination.

The computer is cold; it rattles and moans when I turn it on. Putting in passwords, watching as the desktop loads. Finally online.

It's existed for years. I never looked at it. It never even occurred to me. Why would I look up what sex offenders may live here?

Search by name: Luke Tovin.

I barely hit enter, and there he is.

His name. First. Middle. Last. His birth date.

An INCARCERATED banner under his picture. He looks unusually calm in the photo. His eyes are those of the good Luke. His eyes say he is a good person and that we can trust him.

The list:

Sexual battery.

Sexual assault.

Assault with intent to commit rape, sodomy, or oral copulation.

A black-and-white list, right next to his name. Right next to his birth date.

I pull away from the screen, the glaring light. This can't be him. It can't. He couldn't have done all of this. I look at his picture. Name. Birth date. My eyes flickering between the list and my brother's photo, faster, faster. Back and forth. It is Luke. It is Luke.

The proof is all here. Skeleton taps on the screen. Agreeing. It is Luke. Skeleton taps again at the list. He's right. All of these charges can't be from only one incident. My breaths move to the top of my lungs, and I can't force the air down any deeper. Heart beating so fast. The screen is going out of focus. I push the chair back from the desk. I need space.

"What are you doing, Clare?" Mom's voice. I turn toward her, stand up. I am taller than her, bigger than her.

"Why didn't you tell me? Why would you lie? You said he was in jail for stealing. You said he wasn't a bad person; he just made some poor choices. You said he wasn't dangerous." I don't want to be crying. But I am. And spitting. And boiling. The room begins to move, Skeleton spins away, but Mom's face is perfectly in focus. The vein is bulging under her skin, bright blue, icier than the light in my nightmares. Her jaw starts to tremble.

"YOU"—her voice is low and distorted—"are a nosy, spoiled brat. You think that you know everything? You think that I lied? How do YOU know that the people who accused him aren't the liars? How do YOU know what is the truth?"

"They couldn't *all* be liars, Mom." The anger manifests itself into my hands. They curl into fists. My fingernails dig deeply into my palms. "And you know that. You *knew* that. You knew what he was in prison for. You knew. And you kept welcoming him back into our home." I say each word slowly, trying to keep my voice even, although it comes out wavy and thick. "'Come on in. Steal from us. Break a few windows. Pick a few locks. Snort some cocaine off our bathroom counter. Beat up your father. Stick a fork into your brother's arm.'" My voice cracks on the last words, my anger getting tripped up with a surge of grief.

"He is a good brother to you," my mother snaps back. "Remember all the letters. Remember holidays and bike rides and swimming in the lake. Remember him scaring off the kids that picked on you. You owe him so much. Remember that, before you go accusing me of doing something wrong. I ALLOWED him to be a good brother to you."

"No, Mom. You aren't hearing me. It doesn't matter that he was good to *me*. He was *hurting* other people. And you knew how he was hurting them. How could you,

Mom? How could you keep letting him come home when you knew that he could do this?" I point at the computer screen. "What about me? What about Peter? What about every single person who got hurt by Luke because you were so busy keeping him free? Who protected the rest of us while you were protecting him?" The words are coming out fast. I am distorted and ugly, feeling the skin around my eyes and mouth, swelling, reddening. Fat, hot tears blur my vision. She shakes her head at me. No. No. No. She needs to hear me. "How many girls got raped because *you* needed to have your son home?"

She crumbles, limb by limb. I lunge forward to try to grab her, to keep her from falling. I am not fast enough. Her body thuds as it hits the floor, her robe bleeding into the carpet, her face protected by aged hands.

She's sobbing.

And I realize: I've never seen my mother cry before. Not at funerals. Not in the hospital. It snaps my brain.

I didn't have to accuse her. I wanted Luke home too. But that was before I knew what he was capable of. And she had to have known. At some point she *must* have believed he wasn't innocent. At some point she chose him over everything else, everybody else. Skeleton stomps his foot, points at Mom, and raises his hands into the air: Do something to help Mom. Don't leave her crying like this.

"Mom," I say softly. "Mom. You can't change him. It doesn't matter how many times you let him come home. You *can't* change him."

I can't change him either.

My fists are soft open hands now. They sail gently to Mom's back.

"Come on, Mom," I say quietly. "Come on. I'll help you back to bed. I'm sorry. Okay?"

"You should be sorry." Her face twists from her hands, the veins larger, icier, her eyes sunken deep behind swollen lids. "Get away from me. Go to bed."

Dad peeks out their bedroom door. Baffled and half-dressed, he stumbles across the room and wraps Mom in his arms, shielding her from my eyes. And Peter's. I don't know how long Peter has been standing in his doorway. Maybe the whole time. He takes a few steps toward me, his eyes soft with compassion, with worry. But I turn and run. He doesn't follow.

With my room shut tight, and my desk chair angled under the knob in a desperate attempt to bar it, I lie on my back on my bed, staring at the door. Skeleton lies beside me, reaching out to hold my hand.

"Leave me alone. Leave me alone." I push him away. Pull my covers over my head.

I looked for proof. I found it. There is no way to turn around. Ever.

With the sunlight coming in, dancing for a second on the windowsills before being sucked away into the eggplant walls, I wake. Flip, flip, flip, through the motions and emotions of the previous night. Mom can't change Luke. Compassion will not cure him. Luke is responsible for changing his actions in order to change his world. A single beam of light falls on my right arm, and tingling warmth awakens the skin. Luke is responsible for changing his actions in order to *his* world. I'm responsible for the actions I take to change *my* world.

I dress quickly, put a hat on my head. Leave the house without a word.

In the hardware store I pick up all the supplies I need, bring them back. Lean my chair against the knob, once again barring my door.

I mask off the ceiling line and trim with tape. Dip my brushes into the bucket of primer, first cut in the edges, then roll the middle of the walls. But white is too sterile, too clean and cold for my room.

A second coat. This one light green, the color of new apples. Sunlight bursts in through the open window. Reflects and brightens, refreshes and renews.

I shake, just a little, as the job is done. Shake because I'm not sure what this means. I'm not sure what Mom will say or do. I'm not sure of the punishment. Shake because I'm surprised at myself. Happy with myself.

I refuse to continue to let the sunlight be sucked out of my life.

Chapter 53:
Clarity

NOW

I push my furniture around, rearranging it to sit exactly where I want it to be. The wide-open window allows an early spring breeze in. I would love to spend the day in my new room, but the paint fumes are a bit much, and there are more hours of daylight to enjoy.

On my way out I stop at the pile of mail on the counter, unsorted but with a letter addressed to me on top.

The pre-stamped envelope. Luke's prisoner number printed clearly under his name. I'm not sure I want to read it, but I tuck it into my pocket and head out the door.

It's easy to find the trail Luke showed me on the day he came home last summer; hard to believe that was less than a year ago.

I stop at the bush, pull out the jar of vodka. Inspect it, almost choke from smelling it, then tip it over and watch every last bit of it drain out.

At the top of the trail, I look over the valley, admiring the slowly melting snowcaps in the distance, smiling in disbelief at the waterfalls that were only trickles during the summer.

I could burn the letter. Put it into one of Mom's roaring fires, unopened. I could drop it over this cliff and watch it fall through the air, getting smaller and smaller, until it completely disappeared.

Skeleton points at the letter, now in my hands. He's curious to read what Luke has written. I'm curious too.

But I don't open it yet. Looking over the valley, the snowcaps white against the bright blue sky, sitting on this rock, I feel that peace is possible. Why read the letter? What am I looking for? An explanation. An apology. A bit of hope that he is the good Luke, instead of the bad. But is an explanation or an apology, or a tiny crumb of hope, enough when the truth tells me that his past indicates he will continue to steal, continue to assault?

Curiosity takes over. Skeleton and I open the letter together, read it word by word.

Dear Squeakers,

Ma and Pop tell me that the college acceptance letters are pouring in. Congratulations. I'm proud of you. Maybe that doesn't mean so much coming from me, but I hope the sincerity of it somehow comes through on paper. Congratulations. I mean it.

Listen, Clare, I'm kind of hoping that you will write me, occasionally. I'd really love hearing from you, especially since Peter and my friends never write. Only Ma and Pop. I don't know what I would do without them.

Don't give up on me. Please. What I did was wrong. I messed up so big, but I need you to keep believing in me. Sometimes I think that it is easier for me to be here, because at least in prison I understand how it all works. Outside I do things I can't explain. But I've been thinking a lot about what I've done. I know that when I get out next time, I'm gonna do things right.

Squeakers, I'm still your brother. I need you to write. Please. Maybe send some photos of us at Granny's last summer. I think of that trip all the time. It's one of my favorite memories. I love you and miss you. I need you, Squeaks. Maybe you could come and visit. It's so lonely here.

Love,
Luke

I lower the letter and look out at the valley. If it were a cloudy day, I wouldn't be able to see the crystal-clear water hopping from rock to jagged rock, the green tree-tops etched into the backdrop sky, the fingers of snow reaching down the shady valleys. But it's not a cloudy day. I can see every detail.

I fold up the letter, place it in my pocket. Start my walk home on the muddy path, with Skeleton clinking close behind.

In through the front door, Mom is giving me the silent treatment. I say hello; she shakes her head, the bulging vein a permanent part of her brow.

Dad catches me in the hallway. "I see you painted your room."

"Yes, I did," I say.

"Your mother is very angry about it. You should've asked her if you could paint it first. You know, this is our house, not yours," he says.

"So you don't like the color," I say, taking a step to the side, preparing to walk around him into my new sanctuary.

"No, I didn't say that. I said that you should have asked us first," he says, blocking the hall with his body. "You apologize to your mother. Or I'll ground you."

"I think you are asking the wrong child to apologize." Will my parents *never* get it? "Dad, it's just paint. I didn't steal anything. Or rape anyone." I stand up taller. "And I'm not going to. Ever. Painting my room isn't a gateway to violent crime."

He has no response. I spin on my heel and go back to the living room. Mom can be silent all she wants. I have something to say. "I'm not Luke, Mom. You don't have to worry about me like you worry about him. I'm going to make my own decisions. And I hope most of the time they'll be good ones." Like apple-green paint. "So just treat me like Clare. Like we don't have Luke in the middle all the time."

She looks from me to her ornaments, and for a moment I think I've said something that has reached her. But she responds, "I always know what's best, Clare. I always know what's best."

I throw up my hands. "Fine. I tried."

Dad's now blocking the entrance to the hall. I push past him and throw my room door open. I'm greeted by my window beautifully framing the apple tree. Tiny leaves are sprouting from each branch, white blossoms beginning to emerge.

It's spring. A pang of guilt hits me. There are four

blankets that wasted a winter under my bed. I decide I'm not going to dwell on the guilt. Peggy won't care. She'll be happy to see me, and they'll always have use for the blankets.

An excited jitter runs through my body as I pull the box out. I love knitting the blankets. I love delivering them even more. In fact, the only thing that will make it better is sharing it with a friend. I text Drea, and in ten minutes she's in my car.

As Drea watches me hand the blankets to Peggy, I realize how weird and ridiculous it was to keep *this* part of my life a secret from everyone. I can't explain why I did that, why it felt so right at the time. All I know is, now I'm seeing everything with clarity.

Chapter 54:
Making Peace

NOW

That night, on my bed, relaxed, I watch the fish in the tank swimming slowly, in and out of the log, under and above the castle. It's all very peaceful in my apple-green room.

I open the letter again, read through slowly. Luke wants someone to support him, love him, believe in him.

But what do I want?

Let me try to analyze this, like I am analyzing a branch of government or a famous piece of literature.

What do I want?

I want the lake, without the swamp, without the poisonous snakes, without the thin ice. I want peace.

I pull down my wooden box, open it to see all the letters, and the photos, and my locket. Add the new letter to the box and leave the house for the third time today.

Around the lake, I walk by moonlight to the deepest part, steps before the swamp. Standing with my bare toes curled around the edge of the cement rim, I put the box out far, far in front of me.

"Good-bye," I say, sticking to my decision, unclamping my fingers from the sides, releasing the box for my treasures, every memory of Luke, good and bad. Releasing it. Watching it sink slowly down until it disappears. I imagine it hitting the bottom, the swampy silt swallowing it.

It's a good decision. I am sad but relieved. My memories of Luke will rest here, in the lake that can't help but have equally good and bad sides to it.

When I turn around, Skeleton is behind me, watching with big empty eyes. He tips his hat at me, gives a nod of approval. But he still doesn't leave.

Chapter 55:
Mom's Family Skeleton

NOW

Spring break. My senior year. There are one million things I'd rather be doing, but Granny needs help, and offered to pay me for my work, which is fantastic, since I *still* haven't been able to get a job in town. The farm has sold, leaving Granny thirty days to sort everything she owns, take a few things with her, give the rest to family, donate anything left to charity.

The farmhouse is empty now. We've been working all week. My suitcase is upstairs, waiting for me to pick it up, so I can fly back home.

I stand at the foot of the staircase, looking up, watching the splintered bowing wood, the nails pulling up on either side. I stand watching nothing. Nothing stands on the stairs. Nothing strolls or thumps or squeaks. There is only me, me and my tightened chest, my sweaty feet, my hairs on my neck slowly rising, one by one.

I look up these stairs, knowing I have never seen a ghost, never watched doors open and close on their own, or lights flicker on and off without a finger on the switch.

Here I am, eighteen years old, a senior in high

school, technically an adult, and I am hair-raising scared because I can't explain or understand my body's physical and emotional clues: get ready to fight or run. Something is askew.

Is it possible, I wonder, for a house to retain the memory of something bad that has happened there? Is it possible for skeletons, still locked in closets, to cause my body to react like this to these stairs?

Here on the steps it feels like broken windows, like bloody trails leading through the living room, like a metal utensil sticking out of a human limb.

It feels like, if I were to guess, something terrible might have happened to my mother on these steps, in this house. An extra chill runs along my spine as visions of my grandfather swirl around me. He's angry drunk, violent. And he is on these stairs.

Mom's family skeleton peeks out of the upstairs hall linen closet, only its skull and bony fingertips. The vision of Papa slips away.

I'll never know what happened to Mom. What makes her protect Luke, even after he did awful things. What makes her mood change like someone has hit a switch. What makes her feel the need to keep her ornaments perfect. Because Mom will never tell whatever happened to her when she was growing up that causes her to need so much control. She'll continue to weave and spin a story of a small-town girl, growing up in an innocent farmer family, complete with eggs for breakfast, collected fresh that morning, and milk still warm from the cow. She'll spin and weave, blocking the closet door with her web, trying to keep her family skeleton tightly locked away.

But skeletons are resourceful. They don't like to be locked up. It'll peek out, rattle its bones, reminding her of its existence at any part of the day or night.

My Skeleton joins me on the stairs. He taps my shoulder, his eye sockets long and sad. Even though Mom can be a complete nightmare, neither of us wants to think of her being hurt.

Together Skeleton and I start up the steps. Slow, deliberate strides. We will not run. We walk to her family skeleton. We do not push the closet shut, do not try to lock it away.

Skeleton extends his hand to me, and for the first time I take it, feeling a strange gratitude. He is part of who I am. A result of experiences. He has given me sharper intuition, the ability to feel fear, love, hate, sadness, all at once. He has allowed me to see the truth about my family.

Chapter 56:
Protection

NOW

Gummy bears fly from Drea's hand onto my lap.

"Shut up!" she squeals. "You are not telling me the truth."

"Oh, yes," I say, ignoring the gummy bears. Carefully steering each S-turn. "It was amazing. As she was going out the back door, Mom's bedroom door was opening. Two seconds earlier, bam! She and Peter would have been caught."

"Good thing he's moving out," Drea says. "That boy is almost twenty-two years old. It's not right for him to still be living at home."

"Speaking of moving. I got the sheet from UCLA—" I start.

"Wait. What did your mom say?" Drea interrupts.

"She gave me a speech about how the Ten Commandments command me to honor my father and mother, and therefore I must stay at home and commute to Shithole State. Then she added that I will have no support, emotional or financial, if I still choose to disobey her and go to UCLA."

"Is that supposed to be a threat? Tell me how that is

different from the last eighteen years of your life." A gummy bear angrily bounces off the dashboard.

"Her threat may not last. I can tell she likes it when people congratulate her on my acceptance to such a good school."

"She should be proud. My mom is. And it hits an eight-point-five on my party scale, so I might just have to come up from Long Beach State to visit."

"What, so you can study on Friday nights with me?" I joke.

"I guess you better come visit me. So what did UCLA send you?"

"All my dorm information. They gave me my room-mate's name and e-mail so we can get to know each other first. I hope she's normal." Even though I have driven this road many times, I flick on my brights to see the turns better in the moonless night.

"Ha. What if she's a clean freak who bleaches the room every morning and requires you to make your bed as soon as you get up?"

"Worse yet, what if she smells? What if she never takes showers?" The headlights illuminate the cliff sides to the right, the metal barricades on the left, lining the edge.

"And has a pet rat that she keeps under the bed." Drea's laughing hard now.

"And— OH, GOD!" Drea and I gasp. We both saw him at the same time.

Covered in blood, he turns and waves his arms over his head. *Stop, stop.*

"Don't stop," Drea says. "Just keep driving."

"You're right." I speed up, taking the turn a little too quickly. Then I slow down to stay on the road. There was so much blood. All over his hands and legs and arms. He could be a murderer who just killed someone. Worst was the blood pouring down from the top of his head. Bright red covering the left half of his face.

He could be someone like Luke, hitchhiking alongside the road, maybe looking for a victim.

He could just be a guy who took a turn too fast and crashed his car.

"Drea, I'm turning around. We need to go back."

"Clare, are you crazy? He could be dangerous."

"We might be the only ones who come down this road tonight. I need to make sure he's okay. I'm just going to slow down. Tell him we're calling an ambulance." I turn the car around, carefully.

"I'm calling right now," Drea says as she dials on her phone. "We don't have to go back."

We are nearing the place now. Slow down. Brace myself. I still gasp when I see him. There's so much blood.

As Drea talks to the 911 dispatcher, I pull over on the opposite side of the road. From a quarter-rolled-down window, I say, "What happened?"

"I rolled my car off the side," he replies.

"We're getting you help. We called an ambulance."

He is our age. Maybe older, but not too much.

"What should we do now?" I whisper to Drea as she hangs up the phone.

"Drive home," she says.

"I mean, should we wait with him? For the ambulance to arrive?"

"Listen, crazy. I don't see a car, do you?"

"No." It could be over the side. Or not.

"All I see is a bloody guy walking on a deserted road through the woods. This is how horror movies start. Two dumb girls who were just talking about their great futures pull over to help someone. He pulls out a knife and cuts them up into little bits, drives away in their car with their body parts locked safely in the trunk," Drea says.

"What if he's just a teenager like us who got into a car accident? Wouldn't you want someone to wait with you? The woods are scary."

"Yeah. The woods are scary. Especially when there is a bloody man walking around in them."

"I need to know that he is going to be taken care of. I'll have nightmares for months if we don't. Besides, I don't want to live thinking there's a criminal inside of every person I come across."

She's processing what I just said.

"Okay," Drea says, "but we do it safe. We keep our distance."

"Thanks for calling," the guy says. "I have no idea where my cell phone flew. Man, this sucks. Do you have any cigarettes?"

We all laugh, uncomfortably. But it's still a laugh.

"No, sorry."

"How about some tissues? I tried to clean myself up with my shirt . . ." But it was already too bloody. A strip of gray down the center is splattered but relatively clean, considering the rest of it. Dark red sleeves. Dark red sides.

"We do have a bottle of water, if that helps," Drea offers.

I give her the *What the hell are you doing?* look.

"Yeah. Thanks." He walks step after step toward the car. I check the locks, put the car in drive, get ready to flee.

"I got a bloody nose. Tried to stop it. I didn't realize the turn was there. My car rolled off the side." Closer and closer. Stop shaking, arm. Don't give away how scared you are. He is close enough now. His nose looks broken, twisted to the side, out of place. Streaks of dark red smeared when he tried to wipe his face clean.

"I think there's a big cut above my eye," he says. Drea gives me the bottle and I stick it out the quarter-rolled-down window.

His hand takes the water bottle. He backs up as slowly as he approached. I think he knows how frightening he looks.

"Thanks for the water. And for stopping."

Flashing red in my rearview mirror. As the ambulance parks, its lights reveal a crumpled car. This guy is not a murderer. He is not someone trying to find an easy victim to hurt. He is not someone like Luke. He is someone who got into a car wreck and needed help.

Later that night, on the trundle bed in Drea's room, I try to get comfortable, telling my brain that I don't need to see the guy covered in blood every time I close my eyes, that I don't need a nightmare.

• • •

I wake up, confused, surprised. Morning's pale gray illuminates the edges of the window, the light barely creeping into the room. Not one nightmare. I nestle back under the covers and fall back to sleep to the *tick*, *tick* of the grandfather clock in the living room.

Chapter 57:

Distance

NOW

The scene is almost the same as it was one year ago, bonfire crackling and reaching to the sky, peers idly ingesting their substance of choice, Drea's dark skin almost blue in the full moonlight. And Peter, next to the beer cooler with a new blonde.

"Little Sister," he says, "you're here later than I expected for someone who doesn't have to sneak out because she has Mom's permission."

"More like we agreed to disagree," I say. "She let me leave but first gave me a lecture about being responsible that ended with some crap about hoping I do the right thing and stay in. Enough about that. Beverage, please."

Drea and I hand our five-dollar bills to Peter, but he waves them away. "Happy Graduation," he says, handing us each a beer.

I spot Ryan out of the corner of my eye, his wavy hair peeking out of the beanie I made. "I'll be back," I say to Drea.

"I'll be over there." She raises her can in the direction of Omar, Chase, and Skye.

"Hey," Ryan says, his face breaking into a wide smile

as I walk up. Before I can even say hi, he adds, "So. I, um, I kind of have something for you."

He opens his backpack and hands me a hardcover book.

Soul Escape. Mandy's photos.

"I noticed that you kept going into the cafeteria to look at these. Mandy made a bunch of books and gave them to her friends. This was mine. I want you to have it . . . if you want it."

"Thank you." I practically whisper the words, opening the book, taking in one picture after another, then pausing on the one of Luke's arm.

"So, how is he?"

"Luke?" I ask.

Ryan nods.

I shrug. "Lonely, I guess. I really don't have any contact with him. It's better this way. For me. For now. It's better." I pause, then admit, "I still miss him. I still love him. Even if I never talk to him again." I close the book and hug it to my body.

"I get that," Ryan says, even though he doesn't have to. I know he gets it. He gets me.

"Thanks again," I say, then change the subject. "So . . . did you figure it out? How to beat the system and just travel and surf?"

"Maybe." He leans against a tree. The light of the bonfire reflects, making his hazel eyes almost orange. "I'm actually going to college. I'm studying nonprofits, so maybe I can work for an organization like Surfrider Foundation. Something that works with the oceans."

I hold my can up to his. "Congrats."

"What school did you decide on? Still thinking of doing something with marine biology?" He leans closer to me.

"UCLA. I don't know what I'm going to do with my life, but I guess I have time to figure that one out."

"You can probably beat the system. Do something that will get you in the water swimming every day. Speaking of . . . This summer, any chance I'll see you out on the lake?"

"I'm not going to be working there, but I'll be swimming. Most likely in the mornings."

"Your favorite part of the day," Ryan says, tucking a piece of my hair behind my ear. "So it's a date, then?"

"It's a date."

Graduation. The field lights are on, my name has been called, and I am walking across the dais.

Tomorrow is the first day of my last summer at home. It's going to be filled with my friends, secret swim lessons for Chris, and teaching the moms at Loving Hearts to knit. Then, in August—college.

After the ceremony, Drea, Omar, Lala, Chase, Skye, and I gather together, hugging and grinning, arms around necks and waists as flashes spark and cameras click. Ryan makes his way over, slipping in our group photo next to me.

"Watch out, world. . . . Here they come!" Tonight Dad has traded in his typically goofy jokes for his awkward brand of sincerity. Mom has even dropped most of her rules, just for the occasion. My graduation is, in fact, turning out nothing like I had assumed it would be without Luke here to make sure everything is okay.

Luke. He isn't here. It's a quick, passing thought. He's not here. And that's fine with me.

"Let's get a family picture," Mom suggests as she hands her camera to Ms. P. Skeleton squeezes between Peter and me, his bony fingers somewhat comfortable on my shoulder.

As Ms. P wraps her arms around me and says, "I am so incredibly proud of you," I feel a sudden pang of sadness mix in with the evening's exhilaration. It takes me off guard. Leaving my parents behind, and the fresh start that college promises, also means a physical distance between me and Ms. P . . . and my friends . . . and Peter. I hug her back, extra tight, part of me never wanting to let go.

But a bonfire is waiting, and if my friends have mixed feelings, they aren't showing it. We walk away from the field, from our parents and our past, laughing, speculating about things our futures will bring. With Ryan's arm around me, Peter and my friends at my side, any sadness I have dissipates. I look back, watching my parents becoming more distant. Skeleton stands with them, raising his glass of brandy in a toast to me. Tonight is a celebration, and he knows he's not invited. But he doesn't mind staying behind. He'll wait, knowing I won't try to lock him in a closet. And I know he won't lock me away either.

Check out these gripping stories from *New York Times* bestselling author

JASON REYNOLDS

"An unexpectedly gorgeous meditation on the meaning of family, the power of friendship, and the value of loyalty."

—*Booklist*
on *When I Was the Greatest*

"A vivid, satisfying, and ultimately upbeat tale of grief, redemption, and grace."

—*Kirkus Reviews*
on *The Boy in the Black Suit*

★"Timely and powerful, this novel promises to have an impact long after the pages stop turning."

—*School Library Journal*,
on *All American Boys*,
starred review

Skint's in the Pit because of Dinah. So she figures she better get cracking and affect his speedy release. Dinah would go to the **ends of the earth and back** if it would help Skint.

But is it possible to try too hard to save your best friend?

A NOVEL BY N. GRIFFIN

THE WHOLE STUPID WAY WE ARE

"So furious, so heartbreaking. . . . A thing of beauty, that's what this is."
—Kathi Appelt, author of
The Underneath, a Newbery Honor book